'As a detective, I very often deal with the bizarre. Sometimes involving murder. Always involving mystery. Deep down though, I'm a Pragmatist, bent on finding practical solutions to claims of perculiar activity.
Even when I fail, I think I come pretty damn close . . .

. . . I'll let you be the judge.'

Cameron Josey

Book 3

ZerOzone

James William Davis
©

ZeroZone

ZerOzone ©
Written by James William Davis

Published by James William Davis
17 Wedgewood Crescent, Beacon Hill NSW 2100

Copyright 2020, James William Davis
International Standard Book Number
ISBN 978-0-646-82836-7
©

National Library of Australia Cataloguing-in Publication entry
Author: Davis, James W.

Title: ZerOzone James William Davis.

Draft: 024 Book 3 ZerOzone V6 Draft 003.docx
Cover: 010 9780646828367 – perfect. pdf

©

Cover Design and Layout by James William Davis.

In this fictional book, names, characters, businesses, organisations, places and
events are either the product of the author's imagination or are used
fictitiously. Any resemblance to actual persons, living or dead, events or
locales is entirely coincidental.

James William Davis

Born in 1944, James William Davis first branched into writing during his time in the film and television industry. Story telling became a driving force in his working life, albeit with a camera or an editing device.

Now he likes to hone his craft using the written word—that essential step prior to all other forms of expression.

Professor Verg warned the world it would happen – no one listened, except those who wanted him dead.

Detective Cameron Josey is drawn in by a long-time friend to find the perpetrators, but finds himself being forced into battle with his own demons instead.

Ancient myths and superstition confound his task, taking him deep into the hot zone in the spiritual heart of Tibet.

Prologue

Crawling on all fours, a bedraggled archaeologist emerges from within a tight dugout, anxious to see what all the fuss is about. He pulls away a red scarf that has protected his lungs from the harsh shale-dust. Wiping sweat from his eyes with the sleeve of his shirt, he strains to focus on the frantic woman running toward him.

'Mr Leung, come quickly.' Her breathless urging for him to hurry is to no avail.

With his back set in a painful arc, the elderly man is quite incapable of hurrying. 'All right Lui Jie,' he grumbles, 'Beijing was not built in one day.'

On reaching her mentor, she respectfully encourages him to reach full stance, which is clearly not easy. Once on his feet, impatient with his unavoidably slow pace, she repeatedly runs ahead, frantically waving at him to follow. Her heightened elation does seem to give him extra strength, his posture improving with each passing moment. By the time they have stepped onto the trestle that will lift them, his heart is racing madly from the exertion.

'Take us up!' she shouts to excited workers that have

gathered at the base of the dugout.

Manned ropes tighten, lifting the platform with a jolt. She wraps her arms around the trembling fellow to steady him. In her eyes, he recognises the enormity of her find, yet he knows there is no point in asking what it is; he understands he must see it for himself.

The platform bounces to a stop, presenting a dark cavity. She gestures for him to enter. To abide, he must crawl crab-fashion. He pauses in the pitch dark space, reaches behind for the lamp made ready by the young woman and moves it carefully out in front.

The irregular walls dance, the lamp taking a moment to settle in his unsteady hands. The resulting glow reveals what the archaeologist has so far only partially unearthed, the remainder tantalisingly hidden from view. His etched face twists and trembles, illustrating something truly extraordinary lies before him.

Still breathless when he turns to meet her gaze, Mr Leung lowers his voice, his comment meant for her ears only. 'You have *really* found it,' he whispers from a dust dried throat. 'Just as you predicted you would, my darling girl.'

Reaching for her cell phone she tells him excitedly, 'I must call Professor Huang immediately.'

'Yes, yes – give your uncle my best wishes, he will be beside himself when he hears your news.'

'Oh yes, he will be - *very* excited.'

CHAPTER ONE
The attack

Professor Aaron Verg fidgeted nervously. 'Look, I know how c-confusing this all must sound,' he said with a mild but incessant stutter, 'but you're getting ahead of me, Detective. Can I just tell my story from the beginning?'

Josey was eying his visitor with a measure of disquiet, an attitude he knew he'd have to quickly conquer if he were to remain friends with Belinda Baxter, a woman he'd known since high school, and the reason the man had come to see him – and now goddamn it, she was about to marry the guy.

The ill at ease scientist was projecting an awkward social ineptness, uncertain of himself and others it would seem. But then, the fact someone had recently tried to kill him, might be a good reason not to make too hasty a judgment.

Verg had already explained he was in the employ of a science organisation called SciCore, whose job it was to monitor disruptions in Earth's upper atmosphere. The high level of secrecy set in place for their work, meant that Professor Verg's sworn promise not to disclose information pertaining to the research centre, was legally binding - problem was, in recent times he had broken his silence, inclusive of his now talking to a private detective about it.

The attack on his life wasn't even close to being the most bizarre aspect of his story though, but it was the only part that came close to a reason for his asking for help. His story began at the Research Centre . . .

*

Driving through SciCore's rain lashed Garden of Eden, Professor Verg can't help the feeling a serpent is loose in this perceived scientific paradise. He concedes having nibbled on the financial fruits himself, evidenced in part by the late model Corvette that he drives.

At the exit, the security guard steps into the downpour, to note the vehicle's number and its time of departure.

Through the wiper-swept windscreen, Aaron Verg distractedly watches him check everything with anal diligence. Not until he has predicated Professor Verg is in fact the driver, and alone, does he activate the iron-gate.

An unexpected lull in the storm produces a small break in cloud cover, releasing the setting sun as it melts into the canopy of the surrounding national park. The blinding light easily penetrates the steel bars, animating a striped shadow across the Corvette's contours, the strobing glare forcing its driver to turn away. He doesn't see the group of demonstrators cramming through the gate's widening gap at first, but sensing increased movement in his peripheral vision, he pivots his head and squints into the light—

A placard crosses the path of the sun and slams against the driver's window:

SCI-CORE-UPTION!

At the clang of the gate's concluding journey, he attempts to drive through, but a dozen people block his path. Police with weapons drawn, encourage the unruly mob to back off.

Conversely, a man built like a wrestler—and with just as much theatrical fire in his eyes—appears out of the crowd and leaps onto the Chevrolet's bonnet. Tattooed arms swing a mallet at the bullet proof glass. Driven wild by its failure to break through, the illustrated man swings all the harder. A high pressure water-canon sweeps in, trying to remove him, but he hangs on defiantly - while some others are successfully forced to retreat.

Dealing with the wild eyes of the man glaring at him through the windscreen, the professor cautiously nudges the Corvette forward to intimidate him, and the mob into moving, instead they close ranks, rocking and thumping at the car's pristine body with their fists. This invites a more concentrated jet of water, successfully knocking them from their feet and sweeping them aside.

The corvette's engine roars, spinning the wheels into a solid grip, catapulting the car through the resulting gap and through the open gate. A sharp broadside onto the road dispatches the stubborn bonnet surfer to the asphalt, leaving him to cope with discarded skin.

In the rear mirror, the research centre recedes into the distance, as nature's garden plays host to the speeding car's getaway along the undulating carpet ahead.

The familiar traveller relaxes, looking forward now to his destination in the distant haze beyond the city lights. The wooded park flicks by unheeded. Not nearly as unheeded, are the thunder clouds up ahead, threatening to return the heavy rain that had burst from the sky earlier. Cumulonimbus clouds with a pale green tinge to them have become a familiar sight. Although spectacular, when this sort of visual phenomenon appears, the ensuing storm promises to be a dangerous one.

He slows; storms in recent times have been more intense, more unpredictable. Lightning strikes in and around the city have killed fifty four people in the past year. The timing of these storms cements home the essence of the many recent conversations about climate change.

He flicks on the radio in time to hear the usual warnings about the approaching instability, but the announcer's voice is predictably buried in static. He doesn't need a commentary anyway; he can plainly see the atmospheric upheaval is coming straight at him. The thought crosses his mind to turn around and outrun it back to the research centre, but somehow the idea makes him feel lily-livered. Any further conflict with angry demonstrators prompts him to continue into the storm.

When the edge of the rain-bomb finally looms closer, he judges it to be even more extreme than expected, even by the grim broadcaster. Now caught in the car's high beam, a wall of water—falling as though from a bursting airborne river—races toward him. Inside its veil, ribbons of lightning dance to the beat of thunder, heard even over the sweet rumble of his V8 engine.

He reduces the Corvette's speed even further, in the hope of softening the unavoidable collision, but the resulting smash amounts to a minimal saving - the vehicle autonomously brakes against the eventual impact. Wipers submerge into a surf-like wash, instantly rendering them useless—

He flinches away from a deadly ribbon of lightning that explodes just outside his window, its intensity exceeding anything he has ever witnessed.

Seconds later his tiny cocoon is enveloped by powerful cyclonic winds and rain, the speed and ferocity locking the Corvette within its grip as surely as if it had sunk beneath the waves of a massive storm at sea. His vehicle has lost all sense of control, the concept of driving on; wiped from consideration.

He leans his foot on the brake with the blind goal of keeping his vehicle somewhere safe in the circumstance. Finally stationary—but far from still—all he can do is sit and wait for the mad storm to pass; and hope he will be alive when the event is over.

As fearful as the lightning is, it's the leviathan power of the wind that scares him the most. The vehicle rocks insanely, sliding on the wet road. The slipstream has positioned the car head-on into the monstrous gale. He fantasizes that the sports car's sleek wind-cheating contours may hold it to the ground as it is capable of doing at exceptional speed. But, he's not convinced this is the way it will play out. If the Corvette were to be lifted and swept away, its structural integrity would be his only remaining defence against the elements—and, against probable death.

This morbid thought is compounded when his dubious cocoon is savagely penetrated. A branch, or something, has hit the windscreen hard, solidly enough to invoke a small but alarming fracture in the glass. Beyond the cracked windscreen, nothing but the black curtain of night is visible. The leak is threatening to worsen. He reaches to the glove box for duct-tape—

Three hard knocks at the driver's window brings him to a chilling realisation.

That sounded deliberate, but he chooses to believe they are nothing more than strange flukes of nature; debris loosened by the gale. He waits, hoping his assumption bears fruit.

He manages to convince himself that a repeat of the evenly spaced sounds is highly unlikely, but an instant flash of lightning reveals a frightening glimpse of an unnatural movement.

Is someone outside in this madness?

A glint from a metal object spearheads a collision with the windscreen - an impact massive enough to break any normal glass.

The strengthened shield on the Corvette can only take so much he imagines, especially now that it's already damaged - another hit might succeed. He has no intention of hanging around to find out if this is true.

He thrusts his foot on the throttle, invoking too much power, and instantly realises the car's wheels have become deeply embedded in mud, having slipped onto the soaked shoulder—

Another massive bludgeon impacts the side window inches from his head, the strengthened glass withstanding the onslaught once again; and once again, lightning reveals the scope of the windswept torrent surrounding the car. But, that's not all, in the temporary glow he sees the distinct figure of a person heavily clad in motorcycle gear, leaning into the wind and rain like a sailor on the deck of a stranded ship.

As might a ghost, the figure's image remains when the light fades, leaving the perpetrator's whereabouts and intentions to imagination. There is no need to *imagine* the stick or *metal bar* that had been wielded.

The Corvette's wheels are spinning wildly on the spot with little to no effect - its engine is revving at maximum, producing a robotic-like scream that competes with the incessant roar of the storm.

Is the car moving forward at all?

He can't be sure.

Lightning irradiates the area where the ghostly-rider had a moment ago stood. Who or whatever was out there is gone. He cranes his neck in the precious few seconds of light that remains, failing to locate the assailant.

Headlights incapable of penetrating the storm are no help.

Again the area sinks into complete darkness.

The car's intense tossing to-and-fro wrenches the steering from his hands, provoking a curse, a personal affront to his inane driving skills.

For an instant, he imagines his fate is now left in the hands of a higher power; not the creator, but someone close to him, his ex-partner; *Fredie Faraday.*

'I could do with a little help here Fredie,' he prays aloud.

Faraday prematurely left the planet close on twenty

years ago while saving Josey's life in a shootout. Josey's never forgotten it, and still calls on his deceased partner whenever he needs help – *as if you haven't done enough already* he often jokes to the incarnation.

He pushes the comforting thought from his mind; convinced that if he is to survive he will need to fight to gain control. Not an easy task with wheels still spinning in traction-less mud—

Something rips through the driver's door as suddenly as thunder, becoming wedged. Glancing down, he sees the weapon is a common garden axe, smeared with blood; *his* blood.

A red stain seeps onto his shirt, indicating he has been hit just below the ribs; as yet, no pain.

The blade withdraws as the axe is retrieved by the attacker. Just as quickly it returns, hitting the side window with penetrating success. A whirlwind of fractured glass and rain erupts into the cabin, forcing Aaron to bury his eyes in the crook of his elbow, leaving him to battle the car with one hand.

He feels the wheels skate from the mud and grapple with the ice-like tarmac. The car jerks forward as spinning wheels ostensibly gain footing.

Blindly fighting to maintain grip and acceleration he spins the steering left and right repeatedly, to keep on a road he can't even see.

Getting away from the crazed attacker seems possible now, if only he can avoid crashing the car.

A mix of relief and anger consumes him as the axe can be heard hitting the rear of the vehicle; the assailants last ditch attempt to express unsolicited rage.

A half kilometre away from immediate danger, a single

headlight appears in the blackness of the mirror, confirming the attacker is indeed a motor cyclist and more than likely capable of catching up. The chill and heat of adrenalin throbs in his back as the receding point of light is growing again, rapidly closing at high speed, seemingly without sufficient passage of time. His eyes dart fore-and-aft in panic. The blazing glare at the back window forces him to draw his eyes away for fear of being blinded to the road ahead. The glare of the headlight slides from view, sending shadows dancing across the instrument panel as the motorcycle rounds the car and pulls alongside; whining gears shaving off speed to bring the biker once again level with the car's window—

A blaring harmonic horn announces the rapid appearance of banks of lights stabbing out of the storm, forcing the unsteady biker to accelerate as if drawn away by a sudden and powerful vacuum, miraculously avoiding what could have been a certain collision between the bike and a B-double truck. The blaring horn descends back into the sound of the storm and the Corvette's racing engine.

The professor notes the speedo is hovering around two hundred kilometres per hour, and yet seems motionless in the wake of the powerful motorbike.

He draws a palpitating breath in a valiant effort to recruit some semblance of relaxation, but a hundred yards ahead, more lights grow in the storm, very low to the road; stationary, yet closing fast.

'Shit, here we go.'

A gentle squeeze on the brake this time, and a triple fishtail, brings the bike into the Corvette's stationary beams, the powerful machine now lying helplessly on its side, the maniacal rider spread-eagled on the road beside it.

Unable to determine if the stricken perpetrator is moving or if rain splatter on the windscreen is creating the effect, the professor waits.

Possibly dead, he hopes with a hint of guilt.

Dismissing all instincts to drive away he steps from the car. Common sense tells him its madness, but when the rampant wind blows him to the biker's side without taking a single step, he has little choice in the matter. He can't help marvelling at the motorcyclist's resilience in standing up to the storm on an open motor bike.

As hoped, there is no sign of movement, and with pounding rain exploding against the biker's opaque face-shield, there is no way of telling if the man, or woman, is conscious. Blood seeping from beneath the damaged helmet is creating a pink smear, only to be washed away in an instant.

Crouching and leaning closer, Verg raises his voice to be heard above the deafening downpour. 'Hey, arse-hole, can you hear me?'

No response.

He looks over his shoulder at his waiting car and imagines the most sensible thing he can do right now is return to it.

What the hell am I doing? Do I really want to help this bastard?

The victim groans - a man's voice.

Cautiously rolling him onto his back, Verg reaches out to lift the faceplate to reveal who is behind it, vaguely wondering if it is someone he knows—

The rider's gloved hand shoots up and grabs his unlikely rescuer by the throat!

Held in the focus of headlight beams, rain smashing against bitumen, creates a white haze that all but hides the attacker from view as he begins struggling to his feet. Disadvantaged by gravity and lack of balance the biker loses his grip, allowing Verg to pull away from the stranglehold. He sprints to his car fumbling for keys in his pocket, wishing he'd left them sitting in the ignition for a quick getaway. He practically swings the door off the Corvette's hinges to reach the driver's seat, but drops the keys to the roadway—

Shit!

Rummaging beneath the vehicle on his hands and knees in almost pitch darkness, he can hear the assailant's running feet splashing toward him—

His hand touches the keys - he has them in his grasp as he retracts from beneath the car, but it's too late—

'This is a gun at your neck, Verg, don't make a damn move.'

He does the exact opposite, but the man's powerful clasp on his collar thwarts an escape. Before he knows it, he's being dragged to the middle of the road and dumped there. When he rolls over to face his attacker, he comes face to face with the muzzle of a silenced gun, pointing at arm's length. Believing he is about to die, Professor Verg searches for the words to plea for mercy; again too late.

The man's helmet takes on a new shine as the weapon spits out its projectile.

What little sound it makes is drowned by the storm.

He doesn't feel the bullet hit. There's no pain, just a cold sense of descending consciousness. He falls, hitting the drenched bitumen hard – face down. Rolling his head to the side in order to bring his mouth clear of the pooling rain; to breath, he hears the motorbike start up, idle, then power away.

He tastes the blood that's streaking from his mouth, sees it thinned by rain, and feels the sting in his side brought on by rain seeping into the open axe-wound. He knows he must have been hit by the bullet, but has no idea where.

The last thing he hears is the deluge exploding on the surface of the roadway; the last thing he sees, is a pinpoint of light bobbing toward him . . .

*

The frown on Josey's face wasn't promising. 'You l-look confused.'

'Were you shot or not?' Josey wanted to know.

'This only happened a few days ago, so, obviously not. I heard a shot, and the b-biker rode away. What else can I tell you?'

'You could tell me how this guy, the way you tell it, somehow magically managed to weather a storm that even your Corvette could hardly cope with.'

Verg put his head in his hands.

This was getting very uncomfortable for Josey. 'Are you okay there?'

The distressed prospective client lifted his head, displaying a deep furrow across his brow. 'I'm trying to explain. Do you want to hear my story or not?'

Josey softened his stance, but only a little. 'Go ahead.' *Make it quick,* he thought.

'Anyway, I came to the conclusion the attack must have had something to do with my r-research.'

Too early to make that call, Josey considered, *does this guy need my help, or is he trying to work it out for himself?*

Now he looked decidedly uncertain about continuing. He finally gathered himself and said, 'The rest g-gets even weirder.'

Josey figured his story was already weird, but wasn't convinced it was the kind of weird he liked, that aside he couldn't help wondering what his friend Belinda saw in him. His untidy dress-sense did little to provide an answer. This nervous and edgy man didn't seem her type. Now, in spite of the scientist being fifteen years her junior, they were engaged to be married, *bloody hell.*

Conversely, Verg didn't know what to make of his fiancée's choice of sleuths. Maybe it was Josey's illicit history with her, a detail she had courageously divulged before trundling him off to tell his story.

Touching the other side of forty, Josey had a calm assuredness about him, his casual persona gave a sense of experience that comes with maturity, but no amount of experience was going to help him deal with the professor's odd appearance and manner.

Although managing a neutral expression, Josey regrettably brought an involuntary negative tone to the surface. 'What exactly is it you want me to do?'

Verg was taken aback, so much so that his stutter worsened. 'I was t-told you *protect* p-people without involving the authorities. Have I b-been g-given a bum-steer?'

Josey humoured him amicably, 'Belinda's not that sort

of person; and you can trust that I'm here to help, simply because she asked me to. I'm not sure if she's told you, we go back a long way.'

Verg didn't know how to respond to Josey's watered down reminder of his adolescent romance with Belinda.

In fact, it was much more than a simple romance, Josey well remembered the intimate fling he'd had with the gorgeous Belinda in their last year of high-school, It had taken place beneath the grandstands during a game of handball that was being played in front of Josey's classmates. Mr Mathews, Belinda's maths teacher, showed up under the seats and literally caught them in the act. They were both expelled on their very last day of school.

Blissfully unaware of Josey's secret thoughts, Verg recommended his story. 'You'll need to hear this if you're to form any sort of picture of what this is about. As I've told you we're involved in matters relating to the atmosphere, a big part of that takes place in Antarctica.'

Josey lent back deep into his chair, signifying patience.

Verg wrung his hands, draining the blood from his knuckles. 'I arranged for an investigative team to go out on the ice and conduct some t-tests. Problem was - I made the mistake of not clearing it with Davenport, my boss . . .'

CHAPTER TWO
Discovery at the South Pole

Snow sweeps across a vast frozen prairie pushed by an unremitting wind, the sun, adhered to the horizon; perpetual day, a day bitterly cold like most days on the bottom of the globe.

Only sea-lions and penguins should consider an outing in such a time and place. Yet, two scientific researchers ignore this sensibility, clumsily reading instruments that are constantly being smothered by a fresh layer of snow. Their bright yellow helmets, gloves and snowsuits, accented by green emblems graced with the southern-cross stars, and the bold blue letters ASGF - identifies them as SciCore's southernmost Ground Force.

A needle swings off the face of a gauge one of the scientists is watching. He anxiously clears away ice with a gloved hand to make sure he isn't seeing things.

'You completely covered, Ray?' he calls.

His companion, who is working nearby, hears the

urgent comment from within his helmet. 'Andy, you got something?'

'That's a bloody understatement. See for yourself.'

Ray pads across the compacted ice to check the instrument he has been invited to see.

'It's right where Verg said it'd be,' Andy points out as he reaches him.

Ray lets out a whistle, portraying equal surprise at the reading. 'Right, I'll send it through.'

Without delay, and as quickly as the wind allows, he negotiates the slippery ice to reach a fabricated igloo. The tiny refuge is the only other feature on the ice that can be seen, and although the white limbo seems void of landmarks, he knows his exact position on the map. He knows that to the south-east stands a permanent base camp housing at least thirty other SciCore staff, none of whom have a clue about the tests the two men are conducting. Ray is also very aware that to the north in Australia, half way between the pole and the equator, Aaron Verg waits for confirmation. He understands just how anxious the scientist will be to hear the news, because Verg has not only backed the expedition with his own money, but done so without the knowledge of the company. This fact actually sits well with the *field op*, because support for the professor down the ranks is high. Even more satisfying is that Professor Verg has now been proven right, that is if *satisfying* is the right emotion for news this bad.

Within the Igloo he removes his helmet and outer jacket, allowing access to a cell phone he has tucked away in a warm pocket close to his chest. He thinks for a moment about what to write; clips the phone to a long distance transmitter that provides him with a keyboard connected to a large monitor; and removes his gloves to type:

Ray Helms reporting from ice-down. Spot-on professor, we've recorded a rapid 50% depletion.
100% increased stratospheric cloud cycle, springtime decrease highest on record.
Sorry, not exactly good news. RB.

Five thousand, four hundred and seventy nine kilometres north of the igloo, the tiered seats of SciCore's closed university are amassed with keen young minds, ready to absorb the latest in science. Professor Aaron Verg is barely more than a decade older than many of the young budding scientific minds in attendance. He could easily be mistaken for a student himself.

A massive flat-screen monitor covered in complex equations provides written depictions of the gas and chemical concoctions being discussed.

With his signature stutter shelved by his knowledge of the subject at hand, and the respect bestowed by his faithful followers, the professor pontificates on rights and wrongs of climate change, not the least concerning aspect, Earth's problems in the stratosphere.

'The polar vortex is assisted by the polar winter,' he tells them, demonstrating his point by drawing on a white board positioned beneath the large computer screen. 'Cold temperatures form inside the vortex, making these stratospheric clouds.'

He turns back to the class, checks they are keeping up and adds, 'Heterogeneous reactions convert the inactive chlorine and bromine, allowing the catalytic ozone destruction cycles. Ozone loss can be extremely rapid, this's the scary part.' Studying the blank faces, he waits for questions, but gets nothing.

Returning to his desk he begins packing papers into a small bag. 'No questions. Good, you must have all been paying attention.'

A question finally comes from a female student. 'Professor, can you tell us if you think the ozone holes are our fault?'

It's a loaded question. He closes his bag and heads for the door. 'If I told you what I think, you might repeat it, and I'd be out of a job.'

A gentle laugh resonates from the class.

As the professor makes it to the door, his cell phone vibrates in his coat pocket. He gestures for the class to hold while he checks the call; it's *Ray Helms*'s message from Antarctica.

Even from the back row, students can make out that the message is causing him to hesitate leaving. He turns back to the student who asked the cheeky question, holding her gaze with unnerving intensity. He can see that she thinks she's in trouble.

Glancing at the message again, then back to the girl, he makes a decision. Noticing she has a phone on her desk, he asks, 'What's your number?'

Becoming self-conscious, she nervously looks around at her peers.

Verg points his phone at her. 'Yes, Brook, I'm talking to *you*. Number please and I'll answer your question.'

'Speak up Brookie!' a male voice shouts from the back row.

The class swivel their heads on mass, and on seeing the outspoken young man preparing to place the girl's number into his phone, they let out a chorus of hoots and howls.

To ease Brook's embarrassment, the professor walks up closer and acquires her number in private, after which he forwards a text message—

If nature gets its way,
Antarctica will be the least
of our problems.

'Does that answer your question?'

When she lifts her face from the glow of the phone he sees surprise - and a smidgen of confusion. 'Have fun with that,' he tells her.

On recommencing his exit without explanation, the class erupts with a choir of questions, aimed at both the girl and the professor. He motions for them to hold it down and announces, 'As you've probably guessed, our topic for tomorrow will be based on Brook's text.'

The class voices mixed approval and disapproval. Brook's intention to ask another question is thwarted when he raises a hand to encourage her to hold onto the thought - 'Tomorrow.'

He gives the class a dismissive wave and leaves them to mob the recipient on tomorrow's hot topic, and to discuss the implications amongst themselves . . .

*

Professor Verg could see that the detective was finding it

hard to equate any of this to someone wanting him dead.

Josey didn't want to sound cynical, and he knew he'd have to explain his decision to Belinda Baxter when he spoke to her later, but that's just the way it was. He didn't get as far as informing Verg he wouldn't be taking the case, the unlikely professor inexplicably spat the dummy. 'I knew this w-would be a waste of time,' he grumbled as he stormed from the office.

When the coast was clear, Josey's partner Maxine slipped her head through the door to have her say. 'That went well,' she said, '*not.*'

As he punched a number into the phone on his desk, Josey unashamedly gave her the key reason the case was on the nose. 'Max, he needs to talk to the police. Maybe then I can take a look at it.'

'Hmmm, might be a good idea to talk to Belinda before *he* does.'

Josey raised his index finger to have Max hold as his call connected. 'Belinda, Hi –'

Maxine swivelled in the doorway and left, and now of course would come her boss's unenviable task of explaining himself to the one partner he had never really gotten over, Belinda Baxter, his first love. Maxine knew a lot of personal stuff about Josey; she had been with him for more than a decade. They were almost able to read each other's minds.

In less than twelve hours, *both* their minds would be changed about the case not going ahead.

CHAPTER THREE
The Case as told to Molly

From the couch where he had been chilling, telling the Professor Verg story to his thirteen year old daughter, Josey opened his eyes and saw she was screwing up her face. 'What's that look for?'

Molly's frown deepened. 'I'm trying to understand why you're telling me about the case if you're not planning to take it.'

'Who *says* I'm not?'

She was considering herself lucky that her stepfather saw fit to tell her anything at all; in fact this was the first time he had ever given in to her pestering about his work.

He eventually—and reluctantly—agreed to talk about this particular case on the basis she had once met his long-time friend, Belinda Baxter.

'So you *are* taking the case.'

He feigned defeat. 'Belinda can be very persuasive.'

Molly grinned knowingly. 'She's very pretty isn't she.'

Josey's wife slid into the room and folded her arms, waiting to see how he responded to their daughter's emotive question.

He caught Rebecca's eye, responding with dangerous honesty. 'No argument from me.'

'Hmmm,' her lips curled, considering him from the corner of her eye.

Mother and daughter were aware of his adolescent affair, albeit with all mention of the specifics omitted. They were eighteen at the time. Rebecca understood there might have been some intimacy going on; she probably would have been surprised if there weren't. Her quirky expression enlightened Molly as to the comfort and openness her parents had with each other.

Josey kept his eyes on Molly's mother as he continued. 'Although we've stayed in touch on and off since school, on the day she rang and asked for my help we hadn't spoken to each other in a couple of years.'

Leaving her husband and daughter to continue their quality-time together, Rebecca disentangled her folded arms and glided from the room, holding a smirk.

Molly's eyes followed until she was out of sight, then, turned back to her dad as he returned to the story.

'On the face of it, her request for help had seemed reasonable enough. It wasn't until her fiancé came to see me that I considered not taking his case. At first it wasn't clear what the case was really about. Between you and me, I can't see what she sees in him. The age difference is something like fifteen years. She's *my* age, right.'

Molly rolled her eyes. 'Do I detect a hint of jealousy?'

Josey's daughter was growing up. She was growing into a very attractive young woman with a personality to match. She had Josey's height, placing her a few inches taller than her mother.

'Anyway, none of that seems to worry Belinda. She made this plainly obvious when she rang. *I really need your help* she says - you know, sounding quite stressed. Without her saying so, I knew the call was about my refusal to take the case. So, I tell her, *I'm sorry; Aaron's case is for the Cops*. I thought that would get me off the hook. I was wrong. *I'm not buying that*, she tells me, but hey, *I'm not calling to bust—*'

Molly recognised he was about to say *bust your balls*.

He faltered and put it another way. 'She wasn't calling because she was angry; she was calling to invite me to dinner.'

'Oooooow, dinner with the beautiful Belinda.' Molly became all artificially serious. 'Don't worry, Dad, your secret's safe with me.'

Her reaction raised a grin; not being her biological father made him more like a friend, and less like a parent. 'Don't be an idiot young lady;' he quipped playfully, 'the invitation is with her and her fiancé. Can I go on?'

Keeping up the charade, she took a quick glance over her shoulder and back again. 'Of course,' she whispered.

'Thank you.' He shook his head in mock disbelief. 'As I was saying, an invitation to dinner wasn't exactly what I was expecting. I told her so. Obviously it was another attempt to change my mind about taking the case. What better way than face-to-face. I knew I was walking into a sticky web, but what's a man to do when a friend invites you to dinner.'

'So you're going.'

'I am, but I'm thinking it could turn into a complete *railroad*.'

'Can I come?'

'So you can keep a check on me, not a chance.'

'You're treading a fine-line, Dad.'

She really was growing up. Of course the story that Molly was being told had sensitive issues that had to be omitted, such as the ozone depletion, and the company secrets. He had only told his step daughter the story at Rebecca's request, a way of connecting with his rapidly changing daughter.

Josey diplomatically sent her on her way to help her mother in the kitchen. He needed to get ready and only had an hour and a half to get to Belinda's property. If Josey thought Verg's story was already strange, it was about to get a whole lot more so. The extent of its eccentricity would turn out to be way beyond his expectation.

CHAPTER FOUR
The plot thickens

Set on five and a half acres on the outskirts of the city, Belinda's ranch-style home was three country miles away from her nearest neighbour. She used the land for nothing more than solitude, a place to rest and clear-the-cobwebs. It was mandatorily surrounded on all four sides by a double-strand barbed-wire fence, intended to confine livestock that in this case had never set foot.

Her time of peace in this place was passing. A web of fear was spinning inward, seeping into the calm that she once knew. A lot of things were causing this disquiet, chief among them her job. The problem wasn't the work, it was the people. Not all, but some. She began to see them for what they really were, enemies of her fiancé.

Painfully aware Aaron unintentionally lacked social graces and at times professional ethics, Belinda tried her best to convince him to be careful when speaking publicly. He wouldn't listen. It was the attack on him that finally frightened her the most.

This wasn't the first time Josey had visited her property, but it was the first time since Belinda took up with Verg. It was the first time he would see the two of them together.

He stepped onto the veranda, greeted by an open screen-door held wide by his very anxious friend. She threw her arms around him as easily as any friend might, but her body against his was not the same as hugging an aunt, or a sister. He let her think that's how things were, but wasn't sure she was buying it.

Slightly shorter than him, Belinda looked a very comfortable fit; their casual dress sense was enough to create the illusion the two of them might possibly be partners.

At most times, she filled out her outfits in all the right places, yet, it was her fine facial features that demanded attention from all new admirers. Lengthy honey blond hair cascaded in large wavy folds to her shoulders. Her brown eyes, by any measure were large and truthful, and lips, a natural blush.

These were the superficial things that Josey saw in her, but there was much more to this woman than that.

'You're looking well,' she told him when they'd finished hugging.

'You too,' he returned with no shadow of doubt.

She knew what he meant.

She looked past him and took in the expanse of her property appreciatively. 'It's a nice evening; we can take a walk around the property if you like.'

'Sure.'

Early dusk was making way for a moonlit night. They

stepped onto a veranda, momentarily holding hands.

He liked the feeling of being around Belinda. At school they had often walked and held hands; and much more. He wanted to again, but he knew it wasn't about to happen, but it was still nice to afford the luxury of imagining, and remembering.

'Where's Aaron?' he asked as nonchalantly as he could.

'He'll be along; I wanted to talk to you about a few things first, on our own if that's all right.'

'Sure,' he accepted, yet unavoidably wondering why.

She shook her head despondently and asked, 'Did Aaron mention *Boz Shannon* when he spoke to you?'

'No, but judging by your tone I'm guessing he should have.'

They stepped down onto a gravel pathway that wound around from the front of the house, the crisp crunch the only sound other than the occasional cry of a late flying black-crow.

In beginning to reveal her story, her light smile wasn't projecting happy thoughts. 'Shannon is a journalist that I work with at *Easi.*'

Josey knew, *EASI*, which Verg told him stood for; *Earth and Atmospheric Sciences Institute* – is a journal for the world of environmental sciences, the rag that Belinda had been with for about eight years, working as a digital layout artist, having very early on taken to computers comfortably.

'He's somewhat of a climate-change activist himself,' she said, 'and a dog-with-a-bone when it comes to a good story. Not one of Aaron's favourite people you might say.' She took a folded document from a pocket in her

Jodhpurs and handed it to Josey. 'I borrowed this from the editor's desk.'

He unfolded it and read out loud.

'*Research Scientist, Professor Aaron Verg, made claims today that Man's Carbon Footprint is not where we should be looking for the real reason Earth's ozone is depleting. He claims the depletion, along with Climate change, is just another one of nature's natural cycles—*'

'That's the gist of it,' she offered.

They left the gravel and continued their walk on the manicured lawns that stretched to the barbed-wire fence.

'Are you thinking Shannon is a possible suspect?'

'No, not as such,' she told him as she dabbed at her moist eyes. 'But I believe his column would have contributed if I'd let it.'

'*If you'd let it*?' He handed her back the document, but she gestured for him to hold onto it.

'I'd like you to read the rest later if you wouldn't mind.'

'How'd this guy get hold of the story?'

'From one of his students at the SciCore campus university I'm told.' She tilted her head. 'Okay, I admit what Aaron said to them was fairly cryptic, but ostensibly it said the same thing. I suspect Shannon just took the liberty of filling in the gaps.'

'Does Shannon know about the attack?'

She nodded. 'Let me fill you in on his reaction when he saw Aaron right after. It'll give you a heads up on where the little rat is coming from . . .'

*

Entering his cluttered office in a hurry, Shannon heads straight for the computer. He instinctively senses Belinda's presence at the door. Without turning he says, 'Your boy has really flipped his lid this time, Baxter.' He cracks his knuckles and starts typing, adding to the text that was already sitting on the screen before he sat down.

Belinda's dislike for the little balding journalist visibly deepens. He points at the screen, inviting her to come take a look at the first paragraph of his story.

One glance raises her sudden urge to push his face into the keyboard. Instead she reasons, 'you do realise this sort of rubbish jeopardises Aaron's safety.'

'He should've thought of that before shooting his mouth off in front of a room full of students.'

Scooping his phone off the desk he brings a video to its screen. 'It's on camera my-love,' he chuckles. 'Has your guy not heard of mobile phones?'

She leans in close enough to focus on the tiny movie of Aaron speaking to the students at the university. The footage shows a group of students surrounding a young female whose phone had become the centre of attention. They can be heard discussing Verg's cryptic text and forming their own damaging opinions about it.

Close enough to the computer for Shannon to smell her hair, she senses him subtly edging in – and snaps. 'When you're quite finished,' she says turning to look him in the eye.

Caught-out, he adjusts the personal space between them. 'Wow, such aggression.'

Rising chatter lifts in the outer office.

They both turn in unison to see Aaron standing in the

mouth of the lift looking like he's been through a war zone.

'Now *there's* a picture,' he observes with an annoying giggle.

Ignoring Shannon's far too accurate depiction she makes a hasty exit, pacing over to where Aaron is holding open the lift door with his shoulder, embarrassed by the attention he's getting.

'Can-we get out of here,' he pleads.

She thinks to abide, but notices Shannon enjoying the show from the protection of his glass cage. 'Hold that thought, professor,' she suggests as she leaves him.

Re-entering the reporter's office with the demeanour of a storm trooper, Belinda finds the annoying reporter leaning back in his chair wearing a Cheshire-grin.

Her raised foot launches his caster-chair across the room, taking it to an abrupt stop against a filing cabinet.

Heads rise in the outer office.

Shannon's eyes are popping out of his head; she's now helping herself to his keyboard, and his cell phone.

'What th' – Hey!'

He's complaint falls on deaf ears, jettisoning him from his chair to prevent the intrusion.

'Don't even think about touching me, Shannon.'

If this isn't a big enough slap in his face, he sees on the screen that she has just deleted the video file from his phone and the story from his computer.

'Too late, Baxter, I've already sent the story to Gerard at the Herald.'
She explodes with rage, her eyes ablaze with a warning. 'Call him! Do it now, Shannon! Or I promise I'll see you're sued for aiding and abetting an attempted murder.'

The reporter's mooned eyes expel fear that she might not be bluffing; her fiancé clearly appears to be beaten up. 'What the hell happened to him?'

Without further argument she leaves, grabbing her bag from a desk in the outer office on her way to help her man back into the hijacked elevator, which has begun pinging impatiently.

The bothersome journalist nervously floats his hands above the keys, ready to continue his story, but suddenly loses all determination to ignore Baxter's warning.

Before the lift doors have mercifully wiped him from view, Belinda recognises her threat has sunk in . . .

CHAPTER FIVE
A moonlight chat

Under the light of a full moon, they circled the property for fifteen minutes, returning to the house to sit side by side on the expansive veranda. As they looked out across the moonlit grass paddock, Belinda became very distant, appearing anything but happy.

'It sounds like he took your threat seriously.'

'He was pulling my chain. It's something he does. He hadn't even been in touch with the Herald.'

'I'm surprised someone hasn't.'

Something had her rattled, something other than the altercation with the reporter, 'What is it?'

Tears freshened. 'Aaron's boss has gone missing.'

Josey responded with a touch of impatience. 'That might have been a good place to start if you don't mind my saying.'

'I was afraid to mention it earlier.'

'Why?'

'Because he and Aaron had a big argument.'

Josey began to wonder if he was getting through to his friend. 'Tell me about the argument.'

Feeling reprimanded she released a tense sigh. 'It was at the research centre, just after he leaked information about what's happening in Antarctica . . .

An ominous storm barrels across the research centre, turning night to day, an unnatural twilight, interrupted only by the electrical light show that randomly reveals SciCore's innocuous seal.

Tucked away from this atmospheric turbulence, Ral Davenport stands at a broad window with his back to the room, studying the storm's intensity. In his mind he rehearses what to say to his young friend, how to phrase it. Once facing him, his resolve to *spell it out* falters, his course of action unclear. Verg's scruffy appearance stands at odds with the boardroom, and the director himself. Their clashing personas are as polarising as the subject at hand.

Davenport drains the remnants of his whisky glass and moves to a wall mounted mini-bar, camouflaged behind a shelf of neatly stacked scientific journals. With his glass replenished, showing no hurry to continue the conversation, he returns to his desk, sits and peers into the potentially calming drink, finally saying, 'You've put SciCore's credibility in jeopardy with this stunt.'

In his early fifties, Ral Davenport projects the persona of a very successful man. His credentials, etched into marble on his desk, suggest permanency.

RAL DAVENPORT

Manager - SciCore Australia

The sound of the milling ice cracking in the warmth of his glass somehow characterizes the rift that holds the two men at enmity, a reminder of their differing opinion on what climate change is doing at the poles.

'We can be thankful this hasn't gotten to the general media.'

'Maybe it should.'

'For Pete's sake, Aaron, the last thing we need is to be drawn into the Global Climate Change row. Local protesters are already heading that way.'

'Then let's t-talk to them, explain why the twenty-twenty-five emissions deadline is impossible.'

'You don't know that.'

'I know a deadline won't help if the alternative happens.'

'Stop!' his boss shouted angrily, 'The government would screw us. They want climate models. I haven't got them, and neither do you.'

Davenport isn't making Aaron's day, but the young man realises his boss is right about the missing *models*, forcing acceptance of the criticism. In spite of this he persists with his argument. 'The p-possibility our carbon footprint isn't the only villain, is reason enough to continue stratospheric tests. If nature d-does its thing before we do, there'll be no turning back.'

'Are you hearing yourself? That argument sits both sides of the fence. All the protesters hear is that you deny climate change.'

'I've never said that.'

'I know, but try and explain that to them. You'll get

crucified. Let it go. For us, it's very easy to appreciate depletion only forms in extremely cold conditions like Antarctica, but to try and suggest otherwise would seem farcical to those people.'

'Only a f-few decades ago it was considered farcical in the Arctic.'

Davenport has no intention of giving in. 'The North Pole isn't the goddamned equator.'

Aaron moves despondently to the window and looks over the research centre's well-kept gardens. Below, he sees people in white protection gear presumably spraying trees with some sort of pesticide. Their activity is not where his mind is. Undaunted, he pushes on with his argument. 'I've never said it'll happen; only that it could. These naturally occurring adverse cycles have happened before.'

'Okay, smart-arse, We all know what drives these cycles. And by *we,* I *include you.*'

'Yet here we are, in the m-midst of a modern day upheaval, a cycle that's out of step, destabilising our climate - rapidly.'

'Caused by us, Aaron - until proven otherwise; the people who pay our bills believe we're to blame – and until they change their minds, we believe that too.' Davenport releases a long frustrated breath. 'Natural or not our hands are tied. We can't go near the stratosphere, and that's that.'

'We may have hell to pay if we don't.'

His boss's shoulders visibly slump, done arguing.

At the window, Aaron's eyes fall on the usual small band of protesters gathered at the other side of the security gate. The storm has eased to a splattering of light rain. A flock of Pigeons released from a parked van, rise and drift like a puff of grey smoke toward the research centre. A few feathered allies of the protesters land on the sill outside Ral's office, where mounds of droppings denote their previous perching platform; innocent messengers doing the bidding of a small unhappy mob called, *CorpCause*, their aim being to target Corporate Corruption. Placards held by the protesters, too distant to read, are alternatively replaced by tiny notes born around the necks of the carrier pigeons, messages of mistrust and outrage.

Ral settles in at Aaron's side, almost reading his mind at seeing the winged envoy outside the window, their sarcastic cargo clearly aimed at the young scientist.

'I g-guess I asked for this,' Aaron admits.

Unable to differentiate himself, Ral moderates his tone, bringing to mind that the young scientist has recently had a close encounter with cancer. 'I'll smooth things with Sleeman,' he offers, 'you deserve that much.'

Aaron realises *smoothing things* is what his boss does best. 'Fine.'

'Promise me one thing. No more talking about this with students.'

Aaron shows little emotion as he walks from the room, leaving Davenport to wonder if it will even be possible to defuse Director Sleeman, SciCore's Top-Dog . . .

*

It wasn't hard for Josey to understand the rift between Aaron Verg and his boss, Depletion of the ozone layer at the South Pole had been known of and spoken about in the press for years, and the cause of it argued over for just as long.

He was beginning to think Verg may easily have made a lot of enemies with his outspoken beliefs; these days, anything that didn't point at man's carbon footprint being the cause of climate change, was politically unpopular.

'I must admit I can see why blaming nature for climate change would be problematic for Aaron.'

'Maybe it is and maybe it isn't. But, he says he'd hate to be the one to have to say he was wrong the day the shit hits the fan.'

On the surface, Ral Davenport's alleged disappearance didn't exonerate him as a suspect, but Josey knew only too well not to jump to any quick conclusions, 'When did Davenport go missing?'

Her expression was weighty. 'I got a call from him here at the house last night; — Aaron was in the shower at the time . . .'

*

'It's me,' says Ral's voice in her ear.

His tenor carries a level of uneasiness.

'Something's wrong,' she guesses, 'I can hear it in your voice.'

His lack of response worries her all the more. 'What's happened?'

She hears him take a cavernous breath.

'*I've* received a threat,' he tells her nervously.

'Oh-my-god.'

'It was a warning to shut Aaron up or next time he wouldn't be so lucky – and I'd be dead if I go anywhere near police.'

'Or end up dead if you don't,' she warns in a shaky voice.

'I didn't know what else to do, so I've told Sleeman about it.'

'What did *he* say?'

'He said the company will handle it.'

'Meaning what?'

'Maybe they'll go to police, I've no idea. He said I should lay low and not to get involved. Make myself scarce.'

'Ral, I'm frightened, this is getting really scary.'

'Tell me about it.'

'Do your family know?'

'Yeah, the letter arrived at Margaret's place'

'God, they must be terrified.'

'They are, but hey listen, I know you've been to see your detective friend, my advice is let him poke around if he's game – make sure you tell him to be super careful, these people are dangerous . . .'

*

'He hung up and that was the last time I've spoken with him.'

'You said Aaron was in the shower when Ral called, have you told him?'

'Of course; he rang Ral back straight away but got no answer. On top of that, No one at the research centre has seen him since.'

Josey faltered. 'So now Davenport's been threatened.' This still didn't exonerate him in Josey's mind, but he had to concede, the vote of confidence and the warning went a long way in suggesting he was innocent of wrong doing.

'I'm really worried, Cam.'

Josey recognised a deep fear, something much more substantial than impartial empathy for Ral's safety.

She sensed he'd noticed and let out a stress filled sigh that was laden with divulgement. 'We were an item, Ral and me; it was before Aaron.'

Josey's lips parted as if to express an obvious thought. It showed on his face as clearly as if the words were scribed on his forehead.

'I know what you're thinking,' she told him, 'but you're wrong. I know you; everyone is a suspect until proven otherwise. Do me a favour and cross Ral off your list, this has nothing to do with him being jealous.'

Josey took in a sharp breath. 'If you say so, but forgive me if I don't dismiss the idea just yet.'

Her lips curled in the corners and she patted his arm in a gesture of understanding and support. 'Anyway, Aaron feels Ral's call proves whoever is doing this is acting directly against the whole research centre.' She once again read Josey's expression. 'You don't agree?'

'I'm not sure what to agree with just yet; the whole thing seems a little cryptic at the moment.'

'Cryptic is the perfect word, you won't believe the rest of what I'm about to tell you.' She stood and paced along the veranda.

Josey noted her body language; arms folded, eyes searching as if recollections were floating out there on the property somewhere.

'I've been hesitant to mention this because it may have

nothing to do with anything.'

In Josey's experience, when a client says *that*, it usually means it's more important than realised. 'Just go ahead and tell me.'

'Aaron's been having hallucinations, recurring, about a Monk. Dreams or hallucinations; perhaps visions, I'm not sure what the hell they are at times.' She took a deep nervous breath. 'The motor bike attack was part of it; I know he told you about the biker because I told him to. And just after that, on his way through the city, he says he couldn't remember how long he'd been stuck in a massive traffic jam. He says that, *somehow*, he had lost an hour of time . . .'

A police officer making her way between rows of cars, pauses to inspect Verg's smashed window.

'What's the holdup, officer?' Aaron shouts above the downpour before she has a chance to speak.

'I might ask you the same question,' she counters noting his condition.

'I'm fine,' he insists. 'P-picked up a stone.'

She considers his explanation and his question, then tells him, 'There's been a serious accident, people are trapped, you'll be here for quite a while, please don't think about getting out of your vehicle.' She continues on her way, walking between the rows of cars that are quickly stacking up behind.

The officer is right about being stuck here Aaron decides. Beyond the rain drenched windshield he picks up the rippling neon sign of *The Coffee Grinder*. Satisfied the diligent police officer has moved far enough away, and despite her instruction, he leaves the car parked in the traffic jam and makes his way across the street.

Getting out of his vehicle isn't making him any wetter than he already is; his clothing is wet through to his underwear, his excessively disordered appearance gains a few strange glances though.

The door to the coffee shop beckons, a place out of the rain and a bathroom to check his injury, ring out his clothes and have a nice warm coffee - if there's time.

A huge crowd has formed a ring on the street twenty deep. Managing to break free at the back of the throng, he finds himself hard up against the window of the Coffee Grinder. Inside the aquarium like sanctuary, the housed patrons can be seen engaging in soundless conversations, which prompt him to call Belinda before heading in. He's in the middle of telling her about the accident and the holdup when directly opposite, where his Corvette is still stranded, a van pulls out of a parking space and makes a left hand turn away from the gridlock, sending Josey into a bolt to his car to take advantage of the vacant space.

'I need to go; I've got a parking spot – right – bye.' He'd made no mention of the attack; that could wait until he got to her at the magazine.

The deep tone of the Corvette's powerful engine rumbles to life, turning curious heads, continuing to attract attention as they see it manoeuvre across the concrete median strip in a hail of sparks, positioning and slipping into the vacant spot.

Leaving the parked vehicle he heads back toward the coffee shop, from where he will be able to keep watch on the traffic. Ignoring the focus of onlookers, including the lady police officer, who he notes has also seen his unorthodox driving, he loses no time melting into the crowd in the belief she may want to talk to him about his driving technique, and his disobedience.

Having lost sight of him, the constable hovers over the Corvette, thinking about writing up a citation. Noticing the rubbernecks have now made *her* the centre of attention, she decides to move on.

The automatic doors of the cafe slide apart, cushioning closed behind him. Inside, there is the relative quiet of human conversation. The coffee house is almost full. As he passes the barista, the look that the fellow gives him speeds up his plan to make it to the bathroom.

One look in the mirror reveals just why people were staring at him when he came into the shop. Blood is running from his nose and he has a dark bruise on his forehead. His shirt has a partly washed away blood stain over where the axe had inflicted a shallow flesh wound. He slips out of his soaked jacket and shirt and does his best to wash away the blood. The singlet, he throws in the bin, then uses the blower to try and take some of the moisture from the shirt. He does the same with his trousers after discarding his underpants. Casting his mind back to the attack, he recalls the man with the gun, and the gunshot. He couldn't remember looking for the wound earlier, but he must have. In any event, with his shirt off he decides to have another look, but finds nothing – not even evidence of blood, other than that on his hip from the axe.

While placing his shirt and jacket back on he hears a noise in another part of the bathroom, presumably made by someone who has been there all along. It places him on high alert.

A man's reflection slides into the steamed up mirror

above the sink. 'It looks like you have had a very bad time,' the voice says from behind while moving past.

Asian, Aaron guesses. He turns and catches a fleeting glimpse of him walking away, enough to recognize he is oddly dressed. A moment later he hears a faucet start at another sink around the corner.

He dries up on the rotating towel and returning to the mirror, combs his hair with his fingers. Thankfully the nosebleed seems to have stopped—

'Would you consider joining an old man for a cup of coffee?'

Surprised he still has company, Aaron turns to face a little old Chinese man dressed like a Monk, smiling.

Two minutes later Aaron is at a table near the window, pleased the Monk is getting all the stares.

'My name is *Zan*,' he says. 'I hope you will forgive me for this unexpected intrusion, because I have something very important to tell you.' His speech is slow and deliberate, as if to be fully absorbed by the listener.

'Have we met – Zan, is it?'

'We have not – *Professor Verg*.'

'Oh, I see, you k-know who I am.'

'Yes, I am aware that you are an environmental research scientist.'

Given the altercation on the highway, Aaron is well wired to recognise stranger danger. He looks around the coffeehouse for any sign of unsavoury characters who might be working in cahoots. Common sense tells him no one could possibly know he would be coming to the shop, he didn't even know himself. But logic doesn't explain how the monk somehow gained prior knowledge of who Aaron is, and where he would be. Of course his driving style may have attracted his attention.

Dramatically, the monk leans forward and lowers his voice, his body language encouraging Aaron to move closer to hear what he has to say. 'In Tibet,' he says intently, 'a brilliant Archaeologist has made a startling discovery.' He snaps from his cogitative state. 'You must understand, following an inherent intuition that took her to the very place she would make her discovery, to the very place she knew to find the *exact* thing she had been looking for, she was faced with great opposition.'

Aaron can't even imagine why his new found friend would think he'd be interested in buying into his story, and asks distractedly, 'And what was this, *startling* discovery?'

The professor's indifference raises a smile in the old man, his fixed gaze suggesting he may not want to be too specific in answering the question.

Aaron adds flatly, 'Who exactly *are* you?'

Ignoring the dismissal, and the doubt, the monk tells him, 'Who I am does not yet matter. But what I am telling you is of the *utmost* importance, your work may be about to take a very dangerous and perplexing turn.' He slides something across the table that has been kept cupped beneath his palm, slowly removing his hand to reveal it.

'What's this?' Aaron asks studying the stone medallion left sitting on the table.

'It is a very special amulet, very similar to an ancient Buddhist symbol of protection, but with a much more profound meaning.'

Aaron turns the amulet over. The opposite side presents a stylised embossed eye, as meaningless to him as the symbols carved into its face.

'If you heed my advice, and go to the Tibetan Plateau; and find the archaeologist working in a place called Kailash, secrets and discoveries will unfold. She knows you are coming, because I have told her so. She will immediately recognise you from this amulet, which you must keep with you at all times. Her name is *Lui Jie.*'

'You say that like you've already decided I'm going.'

He reaches across the table and grasps Aaron's hand. 'The choice is yours, but you must be warned, you have many enemies who will stop at nothing to try and prevent your intuitions from ever reaching fruition. Like you, this young woman has also been threatened.'

Aaron is fairly sure he didn't mention being attacked, although his appearance isn't making it hard to guess.

'I'm sorry, I must leave,' he's told as the monk begins to stand with considerable effort.

Aaron slides the amulet back across the table before the old man even has a chance to achieve full stature. 'You keep this. I have n-no interest in religion or mysticism. I'm certain it means more to you than to me.'

Disappointed and unable to find argument, the Monk reluctantly watches his companion walk away to place an indiscriminate amount of money on the counter, and then exit the shop.

Saddened, the monk retrieves the amulet, places it into his shoulder bag and shuffles across to the attendant at the till, where he's told, 'No need, the other gentleman has already paid. Looks like you're in luck,' he says as he reaches beneath the counter. 'Perhaps you can give him his change.'

He studies the small amount of money that's been

placed on the counter then turns to the busy street. 'I may not be seeing him again,' he says, eventually turning back to present the honest young man with a warm smile. 'I think perhaps you have gained a well-earned tip.'

The bemused barista returns the money to the till, keeping his eye on the strange old monk as he leaves the shop, fascinated by his patience with the gathered crowd that are beginning to jostle for standing rights on the pavement . . .

Imparting all this information seemed to make Belinda uncomfortable. Several moments of uncertainty passed before she finally met Josey's eyes again. 'When he tells me about the dreams, I can see it's stressful.' Emotional tears spilled onto her cheeks. 'To be honest, I think it embarrasses him.'

'I'm really sorry, Bel, I understand this must be very upsetting.'

She waved the suggestion away. 'I let him think I accept they are just dreams. But it's not always easy.' She went to say something else, but had to turn away to avoid being seen shedding more tears.

Josey felt like a cad. 'We can pick this up later if you'd like.'

'No, I'm fine. It's important you appreciate the way he is. You'll never be able to help him if you don't.'

Belinda's story wasn't completely gelling for Josey, if it hadn't been for the account Verg gave him at their first meeting about the shooting, and the fact he hadn't been shot at all, both the biker and Monk incidents might conceivably be real; was Belinda telling him that they weren't?

On her return from pacing, Josey pushed out of the couch as she drew close. He opened his arms and she fell into them with ease.

Although not meaning to press quite so closely to his body, it instantly evoked the memory of how exciting it had been making love to him in the high school gym – the very first time for both of them.

He felt her ease away, and knew what she was doing, welcomed it, because he could easily have made love to her right there and then if she'd stayed against him.

Their choices were made, whether or not they would be regretted remained to be seen.

He forced himself to relinquish the thought. 'I have to ask—and this is just me turning over every leaf—can you be absolutely certain Aaron meeting this Monk actually happened?'

She sobbed against his chest. 'You may not want to help me when I explain what's real and what isn't.'

She had Josey's complete interest now. 'Tell me anyway,' he insisted.

She considered his well-founded stance and said, 'I will, but please don't judge him, will you promise me that?'

'Yes, of course. I promise . . .'

*

CHAPTER SIX
Dreams and Hallucinations

Belinder's free hand irons across his chest, playfully drawing him into a release of sensual tensions.

Throughout, light dances across the walls and ceiling of their bedroom, driven by the wild electrical storm raging outside.

Exhausted, staring vacantly at the ever shifting mosaic patterns, Aaron's mind appears to be drifting elsewhere.

Propped on an elbow at his side, Belinda studies his preoccupied expression and heavily breaths the words, 'Hey; a penny for your thoughts.'

Her beautiful face, moulded in the flickering light, draws him back from wherever he's been. 'Sorry, *what*?'

'You were miles away just now. What were you thinking about?'

He contemplates his answer while regaining his breath, looking set to tell her, yet closing in on recovery begins a backpedal. 'Are you sure you want to hear this?'

'I wouldn't ask if I didn't,' she tells him with a scowl.

He lifts from the pillow, and with lips barely separated from hers he whispers, 'I can't get the monk out of my head.'

Belinda raises herself on an outstretched arm, her palm pressed into the mattress. 'Not in the last hour I hope.'

A light laugh escapes as he drops back to the pillow.

Her playful eyes, wide and framed by the untethered locks of her hair, demand he talk to her.

Instead, he tries to pull her close in hope of a reprise, but her other palm gently presses against his bare chest in denial. 'Speak.'

He turns away his head, conjuring the distracting memory. 'It was the night of the attack. While I was lying on the road bleeding, after the gun went off, I heard the bike start up and drive away. But then, the light I told you about – it was him, torch in hand. The whole thing was bloody surreal, the storm was going off, yet he just ignored it - like it was nothing. How he got there is a mystery. I didn't see or hear any other vehicle, only the m-motor bike as it sped away. He was on his knees, telling me not to worry—

'The next thing, I'm in my car, stuck in a traffic jam, in the city – I looked at my watch; I'd lost nearly an hour.'

Her face carries no doubt, but he feels it should. 'I'm not sure if he was *really* there,' he says hesitantly.

'You were saved by someone, why not him?'

'Don't do that, sweetie,' he pleads.

'Do what?'

'Humour me – you know damn well I was still an hour away from meeting the guy for the first time; at the coffee shop.'

'Of course, I'm sorry.'

Her answer just makes him feel worse. 'So now I dream about people I've never met. Is that what's happening?'

She made no attempt to answer . . .

*

Belinda's account went some of the way to explaining what was real and what wasn't, but not all the way. Josey said, 'So by the time he gets to the coffee shop, he has no recollection of the monk being present at the attack.'

'That's what I say, his recollections are off kilter, and he's aware of it. I just know the confusion frightens him.'

Josey thought for a moment and said, 'Don't take this the wrong way, but I don't think we can blindly accept all of what he says. I mean, can we even be sure the monk *is* real?'

Her face reddened as her eyes began to well, wrestling with the answer. Cameron's scepticism about the dreams and the monk had become a welcome grounding, but he needed to know it wasn't all fantasy. 'I wasn't sure at first, but believe me, the monk *is* real,' she insisted in frustration.

He took her in his arms, more cautiously this time. 'Hey, we'll work this out—'

'Should I be w-worried about you two?' The professor was at the wire-door holding it open.

Josey was unavoidably taken aback by his strange apparel. He seemed grossly underdressed in the circumstances. The budgie smugglers and damp singlet, topped off with leather *flip-flops* seemed totally out of place. The swimmers were definitely odd, since there was no beach for ten miles, and the property had no pool inside or out.

He reasoned Aaron must have just stepped out from a soak in a spa.

Josey wasn't sure what to say in response to Verg's opening statement, because on a certain level there was truth in the suggestive comment. His immediate and unrehearsed reaction was a slightly mechanical laugh.

Belinda got up and gave her man a peck on the lips as they passed each other at the door. She returned with three beers even before the flyscreen completely closed.

'Here! For god-sake get these into you and relax – Professor, sit.' She nudged him into the cane couch opposite Aaron and slid in at his side, giving him a light pat on his bare knee.

They were an odd couple Josey decided.

Aaron pushed back some beer and opened with, 'So, what can I tell you t-that I haven't already?'

'Well, there is one thing I've wanted to understand about you and the company. Am I right in saying you have some sort of hold over them?'

'That's a p-pretty c-cheeky question, Detective,' he said glancing at Belinda with a grin before answering. 'But you're right; I sort of do and don't, it's over a satellite that I designed; a meteorological type, intended to monitor ozone in the upper atmosphere.'

'Do you hold the patent?'

'No.'

'Who does?'

'The founder of the p-parent company in Boston, Jack Pearson.'

'Pearson came to the rescue when Aaron couldn't raise

the money,' Belinda offered. 'In the states they see Aaron as a scientific-god. Pearson likes him, and over there, what Pearson says, goes.'

'Here too I'm guessing,' Josey surmised. 'So Pearson's friendship is pivotal to you keeping your job; is that fair to say?'

'Once again it used to b-be.'

'How do you mean?'

Aaron shrugged. 'My satellite failed.'

This surprised and interested Josey. 'Failed, how?'

'It monitored the ozone, and various other gases, absolutely fine, but I'd designed it to p-prove natural depletion. It hasn't been able to.'

'Right, yet in spite of that, the failure doesn't change your mind about natural depletion, and that's where you came unstuck with Davenport.'

'True, but there's a little m-more to it; he's also one of my greatest benefactors.'

'How is Davenport a *benefactor*?'

'He clinched the building of the satellite – got it off the g-ground in Australia. America wanted to take me back to the states to work on it, but Davenport put up his own money to keep the development—and me—here. He talked it up with the company chiefs. You have to understand t-there are a lot of politics involved.'

'Let's see if I've got this straight. Davenport puts up money, and presumably understands the satellite is designed to prove your theory - am I okay calling it a theory?'

'It is now.'

'And then your theory falls over when the satellite fails. How much money does Davenport stand to lose on his investment?'

'Ten million.'

'Guys, I hate to sound blunt, but people kill for a whole lot less when it comes to money – and loss.'

The professor looked at him sharply, suddenly fighting back tears, and obviously unable to speak.

Josey looked at Belinda for help.

'Aaron's recently suffered a family tragedy.'

'Oh, forgive me, Mate – I had no idea.'

The professor buried his face in his hands and openly wept. Belinda tried consoling him, but his breakdown completely hampered her efforts.

'I'm s-sorry,' he forced out as he got to his feet, 'we'll have to do this some other time.' He swung open the wire door and went back inside.

Josey felt like a complete rake for not recognising the full extent of Verg's stress.

Belinda rested her hand on Josey's arm. 'Cam, don't blame yourself,' she offered with Aaron out of earshot. 'He's hard work sometimes.'

Josey's pangs of guilt refused to go away. If he'd known, he would have given the guy more *slack*.

'He's not dealing with things too well,' she added.

Josey dared to wipe away a tear from her cheek with his thumb. 'Tell me what happened.'

She looked hesitant. 'I apologise in advance, I know how some of this will sound. It was the morning after the attack. We were woken by the phone ringing. It was bad news, the worst kind . . .'

CHAPTER SEVEN
The Amulet

The shrill ring from the living room startles them; the clock on the bedside table showing it's just after 5am. Belinda slips out of bed and puts on a gown as she makes her way out to take the call.

'Stay sweetie,' she tells Aaron leaving him to get some sleep.

Instead, he sweeps away the covers and heads for the bathroom. The early phone call has put him equally on edge.

With his face dripping wet and reaching for a towel, he catches a glimpse of himself in the small mirror above the bathroom basin. Over his shoulder, Belinda's reflection stands in the doorway looking almost afraid to come in.

Swinging around he asks what's wrong, dreading the answer.

'It's your father.'

Aaron knows only too well what this means.

Entering the hospital room, he is stagestruck by the surreal scene before him, irrational concern over what to say, and what to do consume him. Belinda at his side, very conscious of the fact this is his first face to face experience with death.

The nurse at his father's bedside sees the fear, and gestures for him and his partner to come closer, but he stops at the foot of the bed, fraught with a desire to leave.

The young nurse is operating under duress, struggling to administer morphine to his father's catheter, her efforts thwarted by the patients insistent pulling away to prevent it. 'Reverend Verg, you must let me give you your drugs to ease the pain.'

Ignoring her distress, he sets his eyes on his boy, who he sees has already shed tears. 'Son – there is little time.'

'Dad, for Christ's s-sake let the nurse help.' The words tumbled out untethered.

Easing his defiance against the nurse; the reverend's fading gaze remains on his troubled son. 'You say *Christ* so easily now.'

'Dad - don't.'

His desperate father reaches out for him. 'Ask her to leave, I want, to talk to you, in private.'

The unsettled nurse, knowing full well he means her, baulks in the face of her patient's demand, backing away from the bed uncertainly. 'Should I go?' she asks the visitors in a whisper.

His hearing intact, Aaron's father answers, making his instruction even clearer. 'I want to talk, with my son, please.'

The young woman appeals to the distressed visitors for her release, 'I'm sorry; I don't know what else I can do.'

'It's all right nurse,' Aaron breaths.

Leaving the room relieved, yet still a little shaken, she allows the family to deal with the dying man in their own time.

From the foot of the bed, Aaron begs, 'Just let them give you the d-drugs?'

'Son - I'm finished.'

'Come on Dad, you don't k-know that.'

'You, need to listen.'

Beaten by exhaustion, he rests his arm against the sheet, waiting for his son to come to the side of the bed. It takes a cloaked nudge from Belinda to encourage him.

Apprehensively, he positions himself at his father's side, now able to see more graphically the agony that sweeps across the reverend's face as he tries to speak.

He clutches Aaron's arm, desperate to have him hear what he has to say – 'Son,'

'I'm right here, Dad, right here.' His voice shakes. 'What is it you want to tell me?'

A vague lift in Adam Verg's spirit appears to wipe away the pain as he draws a breath through obstinate airways, just enough to be able to say to Aaron . . . 'An – an – angel, c-came . . .'

Careworn, he battles to finish his message, but is taken over by a sudden and uncontrollable explosion from somewhere deep, a vile cough, transmuting into a desperate gasp for air—

But, it seems his fight to explicate his final message is destined to be denied by life's waning force.

Belinda tightens her hold on her unsettled partner,

terrified of what he may now have to witness; she no sooner raises this deepest fear, when confirmation arrives in the form of an alarming whirlwind of movement at the doorway.

'Sorry people; we need to attend to your father!'

The urgent command has come from the specialist doctor, who is already rushing to reach the Minister's bedside, heading up the anguished nurse, compelling the grieving visitors to step back in order that the medical staff might carry out the grim task that has brought them in such a hurry.

The nurse goes straight to the life-support system at the head of the bed to study the patient's status, which has no doubt brought these two medics rushing from their observation posts.

Positioning himself on the opposite side of the bed, the doctor begins listening for the reverend's heartbeat, keeping his eye out for the nurse's reaction to the stats. When she gives it, her body language and a subtle shake of the head – says it all.

Fully aware of the inevitable, the minister's son and future daughter-in-law seek the comfort of each other's arms, awaiting the medico to put it into words. With eyes fixed on Aaron, he tells him, 'I'm afraid your father's organs are shutting down. He has only moments to live.' Locking eyes with the nurse he adds, 'We'll leave you to say your goodbyes.'

Taking their leave, the doctor stops to offer his commiserations. 'Please accept our deepest sympathy.' He draws away to follow the nurse into the corridor.

Carrying the weight of knowing nothing can be done to prevent his father's leaving, Aaron returns to the bedside to witness those final moments.

A struggle to draw breath heralds its arrival. Glazed eyes are drawn to the one window the room offers, to the silhouetted figure standing against the light, the last thing the dying man will ever see. The fixedness of the minister's eye-line induces Aaron and Belinda to follow his gaze, to the man at the window.

In the midst of the minister's one last desperate attempt to speak to his son; the resulting guttural sound regains their attention.

When they turn to face him, death has already come knocking, placing no importance on unuttered words – they hear a final breath faintly leave parted lips, they witness the relentless pain mercifully extinguish. . .

Through wavering eyes, Belinda whispers, 'He was trying to tell you something, what do you think it was?'

Convulsion besets him, drawing him deeper into the sanctuary of his lover's arms. He draws her tightly to his chest, aware of the comforting scent of her hair and the taste of his own tears. Their racing hearts combine in grief.

The man at the window turns to face the shattered couple, knowing he must now console them - after all, that's his job as a man of the cloth; a *Catholic Priest* no less. But, there is much more to his task than mere support for the grieving relatives.

Following their goodbyes to Aaron's father, they meet with the priest in the foyer of the hospital at his request. He introduces himself as *Father Bennett.*

It doesn't take Bennett long to realise, Aaron is in a place where he has serious doubts about his father's beliefs, the distrust is written on his face. 'I promise I'm not here to hassle you,' he tells them both. 'I wouldn't even be involved if not for your father's insistence. He asked that I pass on a message – a message that he desperately wanted to give to you himself.'

Together, on a park bench overlooking the Pacific Ocean, Aaron and Belinda spend time reflecting on Reverend Adam Verg's passing, waiting for the priest to come and bequeath the dying man's message. Truly afraid of what may be running through her fiancé's mind; she worries over how he might respond.

In light of Aaron's way-less than amicable attitude to religious superstition, she has good reason to worry; he's made it clear he has no interest in hearing about angels.

Talking to Aaron moments after his father's death, the priest hadn't used that term; he'd eased into it by calling the visitor a *messenger*. But *angel* is what Aaron took him to mean. And apart from that, he was finding it strange that a staunch protestant minister, like his father, would want to receive the-last-rights of the Catholic Church. The priest had assured him it was his father's wish.

Belinda took a deep breath and asked, 'How are you holding up, professor?'

Tears were in his eyes as he answered. 'I'll be glad when this is over. S-sorry, Bel, believing in God is a b-bit weird for me.'

Although brought up inside a catholic family, Belinda's eclectic attitude to beliefs permits her to make no judgment.

Until they hear Father Bennett clear his throat, they are unaware he is right behind them, and it's presumed he has heard Aaron express his deep doubts.

Understanding their embarrassment, he raises his palm to extenuate concern. 'I promise, the message your father has entrusted with me, has nothing to do with God or religion.'

Aaron glances at Belinda and tells her under his breath, 'I can't do this.'

He makes a move to leave, but Belinda holds him back. 'Just listen; what've you got to lose?'

'I saw him myself,' the priest adds in haste to try and prevent him going.

The ambiguous statement succeeds in postponing the professor's exit. 'Saw who?'

Aware of Aaron's none-too-subtle spiritual scepticism, he's careful in phrasing his answer. 'The man your father *thought* was an angel. I saw him with my own eyes.'

Furrows of distrust sweep across the professor's brow.

'Adam's *angel* was flesh and blood, as real as any living man, a Tibetan monk who claimed you know him.'

Suddenly his father's mysterious *angel* makes annoying sense. 'Why doesn't this surprise me?'

Sensing Aaron is torn between listening-and-leaving, Belinda offers a guarded opinion. 'Just hear him out.'

Aaron eases off, considering her plea.

'You must at least be curious,' she reasons. 'I'm damn sure I am.'

Faced with Belinda's drawn interest he concedes, releasing pent up tensions on a long exhale.

Satisfied Aaron's recalcitrant attitude may be changing for the better, Father Bennett responds with an expression of relief. 'Good. Shall we walk along the cliff while I give you your father's message?'

The cliff-edge pathway that the priest has alluded to, traces a spectacularly rugged coastline bordering the hospital.

'You two go ahead. I'm quite happy to relax here while you have your talk.'

Except for his uncertain expression, Aaron appears settled enough to take a walk with the priest, something Belinda thought she'd never see.

Below the cliff edge pathway, at the base of the fifty foot high precipice, massive rocks hold back the pounding Pacific, as they have for millennia. To their right, pasted on the horizon, a distant container-ship seemingly sits motionless against a gradient blue backdrop. Overhead, seagulls hover effortlessly on salty up-drafts. Without taking his eyes from the scenery, the priest asks, 'Have you never shared your father's faith, professor?'

Aaron encompasses their surrounds with a broad sweep of his arm. 'This is m-my religion.'

Bennett grins affably, pleased with the honesty in the answer. 'Faith comes in many forms.'

Picking up the feeling the priest is approachable, Aaron shelves his unyielding attitude. 'Sorry, I don't mean to give you a h-hard time.'

'Trust me, you're not – belief is a personal thing.'

'Not for my father.'

Bennett jerks his head around, worried his task might still be more difficult than he imagined.

'Don't g-get me wrong, I really did love my father, but he had some strange ideas.'

'Why do you say that?'

'For one, he thought everyone should believe what he

believes.'

This really puzzles the priest. 'I would have thought the opposite of him.'

Aaron begins to sense there might be an abstruse connection between his father and the priest. 'How well did you know the minister, given your age difference?'

Bennett can see his point, thirty years is a big generation gap. 'I didn't know him as well as my father did. But from the stories told to me, Minister Verg was a very diverse individual. Both our fathers were.'

He can see Aaron isn't quite sold.

'Before their mutual, how can I put it, *scrutiny*, of the Christian religions, they flirted with various other doctrines, everything from Hinduism to the Kabbalah.'

Aaron has no idea what the priest is leading up to, but it's beginning to sound like his promise not to mention *God and religion* is marred.

The priest is glancing between the pathway and his walking companion, periodically picking up on his reactions. 'To me, your father seemed just as happy reciting a Jewish Kaddish, as receiving the last-rights of the Catholic Church.'

They walk in silence momentarily, each wondering what the other man is thinking. 'Is my father's *message* in a-any of this?' Aaron finally asks.

'I promise it is, and that it will all make sense.'

Aaron doesn't look convinced.

'You have to understand, they always entered into these experimental worlds jointly. It wasn't a game to them. They gave their hearts and souls, contributing to each and every belief in ways that others could seldom compete with. And it wasn't just the Piety. Like you, your father had a great interest in science. Their inquiring minds eventually came under the watchful eye of a worldwide secret society. It was while studying Buddhism in Tibet, that they were finally deemed to be worthy.'

'Holy shit.'

Bennett is far too liberally minded to be shocked by Aaron's crass terminology, remaining indifferent to it. For Aaron though, the talk is starting to sound a bit too familiar. 'So you're telling me, this is the big important message; my father wanted me to know he belonged to a Buddhist cult?'

'Not a cult, and not necessarily Buddhist, or any other religion, more like a governing body who recognise and award select people who possess extraordinarily percep-tive insights.'

Aaron lets out such an expressive sigh; it can be heard above the sounds of the ocean, but Bennett doesn't miss a beat. 'They can include philosophical scholars, open minded researchers, innovative thinkers in all walks of life. And, scientists like your-self.'

Aaron ceases walking to clarify a point, 'Why the big secret? He could have told me this stuff himself. Why wait till he was on his death bed.'

Bennett gains a few steps before turning to face the professor's incredulous stare, taking a moment to choose his words. 'What I've told you, and am about to tell you, is a well-guarded secret. Only a small handful of people throughout the world are privy to the metaphysical group, known only unto themselves as, *The Observers*.

'They are not a registered organisation, and they have no fixed abode. They communicate with each other without ever meeting in one place. Centuries ago we can only guess as to how they achieved this. These days they use social media, coding their messages to maintain secrecy.'

Bennett reaches into his Cassock, removes a neatly folded black cloth and hands it across to Aaron.

To the touch, it feels like there is a small solid object wrapped inside it. Ordinarily, Aaron would have had no clue as to what it was, but in light of the priest's stories, he's almost certain he knows what he'll find. On peeling back the fabric his gut feeling is confirmed, the monk's stone amulet stares up at him like a bad penny. Why is this Catholic priest now taking over the task of issuing it, and what connection does the Chinese Buddhist have with a Protestant reverend? 'What the hell is this all about?' he is enforced to ask.

Bennett gestures toward the pathway ahead. 'Can we continue walking while I tell you?'

'Sure, it feels a little late to back out.'

The priest manages an affable grin. 'In this case, one side of the amulet is an ancient Buddhist symbol, the other, a badge of honour given by one Observer to another. The Buddhist Monk, who you know as Zan, is the Grand Master of the Observers in China. This is his invitation to you, to accept their offer and to join them.'

Aaron begins rewrapping the stone disk with the black cloth. 'So the Monk came to see my father in the hope he could convince me to take this.'

'It wasn't the only reason. Zan was his tutor, my father's also. When he first came to the hospital your father was completely coherent, because at that stage he wasn't on morphine. I was there too. The Grand Master sat with us for over an hour, comforting your father in ways that I as a priest could hardly imagine possible. He celebrated his life, and that of my own father's.' Bennett gives Aaron a moment to digest what he has told him, and then adds, 'There's something else you should know - about the archaeologist - the Chinese woman that the master told you about.'

Given the priest seems to know all there is to know about Zan, it's hardly surprising he'd know about what's happening in China.

'I suppose you're about to tell me she's one of them.'

'Your instinct is intact, but no - she will be, but as yet hasn't been approached.'

Aaron releases a breathy chortle. 'This just gets better by the minute.'

Still not fazed by Aaron's repudiation, Bennet tells him, 'It does, and it will. Your father knew you were in the running, as is she, and when he realised his end was approaching rapidly, he pleaded with me to pass on the invitation, in the event he died before you arrived, to explain the Observers to you. And, to tell you not to turn your back on your intuition; to accept the amulet—and, Zan's guidance . . .'

CHAPTER EIGHT
Doubts remain

Josey was considering his school friend's involvement with Aaron Verg had grown her two heads.

She saw it. 'I know that look.'

'You have to admit it's a bit, to use your words, *out there*.'

She tilted her head and made no comment.

'So Aaron accepted the Observer story and took the amulet?'

'No.'

Josey was almost certain he would have.

'But *I* did,' she added as she slid the amulet from her pocket and unwrapped it for him to see. 'The priest asked me to keep trying.'

Josey wanted to tell her she was encouraging the fantasies, but instead asked if he could take a closer look.

'Of course you can, if only it was this easy with Aaron.'

He grinned and lifted the stone disk from the cloth on her open palm and ran his fingers across its surface. 'What's *your* take on this whole thing?'

'I don't think there is anything sinister going on.'

Josey screwed up his face, indicating he shared Aaron's caution. 'Let's remember lives have been threatened. Aaron is quite rightly suspicious.'

'Cam, I know you well enough to believe you'll split shit-from-Clay.'

'Within reason,' Josey clarified as he thought about the strangeness of the case, and what it would take to achieve any sort of success unravelling it. 'Is Davenport the only one who knows about me?'

'At this point, yes.'

'That may have to change.'

She jerked her head around at him. 'I don't want the police knowing about what I've told you,' she insisted.

He saw dread in her eyes, 'Bel, believe me I get that.'

Police involvement was looking more-and-more likely though; now that Margaret Davenport had reported the threat on her husband, information that had surfaced in a phone call from the SciCore director. Sleeman told her and Aaron, and not in a friendly way, that Mrs Davenport had poked a hornet's nest.

'Can I please ask you to leave the police to SciCore for the time being?' Belinda was desperate and could see Josey wasn't feeling comfortable. 'I'm asking too much,' she said with a furrowed brow.

He understood why she wanted Aaron's state of mind to remain a private issue, so he pushed the police subject to the side and lifted from the chair. With his hand against the small of her back he took a few steps, easing her forward ready to leave. 'All right, let's start by finding out who rides a high powered motorcycle, and pretty damned well by all accounts.'

The fear that crossed her face prompted him to say, 'Max and I will get to the bottom of this, beginning with letting SciCore know I'm in the picture.'

She gave him a kiss on the cheek as they reached the bottom of the stairs. He felt the peck was a genuine thank-you, but couldn't deny enjoying the brief moment of physical contact.

Back in his city office, Josey relayed the story to Maxine. The strange story about the Observers was so distancing, it was hard for her to take it seriously.

'It's definitely strange,' he had to admit.

She smirked. 'That's never stopped you before.'

He thought about that – 'Good point.'

For the rest of the day, the bizarre accounts played over in Josey's mind, and dispelling all sprinklings of fantasy, and although the scientist's story was undeniably beguiling, taking it *lightly* might prove to be *irresponsible*, perhaps deadly - even if Aaron Verg was proven to be quite delusional.

She came and sat on the edge of his desk, just as she often did. 'So, what's the plan?'

He gently bit on the inside of his cheek while considering the answer, then said, 'Time for some creative thinking young lady.'

The decision was made - and just in time, because there was about to be an invasion.

CHAPTER NINE
The American invasion

SciCore Director Russell Sleeman stood up on the mezzanine watching the group of people studying travellers filing out from customs. Among the crowd of spectators he could see Boz Shannon expectantly craning his neck. Thanks to the magazine's deeply internal connections to the science world, Sleeman knew the reporter was the only member of the press privy to Colin Booth's arrival on the American Airlines flight 426 from Boston.

Clearly Shannon was hoping Booth, who was second in command to Jack Pearson at SciCore's head office, would naively give him a scoop; on the basis he would see no harm in doing so. His assumption that Booth would have no real understanding of the company's local politics, meant there would be no concept of how big a thorn a science reporter could be.

Satisfied Shannon wouldn't be getting anywhere near

the American visitor, Sleeman slipped away to meet the man at another prearranged location. He didn't notice Shannon catch a glimpse of him as he boarded the escalator to come down to ground level.

A moment later, the journalist lost sight of the director and speared off in pursuit. Although he had seen many and varied evasive actions to avoid the press, he had no idea of their exact plan.

He jogged to the observation window and got lucky. A rake-thin white man matching the description he had been given for Booth was striding away from the American Aircraft, while the remaining passengers made their way to customs via the sky-walk.

A uniformed officer met Booth on the tarmac and offered to take his carry-bag, but was waved away with a polite gesture. He was taken through a door that presumably led into the staff-only area on the ground floor. It wasn't difficult to imagine there might be something sensitive in that bag. Shannon also imagined that the visitor would be taken through a private exit directly into a waiting car and expedited away unseen.

Believing there was no point hanging around the airport—because they could be leaving via a half dozen different exits—he bolted back to his parked vehicle, bent on getting his reconnaissance back on track.

Assuming the destination would be SciCore; he travelled to the outskirts of the city and waited on the only road south to the research centre.

Five minutes after pulling over, a limo glided by. He caught sight of Booth sitting in the back seat with Sleeman. Perched in the front seat with the driver was Verg, an unforseen bonus.

Shannon followed at a safe distance. Once the vehicle reached the main gate there would be nothing he could do except wait until Booth left for his hotel, and when he did, he would once again follow. With any sort of luck he might bale up the American to get the scoop on what brought him to Australia.

The trip to the research centre allowed the SciCore trio to address that very question.

The limo driver, who strategically happened to be Detective Josey, hardly recognisable in his cap and uniform, diligently checked the rear-view mirror and warned, 'I think we're being tailed.'

Booth looked at Sleeman to ascertain if his Australian counterpart appeared worried. He didn't. 'It's nothing,' he told his guest.

Verg turned and recognised the car via the back window. 'It's Shannon.'

'I know,' Sleeman revealed smugly, 'I spotted him at the airport.' He glanced at Booth and caught him cringing. 'He's not the mainstream press, don't worry.'

'If I'd known security was a problem down here I'd have brought some guys with me.'

'We have a guy right here – driving.'

Josey looked in the mirror, locked eyes with the American and gave him a nod. It had only taken a day to allow a private detective into the fold, primarily because Josey had spoken with the man at the top in Boston - Jack Pearson.

Booth kept his focus on Verg. 'That was a damn close call you had, professor.'

Sleeman grunted. 'If he'd done what we asked, he wouldn't have been attacked.'

'That was then and this is now,' their visitor told him as he faced the passing scenery. 'I was sorry to hear about the failure with your satellite, Aaron. Have you had any thoughts about what went wrong?'

'Some, but that might be a moot point right now.'

The American smiled to himself and swivelled his head, finding the professor looking at him in the side mirror. 'Not necessarily,' he said to the tiny reflection.

Russell Sleeman was noticeably unimpressed. 'Don't hold your breath,' he told him.

Without moving his eyes from the mirror, he said to the director at his side, 'I assure you Russ, I have no intention of holding my breath, but Aaron; I have to ask, assuming you can fix the satellite, can we do this thing in the stratosphere safely?'

'I b-believe we can.'

'You don't know that,' Sleeman piped up.

Booth ignored him. 'How much time do you need to find out?'

'Conclusively, I can't say, but time is our biggest problem, I don't t-think we can afford the luxury of waiting.'

Booth fell quiet; Aaron's point was close to inarguable, given his predictions at the poles. The man was the only scientist in the entire company who was able to formulate a means of building the SciSats, based on a holistic recognition of the global climatic network. Not a mean feat. And now, in the face of his prediction of future calamity at the equator, he was being hog-tied by political red tape.

Sleeman felt the lapse in conversation was his opportune time to hammer a nail in the coffin of stratospheric experiments. 'You have to appreciate, Colin, if we don't do what's expected of us, we lose our funding. I don't just mean the satellite programme. Our government is threatening to cut us off.'

'Let me make something clear,' Booth pointed out. 'Head Office have no intention of buying into local skirmishes, but what we *can*, and *will* do, is take Aaron offshore where he can better argue his case.'

Sleeman wobbled his head from side to side like someone had just told him it was *he* who had failed, and that his services were no longer required. 'You can't do this, Colin, if Aaron is allowed free rein, SciCore in Australia will never survive – period.'

This warning didn't impact on Booth in the slightest. 'You let me worry about that,' he said eyeballing his Australian counterpart. 'Fact is he's not safe here.'

Sleeman's eyes were darting around uncomfortably, feeling like he was no longer in charge.

Booth thought about the missing scientist, and seized the chance to change the subject. 'You haven't heard from Davenport?'

'Not a bloody word,' Sleeman said sounding like he was grumbling.

Booth nodded and pushed his point. 'Even more reason to get Aaron out of Australia as soon as possible.'

Ral Davenport's disappearance was just as troubling as the potential equator matter. Verg would love to have been wrong about the equator, but in his mind it was closer to *probable* than possible.

Underpinning all of this was the death of his father, and the revelations about his history with the secret society of Observers. Aaron had no intention of mentioning the strange society, or their leader Zan. Verg's inexplicable intuition was already enough for others to deal with. But, emotionally he could no longer expatriate a connection between himself and the strange events that had entered his life in recent times.

As the limo entered through the main gate of the research centre, Verg saw Shannon's vehicle continue on by in a lame attempt to hide the fact he'd been following. He knew the rat would be pulling over half a kilometre up the road and doubling back. He had no idea what the reporter could possibly gain by hanging around, but he figured there must be something.

Sleeman settled his visitors at the boardroom table in his office with drinks, and with plenty more to discuss.

Booth passed on a professional glance to the coffee girl as she set his cup on the table in front of him. 'Joanne, thank you,' he said to the Gothic looking girl with the unnatural coloured hair.

Only one man in the room understood who she really was, and he needed to remind himself not to blow her cover by calling her *Maxine*.

'Can I get you gentlemen anything else?'

There was a chorus of satisfaction, and a wait for her to leave.

'I'm just nearby; please don't hesitate to buzz me.' She was pointing at the intercom at the centre of the round table.

Sleeman and Booth looked to be wondering why she was still in the room.

'She's new,' Sleeman said awkwardly trying his hand at comedy.

Booth offered no more than a polite lift of his brow, evidently more interested in responding to his coffee. Setting his gaze on Verg he said, 'Tell me about the attack, has the culprit been found?'

Under advisement from Detective Josey, Aaron knew not to give out too much detail. 'No, not yet.'

Booth glanced at the professor's jacket. 'Are you carrying?'

This isn't America, Verg thought. He patted the pocket of his coat and turned toward Josey. 'A gun—no. My bodyguard carries a firearm—so I'm told.'

Booth remained deadpan, locking in on Sleeman. 'Who's working on finding Davenport?'

Sleeman said, 'Our people are looking into it.'

'You've been to the police, right?'

With a subtle headshake he explained, 'They came to *us,* after Davenport's family called it in.'

'Do I take that to mean you had no intention of going to police yourself?'

Sleeman drew in a sharp breath and spoke as he exhaled. 'Colin, I don't expect you to understand the level of opposition that exists here. Publicity is the last thing we need.'

Aaron didn't notice Sleeman's disapproving glare flick onto him – but Booth did. Unzipping a small leather bag that he had brought to the table, the all business American removed a folder. He systematically organised groups of documents side by side, then handed Sleeman and Aaron their copies.

Sleeman looked at the documents suspiciously. 'What's this?'

'They're contracts, aimed at releasing Professor Verg

from his Australian commitment.'

Sleeman's eyes rounded. 'You're kidding.'

'Not at all. Under instruction from Jack Pearson, I'm to return to Boston with Aaron in tow, where he will continue his ozone work without political interference. And that - is not negotiable.'

'I can't believe this.'

'I thought you'd be happy, Russ,' he reasoned with mock diplomacy. 'No more hassles with bad publicity. However, while I'm here, we can work together in formulating a strategy for you guys to weather the storm. No pun intended.'

Sulking, Sleeman said, 'I'll be lucky if I've got any *guys* left at this rate.'

'And w-what am *I* signing?' Aaron inquired.

Booth seemed surprised, 'You're coming to America, to perfect your SciSat, I thought I made that clear.'

Sleeman was gobsmacked.

The director's discomfort was a sight for sore eyes, but Aaron wasn't about to be railroaded. 'I'll n-need to read this.'

'Of course, I wouldn't let you sign it if you hadn't.' The American turned to Sleeman. 'Russ, I'll need your fully-read and signed contract before we leave for Boston. I suggest you have a quick browse while we finish our coffees.' And back on Aaron he said, 'When we're done here, if it's all right with you, I'd like to borrow your bodyguard to drive us to my hotel. I can get to meet your guy properly, go over the contract and have a meal together, my shout.'

CHAPTER TEN
The Investigation begins

So far Josey had no real suspects, just a growing list of names, nothing more than those people associated with the professor. To some of Aaron's associates, Josey was his bodyguard. To others, he was an investigator trying to find the bike-rider responsible for the attack. To Russell Sleeman and Colin Booth, he was both. No associates were privy to the true identity of Sleeman's brand new secretary, Joanne, who was operating undercover to expand on Josey's eventual list of suspects, who may-or-may-not have a vested interest in the SciSats.

The case had to start somewhere. He chose the family that had brought the case to the attention of the police, Davenport's wife and only son. He drove down to Lucas Heights, where they lived in a modern two story house in a quiet cul-de-sac. The front garden looked to have been pristine at one time, but was clearly abandoned now, in contrast to the rest of the street.

Davenport's disappearance was little more than a week old. The dilapidated garden suggested his absence had been far longer than that, assuming he'd been the gardener. The extramarital affair with Belinda Baxter was the presumed reason he hadn't been living at home. This was conjecture of course and Josey wouldn't be bringing it up, unless it somehow wove itself into the conversation.

When Mrs Davenport opened the door it surprised him, she looked more than a little like Belinda, just older. *Funny that.*

'Detective, please come in.'

She didn't smile, but her tone was welcoming and cooperative. She closed the door and ambled past him to lead the way to a sitting room. She gestured for him to sit, all very formal. Perhaps she preferred social graces and was most comfortable portraying herself that way.

Josey sat toward the edge of his padded chair, careful not to appear too comfortably entrenched. 'Thank you for taking the time to see me.'

She gave a weak smile and looked toward the foyer. 'Excuse me a moment,' she said lifting from her chair. 'I'll see where David is.'

'Well actually, I wouldn't mind talking to you first.'

Seemingly unfamiliar with being corrected when she first turned, she then immediately relaxed. 'No, that's fine.' She took her seat, notably conscious of making sure the helm of her skirt covered her knees, sitting straight-backed with her hands clasped in her lap.

For Josey, it went without saying; she projected an attractiveness that when in her youth, would have made her stunning. Ten years younger, and taller, she would be a dead-set ringer for Belinda, making Davenport a *class-A fool*.

This woman clearly misses her husband, Josey thought.

'How can I help you, detective?'

'The name's Cam.'

She patted her collar bone. 'Denise.'

'Great.' He decided on sitting back. He knew his first question would regurgitate bad memories. She already looked uncomfortable. Josey didn't need to hear the personal stuff. 'If there's anything you don't want to talk about—'

He could see the wheels turning as she tried to decipher the offer. 'No, it's all right; I'll answer your questions.' She was rubbing her hands together as though they were cold.

'Thanks, Denise. Let's start with when you first believed he was missing?'

'It was when he stopped using our joint credit card.'

'When was that?'

'That was the day after the letter arrived.' The look she handed him was quizzical. 'I think you understand he wasn't staying here.'

He gave her a subtle nod. 'You called him—about the letter?'

'Yes, the moment we got it.'

'Did he come over to see you?'

'No. I sent him a copy in an email.'

'Can I ask how often you'd been seeing him before that?'

'Probably once a fortnight.'

'Any indication he was worried over something?'

'Ask his girlfriend. I have no idea.'

Josey knew she was in dire need of releasing steam over her husband's affair with Belinda. He wanted to tell her the affair had ended over a year ago, but he decided to let it slide. 'Are you able to tell me where he stayed, before he went missing?'

'I can.' From a small table beside her chair, she picked up a scrap of paper and handed it to him. 'You're wasting your time if you think he's gone back there. The police have already checked.'

Josey wasn't displeased the police were now involved, but it was of little help to him.

'The house is empty at the moment,' she told him, 'but I can let the real estate know you're coming if you wish.'

He took a glance at the address and put it in his shirt pocket. 'Where else do you think he might go if he wanted to hide?'

'The only other place is our holiday shack on the river, Georges River. The police went there too.'

'I'd like to take a look round anyway if that's okay.'

'That's up to you,' she said as she half-heartedly began writing out the address. 'That place is empty too, I'm thinking of selling them both.'

Denise Davenport was clearly losing interest in talking. Josey had expected it would be hard coming into the case on the heels of the police, because they invariably ask a lot of the same questions. He decided to concentrate on the threat and to start thinking creatively. 'Was the letter you received sealed in an envelope?'

She felt the detective was clutching at straws. 'No. Why?'

'May I see it?'

She gave a frustrated sigh and withdrew the note from a desk at her elbow, handing it to Josey to help himself to its contents.

He opened out the roughly folded sheet of paper and saw that the message was exactly as Sleeman described it after being shown it by police, typed in large-face capitols. The untidy folds and creases suggested it may have been shoved into a pocket, perhaps a jacket.

Mrs Davenport raised her eyebrows when the detective put the letter to his nose and smelt it.

Not just any sort of jacket, Josey thought – *a leather jacket*. Plus, he detected the unmistakable presence of *oil, or fuel*. 'Did the police ask to keep this?'

'No. They just took photographs.'

Josey held up his phone. 'Do you mind if I take a shot of it?'

She shrugged as movement in the foyer drew her attention. 'David, where are you going?'

Her eighteen year old son reluctantly interrupted his planned exit. Dressed in casual gear, complete with a small backpack and baseball cap, he looked anything but happy about not quite making it to the door unseen.

'The detective needs to have a word.'

His shoulders slumped dramatically. 'Why? I don't know where Dad is.'

A bit insensitive, Josey thought.

'David.' Her disheartened plea changed his mind. He slid the backpack to the floor and came into the sitting room.

The last thing Josey wanted was to have her son pissed off and uncooperative, or to be pissed off himself by the kid's attitude. 'Two questions and you can be out of here,' he promised.

'Okay. Shoot.'

Josey heard pent up anxiety exorcize from Denise's lips. He held the letter out and forced a smile to let the kid feel he wasn't in any sort of trouble. 'Would you mind smelling this for me?'

David's exaggerated frown feigned the suggestion Josey was below par as a detective, but in fact he could have been covering for something.

Josey glanced at Mum, noted her discomfort, then back to the son. 'Humour me. Just tell me what you smell.'

He remained hesitant, holding on his mother to see what she thought about the strange request.

She simply told him, 'Do as the detective says.'

Under duress, he took the letter and smelt it briefly and gave it back. 'Paper, what the hell else?'

Josey gave an unnerving smile, folded the letter and handed it back to Mrs Davenport. 'That's fine David. I don't need to ask you anything else.'

Mrs Davenport patted her knees to draw attention. 'All right, David – go. I'll see you later.'

He shook his head incredulously, turned, swept up his backpack and punctuated his exit by closing the door harder than necessary.

His mother failed to cloak her embarrassment.

'I won't take up any more of your time, Denise. I think I've got all I need.'

Relieved that the interview was over, she stood to see the detective out.

At the front door, she apologised for her son's behaviour, but Josey swept it aside and thanked her for her help.

While driving back to the office he mulled over what had come out of the meeting with the Davenports. There were a few things, the kid was nervous, and either he had no sense of smell, or didn't want to get involved in a discussion about the inarguable smell of oil present in the paper. Josey's hunch about that was thin at best, but maybe a little investigation would thicken it. Of course the kid could be forgiven for not picking up traces of leather, it *was* faint, but the smell of oil was rich.

Maxine sat at the computer surfing the internet with Josey over her shoulder. 'Their web-site doesn't give us anything more than records of past and present events,' she pointed out. 'No contact details.' Max scrolled to the bottom of the screen. 'This's interesting; CorpCause is having a rally tomorrow, it's at 10am outside the Hyatt.' She looked up at him, '*Colin Booth's* hotel.'

His face creased with a grin. 'Well done, Max.'

'So, how do we do this? As a trusted employee I can't be seen at an anti SciCore rally.'

Josey pulled his phone from his pocket and hit speed dial. 'And I can't either, because if the kid *is* involved he may be there.' His call connected. 'Carl, Josey. Hi. What are you doing tomorrow my man, around ten?'

CHAPTER ELEVEN
The Offer

From the twelfth floor, Colin Booth and Aaron Verg watched the growing number of demonstrators milling around on the street below. Assured they would be safe in the hotel, Josey had gone home and left them to it.

Neither man had been advised of Josey's plan to have Carl Norris covertly search for Davenport's tight-lipped son at the demonstration. At this stage they knew nothing of Josey's hunch that David Davenport and the biker might know each other, or might even have been jointly involved in the attempted murder. It was a scenario that Josey wasn't particularly hoping for, but a hunch is a hunch and needs to be investigated, even if it means elimination.

Now in its third day, the wave of protesters had grown in strength and notoriety, thanks to the newly introduced police presence that automatically attracted mainstream media attention. Verg's supposed outrageous climate-change beliefs had placed him all over the front page of every newspaper and every news broadcast. Sleeman had been spending a lot of time getting drunk at the office according to Maxine, alias Joanne, his private secretary.

Josey figured there were two possibilities as to who leaked the attacks and the threats to the press. The obvious informant was Boz Shannon, but an equal contender was Colin Booth, who when he thought about it, had nothing to lose and plenty to gain in getting Aaron smoothly out of Australia. Josey had no intention in pointing the finger at either man; because it advanced his case not one iota. His investigation was also stagnant in that Carl Norris had failed to locate the motorcyclist or young Davenport amongst the crowd over the three days.

Booth had taken out an extra room for the Australian professor in order to get on with planning the scientist's extradition to the United States.

With a goal to having the American contract signed, Belinda had been invited to join Aaron at the hotel, mainly to give the couple time to get their heads around the big life change on offer. If and when Aaron did sign the contract, it was decided Belinda would join her fiancé in a few weeks' time, once she settled-up with the magazine. Booth had clearance from Pearson in Boston for Belinda to be included in the deal.

'I see what Sleeman meant,' he said to Aaron as they viewed the ruckus on the street. 'You guys have real problems.'

'Which could be solved overnight if we just talked to them.'

'I'm not real sure about that. But, not your problem anymore, this's exactly why we're getting you over to the states.'

Aaron moved away from the window and sat on the lounge. 'When?'

Booth looked over his shoulder at him. 'It'll be soon, we have our own people coming down to chaperone.'

Aaron understood he meant bodyguards, and wondered how Belinda would feel about strangers from the other side of the world being responsible for his safety. Personally, losing Josey was of no consequence, but he felt certain it wouldn't sit well with his overly protective fiancée.

Booth shifted from the window to the middle of the room. 'We're drawing up an itinerary that will get us into Boston around the end of the month. What you need to do over the next couple of days is organise your affairs. Massachusetts is commonly a mild climate, not unlike Sydney. You probably know that. Anyway, pack what clothing you think you'll want, we'll deck you out if there's anything else you need once you're up there. Accommodation will be taken care of—'

'You're forgetting s-something.'

Booth frowned. 'Like what?'

'Like, I haven't even agreed t-to go yet. Not to mention I'm engaged to be married.'

Booth swept his arm through the air. 'Bring her with you. This is a long term offer, professor. Jack is deadly serious about you working for us in America. He'll do whatever it takes to get you on-board. He made it clear to me he's still not happy about you leaving and coming to Australia in the first place.'

Aaron looked at booth hard and long. 'I can't promise to fit in with your planned itinerary. I'll have to speak with Belinda and f-figure out if it works for us.'

Booth began pacing, stopping every few feet or so to face Aaron and continue his pitch, failing to find the right words until the third try. 'If you repeat what I'm about to tell you, Pearson will cut my balls off.'

'Sounds serious,' he responded flippantly, 'm-maybe you shouldn't tell me.'

'We're closing Australia down,' he told him bluntly.

This, Aaron was *not* expecting.

Booth nodded slowly in confirmation.

'Why?'

'That's all you're getting out of me right now. The rest you'll learn in good time.'

'I'll b-be honest, Colin, secrecy isn't a real good way to get me on side.'

He pulled his cell from his pocket. 'I can call Pearson right now if you want to tell him you're not interested. But I swear-to-god you'll regret it if you do.'

Aaron massaged his bottom lip and called him on what he thought was a bluff. 'Okay, go ahead, c-call him.'

Now Booth was on the back-foot. 'I hope you're not seriously thinking of knocking this back?'

Aaron rose from his seat. 'Colin, put your phone away. I'm m-messing with you.'

His phone returned to his pocket, and a sheepish smile appeared on his face.

'You've d-delivered your message. Now it's up to me to make a decision. For that I n-need a little time.'

Normally, Carl Norris would have looked a stereotypical

thirty five year old businessman sporting a conventional short haircut, but three days ago at the demonstration; he was a long haired hippy carrying an anti SciCore placard outside the Hyatt. His aim was to carry off his pretence undetected, and to find David Davenport with the help of a picture Josey had forwarded to his phone. Josey's clear instruction was not to confront, simply to identify and obtain photographic reference.

Carl's other task was to keep an eye out for any sign of high powered motorbikes, and or their riders. After four hours of milling amongst the protesters, he had been forced to accept defeat. He'd put his phone onto movie-mode and shot a lengthy video for Josey to peruse later, the result of which was equally fruitless except for one thing; thanks to a photo Belinda had shown of Shannon in the science magazine, Josey was able to recognise the reporter in the crowd, doing some photography of his own. Not being one to miss out on an anti SciCore party, Shannon's presence at the rally didn't come as a surprise.

Undiscouraged, Josey had sent Carl back to the Hyatt over the following two days of protests, after which the demonstrators reluctantly dispersed without getting close to the American visitor, or his controversial guest. Carl had left the scene equally empty handed; having to report there had been no sign of the expected targets.

Unbeknown to anyone, Aaron left the hotel unnoticed via a lane-way on the last day of the demonstrations, in the company of his fiancée.

Upon their return to the ranch-house, they kept themselves locked away and discussed the pros and cons of joining Booth on his return trip to the parent company in Boston.

Belinda was torn. On one hand she thought it was a good idea to get as far away from Australia as possible, a perfect way to escape the threats. But Ral's mysterious disappearance, and not knowing if he was dead or alive, kept her from immediately agreeing to leave Australia. She suggested Aaron go without her, but he refused to do so.

Two days later, when the deadline to leave for Boston with Booth arrived, they finally accepted a temporary separation. It was too good an offer to refuse.

CHAPTER TWELVE
Departure

On the day of departure from Kingsford Smith Airport, two burley bodyguards from Boston stood watch over the party of six as they said their goodbyes. Josey had brought Rebecca and Molly along so that the professor wouldn't get too weird about leaving Belinda alone with an ex-lover. He wasn't sure the ploy was working.

'You t-two have a g-great time together,' he told Belinda, suspiciously flicking his eyes onto the detective.

The off-balance comment raised a round of awkward glances. Sensitive to Aaron's discomfort, Rebecca tightened her grip on Josey's arm and snuggled a little closer to her man. It seemed to work, because the professor immediately gave his fiancée a heartfelt kiss, and strode away toward the boarding lounge smiling and looking generally settled. Trailed by Booth and the bodyguards, the professor gave one last look back before going out of sight through the doors.

'Well, that didn't go too badly,' Josey quipped. When he turned and saw Belinda sporting a few tears, he wished he'd kept his mouth shut. 'Hey, let's have none of that.'

Rebecca comfortably released her hold on Josey, allowing him to console Belinda with a friendly embrace. She joined the two of them, reaching out for Molly to get involved, which she did with a bright young smile. Josey picked up on his daughter's expression and loved that she was enjoying herself. 'All right,' he commanded in an attempt to break up the group, 'let's get out of here.'

They broke apart all smiles; except for Belinda who was left adding tears to the mix. 'Sorry guys, I'm being an idiot. I need to get over myself.'

'No,' Rebecca told her. 'What you need is to come with us for breakfast and a chat.'

Boz Shannon peered across the top of his newspaper at the happy group, now in the canteen. It pleased him to know they had no clue he was there, or what he was up to. No clue that he had tailed them to the airport, and after working out where Verg and his friends were going, had booked a ticket on the next flight, a flight that had the same stopover in Hong Kong. His aircraft, which was only six hours behind theirs, would arrive in time to pick up the same plane heading out to Boston, the location of SciCore's head office.

Following a good breakfast and a strong cup of black coffee, along with the distraction of her present company, Belinda was feeling a whole lot more relaxed. However, she still felt awkward about Josey being forced out of the picture.

'I think this is for the best,' he told her. 'He'll be a lot safer in the states than here.'

Rebecca rested her palm over Belinda's hand. 'When are you planning to join him?'

Tears spilled to her cheeks so suddenly that she couldn't answer.

Rebecca felt her question was the cause. 'Bel, what is it?'

She sniffed, using the back of her hand to cover the embarrassment of a runny nose. Thankfully, in his usual style, Josey produced a folded handkerchief, which she was glad to make use of. She forced herself to calm down, enough to make a desperate plea. 'Cam – please, I want you to go to Boston.'

Although they couldn't hear what was being said, people nearby were looking, along with Shannon, who wore a smirk on his face as he watched from around the edge of his newspaper. The demeanour of his co-worker, and the surprised looks she was getting from her friends, was fascinating him.

Although equally surprised, Josey trod carefully, not wishing to sound dismissive. 'Bel, he's in good hands. I don't think you need to worry.'

Rebecca caught his eye, her expression exhibiting doubt.

Belinda saw the warning and became even more desperate. 'Money is no object.'

Josey needed to nip this in the bud. 'No, it isn't.'

She looked at him with alarm.

'If I'm to do as you ask, I'll do it because I'm worried about you. But I'll say again—I think you're worrying over nothing.'

Belinda turned to Josey's wife. 'Tell him he has to go.'

Rebecca felt trapped. Especially since in a lot of ways she didn't want him to go. She had a few worries of her own. She put them aside. 'Darling, it's up to you. I know you think he's safe with those people, but what if he isn't?'

Rebecca definitely had a point. 'Tell you what,' he said to Belinda. 'I'll take a short trip to Boston, check things out, if all is well, I'll put your mind at rest and come home. How's that sound?'

She pushed out a breath and forced a weak smile. 'That sounds perfect.'

'Right. Done.'

Her smile deepened as she turned to Rebecca. 'I can't thank both of you enough.'

Molly broke the ice with, 'Great, we're going to America.'

It was the distraction they needed.

Shannon's smirk faltered. What was driving the turna-round to Baxter's stress of a moment ago? If only he could have placed himself within earshot.

After Molly's suggestion they were all going to the USA was established as pure wishful thinking, Josey saw the girls off, then called Maxine to let her know what was happening. 'I'll be going to Boston, Max, but I'll hang out here and make a few calls.'

'No problem. I'll bring down what you need.'

'Lunch is on me.'

Around midday, Max met Josey at one of the Airport cafes, trailing a small travel bag. Shannon had abandoned his dubious newspaper cover and replaced it with a beanie, sunglasses and a surgical mask. Even though the disguise attracted attention potentially, it managed to successfully render the reporter unrecognisable.

Shannon watched Josey and the girl and wondered, was the happily married detective having an extramarital affair? At this point he had no idea the bag wasn't hers. She looked concerned about something from the moment she sat down, like as if she had something important on her mind. Whatever it was, it rubbed off onto the detective as soon as she spoke.

'Was she certain?' Josey asked Maxine.

'Absolutely. She'd put it away after days of trying to change his mind.'

'Why then would he suddenly change his mind without telling her?'

Maxine shrugged. 'She said the amulet's gone and there's no one else who could have taken it.'

Shannon watched them throughout their lunch and the coffees that followed. The concerning news that the young lady brought to the table eventually turned to a more businesslike conversation.

'Talk to Carl and have him stay with *CorpCause*.'

'You still think the Davenport kid is involved?'

'I do.'

'Even though we haven't seen either of them at the rallies?'

'It's their absence that convinces me. There's a chance my visit to the Davenports is the reason they haven't.'

The penny dropped. 'Gotcha.'

'Turns out, David Davenport's girlfriend is the student the professor handed the leak to at the university.'

She thought about what that could mean, but said, 'I

don't see the connection.'

'There might not be one. In any event we'd be remiss to ignore it. Work with Carl to see if there is.'

'You think David's warned the biker.'

'Correct.'

'Anything else you need me to do?'

'Just keep your ear to the ground at SciCore. There may be nothing, but if there is, you're in a good place to hear it.'

'Easy enough.'

'Don't get too cocky.'

She smiled and drained the remains of her coffee.

Shannon watched her leave. *No kiss, just a smile, and no bag. The bag's his. He's the one catching the plane.*

But, why not leave with the SciCore guys? He put two-and-two together and decided that's what the tears at breakfast were all about. *Sweet-cheeks was worried about her precious fiancé, so she's sent her favourite detective to protect him, the reason the sleuth hadn't left the airport with the women.*

It meant Josey would probably be on the same flight to Boston as himself, which also meant they'd all spend a cosy few hours in Hong Kong together.

Although Shannon believed his identity—as far as the detective was concerned—might not be an issue, because as far as he knew Josey hadn't laid eyes on him, he bought a wide brimmed Panama hat to replace the beanie and kept the mask on, just in case someone had shown the detective a photograph.

Seated on the plane, he could just see below the rim of the new hat, enough to establish Josey taking his seat up ahead, over the wing. He removed the troublesome

Panama hat and leant back against the headrest to take in
the overhead air.

CHAPTER THIRTEEN
Into China

Shannon made it off the plane and into the Hong Kong international terminal without being spotted by the detective.

It would be interesting to see if Josey let the Yanks know they were being followed. So far he hadn't. They had a four hour wait for their flight to Boston, but it was no more than an hour before all hell broke loose.

Shannon had his eyes on the detective when he saw him suddenly push out of his seat and stride across to where the American's were, presumably surprising them with his presence. The last time they'd seen him was in Australia, and by all accounts he hadn't been going anywhere. Earlier, the professor appeared to have excused himself before going off to the bathroom. That was ten minutes ago. Now he wasn't to be seen.

One of the bodyguards went on the immediate defensive when Josey approached asking questions. Voices were raised, attracting the attention of airport security.

Shannon left his seat to get closer to the action. He heard the burly American telling Josey to *back-off*. The second bodyguard was nowhere in sight.

Josey ignored the minder that was abusing him and called out to his boss. 'Booth; what's happening.'

Booth turned to the voice, clearly put-out at seeing the Australian detective in Hong Kong. 'What the-frig.'

'Where's Verg?'

'I don't know what you're doing here, but you need to keep out of it.'

'You've lost him.' It was an easy assumption; the American was literally red faced.

'I'm telling you to pull your goddamned head in.'

The second bodyguard appeared from the toilet block in a panic. 'He's not in there.'

Booth's face went even redder. 'Shit, shit, shit.'

Josey saw no point in sticking around while the Americans floundered over the misplacement of the professor.

He manoeuvred through startled onlookers, punching a number into his cell as he went. Faces slid by, but not the one he hoped to see. He didn't let up the pace when his call connected. 'Lou, it's me, I'm glad you're in . . . I'm at *Chep-lap-kok* . . . A friends gone missing and his life may be in danger, I need to know if he's left the airport. I know it's a big ask, but are you in a position to come and help me out? . . . His destination's Boston . . . Right, airport security, I'll meet you there – Lou, thank you.'

Intrigued by the turn of events, Shannon kept his distance as he followed. It was imperative that he not lose sight of the detective, because he was clearly heading somewhere other than Boston. And the new destination would be wherever Verg had gone.

Police Inspector Lou Chen came into the office of airport security, and on seeing the worried look on Josey's face got straight to business. It was awkward asking for Lou's help so soon after the last time; it had only been a few months ago that he had lost another client in Hong Kong. This was different of course, this time he hadn't been the one responsible.

Although Lou was outside his jurisdiction, he bounced orders around in Chinese as comfortably as if he were at the police station. Many influential people in Hong Kong knew and respected Chen, to the point where no one would dare question his authority, even now with the ninety nine year lease ended. He was Josey's greatest Hong Kong champion. Within ten minutes he had the security offices patched into every surveillance camera within a one mile radius of the airport. This, along with a couple of dozen cameras in the terminal, gave Josey plenty to look at. He always carried a picture of a client, which he had passed around to increase the number of eyes watching the screens.

Five minutes later they had a sighting. Aaron can be seen catching the Hong Kong Airport Express bus.

'Your client is very likely going all the way into Hong Kong City,' Lou told Josey.

'That's about an hour, yes?'

'Correct.'

That leaves Verg time to get back for the flight, Josey thought. It was anyone's guess how he managed to get through security carrying a Boston ticket. But, given he left without telling anyone, it was unlikely he'd be back, which could only mean one thing. 'Lou, I think my man is heading deep into China.'

'I thought you told me he was flying to Boston.'

'That's what everybody thought.'

'So why do you think he is now going into China instead?'

Josey didn't want to bore Lou with the story of Zan and the Archaeologist, but suffice to say he had to tell him something. 'If I'm right, his destination is Tibet. Fact is this guy may be in danger still.'

'There has been a threat against him?'

'There has.'

The Inspector recognised the story might be a long one so he left it. He looked around at the men and women who had helped with the search and thanked them. 'I think our work is done here,' he told Josey. 'Are you planning to abandon your journey to Boston to try and find your client?'

'If it's possible.'

'Come, I will take you to Hong Kong.'

'I should let the airline know.'

'Forget it; I will ask security to explain.'

'Lou, you're a gem.'

With the use of a police siren they were able to reach Lou's police station almost as quickly as the airport train.

Lou had radioed ahead to have his staff search the CRH data bases for Australian departures into China, explaining to Josey that unless the subject had originally planned travelling into mainland China, getting across the border could easily take weeks, which would allow time at least to locate the subject before he left. This safety valve was quashed the moment they arrived. An officer approached the inspector and spoke to him in Chinese.

'Something?' Josey asked Chen when the officer was done.

'Yes, your man has obtained a ticket to Tibet already.'

'He must have known all along he was headed there.'

Lou tilted his head. 'Hmmm, not necessarily, it is possible to organise a visa on arrival, a simple matter of filling out a VOA form. However, this type of visa limits how long you can stay in mainland China, and he still may have to wait for permission. But, if you know the right people.'

Josey couldn't imagine who the right people might be, but was hoping Inspector Chen was one of them.

'The answer's yes,' Lou told him reading his mind. 'I can get you on the trains to Lhasa.'

'Lhasa?'

'The capitol of Tibet, this is the destination on his ticket.'

Josey simpered. 'Lou, your powers astound me.'

'This is not to say it will be easy, you must pass through security and immigration at the West Kowloon station before you even leave Hong Kong. The fact the man you are looking for has obtained a ticket would tend to indicate he has substantial powers himself.'

Josey rang Max and gave her the news, which he then instructed her to pass on to Belinda and his family. He had less than an hour to reach Kowloon and go through the processes, thankfully made easier with Lou's help, having been set up with Chinese Yuan, enabling him to pay his way once across the border; Lou had even loaned him Hong Kong dollars to purchase his train ticket to

Shenzhen, at which time he could buy some warm clothes and some solid boots.

Two hours after the high-speed train carrying professor Verg departed, Josey was boarding the following train bound for Shenzhen, a trip that would take as little as fifteen minutes, which would then transport him via Xining and Golmud to Lhasa, a tourist destination that sits close to four thousand metres above sea level. The journey from Beijing to Lhasa by train was to take forty one slow hours. He would have opted to fly in less-than-three if not for establishing Verg had preceded him by train, he wasn't to know that flights were on the verge of being cancelled.

When the train reached Xining, an announcement was made informing passengers that all flights between Golmud and Lhasa had indeed been cancelled until further notice. No reason was given, which was sufficiently alarming to form a worrying knot in the pit of Josey's stomach. This sense of foreboding was amplified when all further attempts to call Australia were prevented by the sudden loss of the train's usual Wi-Fi service, something else that was yet to be explained.

A far less troubling announcement, which was made just prior to departing from Golmud, was that warm clothing and snow gear would be required by people leaving the train in Lhasa.

They were right about the need for warm clothing, because even though it was only mid-autumn, it was already extremely cold. Josey definitely needed to purchase something more appropriate to wear than the jumper and corduroy trousers that he'd purchased in Shenzhen. He was directed to the Shanjing Sweater Shop near Lhasa railway station.

If Josey hadn't been so quick leaving the train to get his new clothes, he would have heard the announcement that all further train services to Lhasa were to be cancelled, and that the returning train would be the last.

Shannon managed to hear it from the platform; he'd alighted from the same train as Josey and now stood watching from a distance as the detective entered the clothing shop. If not for his international-press visa arrangements, Shannon's passage out of Hong Kong, and his subsequent journey into Tibet, would not have been facilitated so quickly. As for the train and flight cancellations, he put them down to the inclement weather that was building on the mountain. Keeping up with Josey now would present an even greater challenge.

The proprietor of the sweater shop that Josey had gone into spoke English, a chance for him to enquire about the archaeologist, Lui Jie, the only lead he had as to Verg's presumed destination.

He hit pay-dirt. Not only did the man know who she was, but knew the location of the exploration site. He was also able to inform Josey that another Australian tourist had been asking after her from the previous train. Josey showed him Verg's picture. The man nodded curiously when he saw it, probably because the smiling face in the picture presented a very different image to the one he remembered.

The helpful shop owner gave Josey a detailed map and a running commentary on how to get to where the Archaeologists were. The proprietor concluded with a very troublesome warning. 'Colder than usual,' he said gesturing toward a rack covered in thick woollen beanies, ski-suits and snowshoes. In spite of not comprehending why the shop owner should emphasise Lhasa's unseasonal weather, he bought all three, plus a sizable backpack. He was already on edge over the messages received on the train. He asked about food on the way to Kailash and was told there were shops and makeshift stalls with local food on sale. The shop owner made one more sale, suggesting a couple of airtight metal containers would be advisable; one for food and one for water – both could be fitted into external compartments in the backpack. Josey spotted a small personal oxygen bottle, and having been conditioned on the train to accept their use as normal, he added it to his purchases.

As the transaction was being completed, he was put on further alert when the man went to a front window and carefully looked out to the street.

Josey thought he looked to be on edge. 'Is something wrong?'

He pointed and stepped back so Josey could see for himself. Outside, tourists were being turned back toward the station by official looking people in white snow-suits.

'What's going on?'

The shop owner waved Josey toward a back door and opened it for him. The door led to a snow covered laneway. 'You go this way,' he suggested.

Josey held his gaze as he exited, hoping he might obtain further explanation. The man politely closed the door on him.

A moment later the shop owner reappeared at the partly opened door at the front of his store, watching the intrepid traveller re-enter the main street and meander away in the distance with his purchased shackles, all tucked away inside his bright yellow backpack. He shook his head incredulously and returned to the warmth of his shop, satisfied his customer was on his way and wouldn't be forced to return the purchased goods.

Josey's next port of call was a place to hire a vehicle. He was half expecting to be stopped by one of the officials that were presumably herding people back to the train, but after acquiring a black SUV and another map – plus a further running commentary on how to reach the dig, he drove away from the capitol without being stopped.

Lhasa had plenty to satisfy the eye of the tourist, a lot of whom were Chinese. The Tibetans stood out, with their brightly coloured traditional clothes and religious customs, which they openly exhibited in public squares, roads and laneways. Their prayer wheels could be seen spinning on the walls of buildings, set in motion by hand, always in a clockwise direction Josey noticed. He promised himself he would find out why before returning home. Sharing the road out of the city with people, animals and all forms of bikes, including mopeds, was slow going. Out the window of his high vehicle, he saw a disabled man, presumably in prayer, making a clapping noise with some sort of hand held implement. Ladies with plaits and gentlemen with wide brimmed hats glided by, taking the time to glance his way approvingly. Many women wore colourful scarfs across their faces, or let them rest as collars.

In amongst locals and tourists that were milling in a square, he saw a young child being carried in a cloth that his father had slung across his shoulder, the child clearly fascinated by a massive group of Monks, who appeared to be arguing with each other in pairs. But close scrutiny convinced Josey they were following some sort of organised ritual, given that some of them were sporadically shifting between anger and laughter.

Outside the city, a thinning number of buildings grew from hillsides as if fashioned from the black rock, and the sealed road eventually gave way to a yellow swath of gravel surrounded by pinkish coloured hills. Through the snow he saw a persistent patch of blue sky that never seemed to get any closer.

As all these sights slid by, Josey had been trying repeatedly to call Max on his cell to let her know where he was. Once again there was no signal. The fault this time had to be something other than Wi-Fi; he figured communication in this remote area was most likely via satellite. An irrational-chill skulked through him as the thought arose, he couldn't dispel the feeling the unusual weather, and the strange behaviour toward the tourists at the station, were somehow connected to Verg and his bizarre stories.

Must be the altitude, he thought, realising he was beginning to feel a little light headed.

Taking stock of his wandering thoughts, he took a few breaths from the oxygen bottle, pushed superstition from his mind and forced himself to concentrate on the immediate task at hand – finding the professor.

CHAPTER FOURTEEN
Mount Kailash

One hundred and fifty million kilometres away, Earth's life force silently explodes in its vacuous abode, radiating across the vastness of space at two hundred and twenty kilometres per second.

If not for the massive gravitational force holding it intact, the nuclear fusion at its core would cause it to explode, instantly destroying it and all of the celestial bodies encircling it.

Tongues of radioactive flame temporarily defy the master, having reached escape velocity, periodically licking thousands of miles into the void. The resulting magnetic storms reach Earth eight minutes and twenty seconds later, raining electrically charged particles down into the atmosphere, reducing the planet's thin layer of ozone for months at a time.

Below this spherical barrier, known as the ozonosphere, warmth and energy provides conditions conducive to life.

The Great Himalayan Mountain Range both tempers and exaggerates these life giving effects, the foothills in the east producing mild summers and cold but bearable winters. Here, October marks the middle of autumn, which at its hottest is by all measure considered and expected to be around six degrees Celsius – *usually!*

Boz Shannon had taken in this wealth of facts and figures and stored them to memory. What he didn't know about Tibet he had researched. This was his first trip to China, yet he came here armed with an encyclopaedia of information, gleaned from the internet while on the train journey from Hong Kong to Golmud. The furthest thing from his mind in the hour prior to his Himalayan cramming session was a journey to Tibet – yet, here he was, travelling on a dusty road in the Himalayan foothills.

The exact translation for Himalayan is *Hima* – meaning *snow*, *Alaya* – meaning *abode* – *Abode of Snow*, and, according to Hindu mythology – *home of God Shiva*. He'd looked it up; he hated not having a handle on whatever part of the world he was in.

Although he possessed this treasure trove of recently attained knowledge, he hoped that by the time he left this place, he would have acquired a whole lot more to add to his encyclopaedia. For instance, so far he remained in the dark about why the climate near Mount Kailash had become so warm, resulting in the complete loss of snow cover since yesterday. By his reckoning, it should have been even colder than down in Lhasa. He was beginning to feel the need to remove the thermal underwear he'd purchased at the train station. For the time being though, he had no reason to suspect that the rays from the sun might be causing him harm. But he sure as hell felt its kinetic heat this day, maximised by the lack of a working air conditioner in his vehicle, which normally he would have had on heat.

Given the lather of perspiration that was creeping down his back and gathering under his buttocks, he welcomed the chance to come to a stop on a ridge, and escape the confines of his mobile pressure cooker.

Even with the naked eye, he could see that the vehicle he was following had also stopped.

The long-lens camera he had picked up from the passenger seat would show him a great deal more detail. He positioned his camera against a rock, steadying his view of the distant scene.

In the shimmering haze of distance, Detective Josey could be seen getting out of his vehicle and moving toward someone laying on the roadside, perhaps a woman, obviously in some sort of trouble, and showing no response to the driver's approach.

Unaware he was being watched in detail from afar, Josey set about determining if the motionless figure was injured, or perhaps worse. The face was hidden behind long black hair. He spoke in the hope of a response, but got no reaction. When he knelt and gently rolled the presumably injured person over, he was startled by what he saw. It was a middle-aged local woman. Her badly injured face had been somehow overwhelmed by unsightly blisters.

Unable to lift her head, she turned her eyes toward the roadside rescuer and spoke in her native tongue, which Josey could only assume was a plea for help.

An unexpected clap of thunder made him flinch. He

jerked his head toward the cause; black clouds were building overhead in an otherwise blue sky.

Closer to the mountains, he could see shafts of laser-like sunbeams stabbing into distant snow. Focusing back on the woman's injuries; a fearful possibility sprang to mind.

He checked his cell phone – still no signal.

Shannon's magnified image showed Josey lifting the woman and carrying her toward his car, his pace suggesting she was in urgent need of help.

He clicked away with his camera, pleased to be already getting early shots for his story. His excitement had drawn his attention away from the bazaar weather event that was forming, but a sharp response to thunder and lightning overhead sent him scurrying back to his car. The unsettling feeling that something was wrong in this place, escalated into panic, along with a sudden urge to get to shelter.

A mile ahead at the Mount Kailash Archaeological site, a lone figure staggered through thick mud to find cover from the explosive weather pattern, now developing into an unseasonable monsoon. Soil laden waterfalls raced down the mountain face, creating knee high rivers just a metre beyond the dark grotto where he stood.

Behind this dubious refuse, away from the torrential rain, workers pushing a track mounted trolley filled with shale, happened to see the figure standing at the mouth of the shaft, silhouetted against the storms blinding flashes. The worker behind the cart called a warning. 'Get back - this is not an entrance!'

Aided by a harness looped around his shoulders, the

worker up front craned his neck and saw the fellow standing on the track, seemingly in defiance. 'Wang, he is not moving!'

'Li Qiang, don't stop! He is not supposed to be there!'

He could see that the man was continuing to ignore the warning, already starting down the track toward them—

'Something is wrong. I am stopping,' Li insisted.

Wang swore and did his job, jamming a wooden peg into the spoke of a back wheel, bringing the heavily laden trolley to an unsteady halt. The cart made a short skid on the downward incline before settling to rest. Qiang freed himself from the straps, uncertain about what to do.

The intruder was moving farther in, now almost upon them and obstructing the track. 'What is wrong with you?' Wang yelled angrily.

'Strap-up, we will run him over if he does not move.'

Getting the trolley moving again was difficult, Li Qiang slipped into his harness, and with steely determination they strained against the weight, pulling the peg, freeing the cart to be hauled upward on a collision course with the intruder.

As they were nearly upon him the obstinate man stumbled and fell against the cart.

Losing his footing, Li Qiang struggled out of his straps to assist, allowing the full weight of the load to roll back onto Wang.

Wang's work boots skated across the timber sleepers in a losing battle to obtain a foothold. Realising the weight could no longer be held, he rolled to the side with no time to reinsert the peg, effectively releasing the runaway cart onto workers below.

The workers on a following cart shouted desperate

warnings, the sound of their voices and the roar of the cart reverberating back down the track.

Those manning a third consignment jumped clear as the runaways picked up speed and shunted into a fourth barrow, carrying the speeding train-like ensemble back down the line.

Inside the cavern, workers reacted to the increasing roar coming from the tunnel, culminating in four heavily laden trolleys shooting into view at breakneck speed, their menacing journey terminated by a sturdy timber barricade that splintered on impact, sending shrapnel into spinning flight. Miraculously, only one man out of twenty in the path of the debris was struck. Several people ran to his aid, their attention drawn away to an urgent cry for help before they could reach him!

They turned and saw Wang standing at the entrance to the tunnel looking shocked and confused.

Lui Jie, the head archaeologist, who had been among those running to help the injured man, stopped and shouted for the others to stay and tend to him. 'Bring the doctor to him,' she added as she ran off to where Wang was standing.

He greeted her with urgency, 'We are also in need of the doctor.'

She looked over her shoulder at the man that had been struck to ascertain his injuries, 'How bad is he?'

'He has hurt his leg,' a man called back, 'but we can look after him.'

'Tell the doctor to follow me,' she said amending her earlier instruction.

Wang led her into the flame lit tunnel, stumbling over rough sleepers and scattered shale that had broken free during the mad roller-coaster ride. On approaching where the events had begun, he pointed to the obscure figure lying on the track. A sickening groan emerged, a sign of life. Li Qiang was waiting ten feet away, afraid to go closer. Brushing past him, Lui moved along the track to obtain a better perspective on the inert man on the ground, his identity veiled in darkness until a handheld flame hovered above.

With Lui Jie's help, the injured man rolled himself onto an elbow and looked around at the people gathered. His damaged face, or what was left of it, was blistered and bleeding. Except for the distinctive *red scarf* worn around his neck, he was otherwise unrecognisable.

The doctor arrived and they stepped aside to let him kneel beside the victim. He knew nothing of the red scarf and asked Lui Jie, 'Do you know who it is?'

She nodded without turning away from the stricken man and whispered, 'It is my mentor, Mr Leung.'

The old man tried to speak, but blistered lips and swollen tongue prevented speech. He pointed toward the dim daylight.

Lui Jie asked, 'Has something burned you?'

He tried to tell her, but collapsed onto his back, he was dying.

In chilling disbelief, she watched him leave, his stricken body swimming from behind a veil of tears.

Puzzled by the old man's condition, Wang Yong turned his head toward the mouth of the tunnel, and the torrential downpour outside, asking, 'How could he be burned when he is so wet from rain?'

When Lui turned to face Wang, the great fear in her eyes told a story. 'Close up all of the exits,' she told everyone in a quiet voice. 'No one must go outside.'

Stunned and confused expressions prompted her to shout in a commanding voice, 'Quickly!'

Wang Yong ran back toward the cavern to carry out the instruction without further question.

She forced herself to look back upon her mentor's frightening injuries, heralding an involuntary shudder, unimaginable grief mercilessly gripping her broken heart.

CHAPTER FIFTEEN
Trouble in Tibet

Thick black clouds forced the use of headlights, allowing Josey to notice he wasn't alone on the road; a vehicle was following about a kilometre back.

With the road churned to mud, Shannon maintained a good distance as the two vehicles slid their way up the mountain slopes. He didn't equate the rain with the facial burns he had seen through his camera, but he was happy to keep his windows closed and dashboard fan off.

From the back seat where Josey had placed the injured woman, he heard she was regaining consciousness, obviously in a great deal of pain. The last thing he wanted was for her to wake up and see she was in a strange car with a foreign man; she may have no memory of his finding her on the road. He needed to get her to help soon. It crossed his mind to stop and see if the person following could help, but decided to err on the side of caution and pushed on.

His concerns about the weather were far more reaching due to the insights gleaned from Verg. It was the distant shafts of sunlight that were scanning the mountains in random patterns that had him most worried.

If he understood the map given to him by the Lhasa shop owner, the dig shouldn't be too far ahead. He checked his cell phone again – still void of the slightest signal.

The next few minutes were heart breaking; the woman was constantly writhing, screaming out things in her language that Josey could only interpret as a desperate plea for the pain to end.

Josey was desperate for the ordeal to end as well, and when a fork in the road swam into his headlights he let out a sigh of relief. At the end of the turnoff to the left stood a collection of vehicles parked beneath a makeshift awning. As difficult as it was to see through the rain, this had to be the place. He slowed and turned in.

Smaller roads and tracks continued in different directions, but this was as far as a normal vehicle could go anyway. He brought the SUV to a stop and strained to assess the scene through struggling wipers. No sign of anyone at first. Not surprising given the ferocity of the storm. He edged the car forward for a closer look and once again stopped. Now he could see a dark shape against the side of the hill, which suggested it might be an entrance to the dig site.

Shannon had stopped his vehicle and doused the lights, close enough to see without being seen. Josey's car was stationary and he wasn't getting out. There seemed to be no one else around.

Hampered by the rain, Josey's headlights weren't picking up any detail about the entrance; but then, like a switch, lightning momentarily illuminated a man standing within a small cavity straight ahead. When the revealing light was gone, Josey swapped to high beam, fetching the man into the augmented glare.

Wang shaded his eyes with his hand, prompting the driver to dip the lights to parkers.

'Can you help me?' Josey yelled as he came out into the rain.

The man made no attempt to move.

Maybe he doesn't speak English. . Maybe the pelting rain is louder than my voice.

Whatever the reason, Josey decided he was on his own. He opened up the back door and slid the injured woman from the seat, cradling her across his arms as he trudged toward where the man stood. Her screams had ceased, which raised concern she might already be dead.

Suspicious, Wang took a step back, wondering who the stranger might be, and why he has arrived with a local woman in his arms. Even in the splashing rain he could see she has been injured in the same way as Leung. He began shouting at Josey unintelligibly.

Sensing the man's reaction was fear, not anger, Josey pleaded, 'I'm sorry. No Chinese,' he told him as he moved in out of the rain.

His plea evoked a completely opposite reaction to what he'd hoped for, the man ran, vanishing into the near blackness of what appeared to be a narrow tunnel, leaving the detective to ponder his next move.

The tightness of the tunnel, and the presence of railway

tracks at his feet, convinced him this wasn't a footway, *there has to be another entrance.*

Stepping back out into the storm carrying the woman, he searched for another way in. The sky turned night-to-day for a few flickering seconds, highlighting the vehicle that had been following him, now parked a hundred yards away with its lights turned off. It was long enough to see the driver was still behind the wheel, but not quite long enough to recognise a face.

Shannon saw Josey looking in his direction, and wondered if it might be time to seek alliance. As he was thinking this, he saw two people appear in the mouth of the cavity. He couldn't quite tell, but one of them might have been the one who'd run away, presumably to get some backup. It looked like he was calling out, because Josey turned around and carried the woman back to where they were standing. Seemingly exhausted by her weight, he placed her at their feet and backed away.

They picked her up and moved into the shadows, peering over their shoulders as if to be sure the mystery visitor wasn't following.

Shannon decided he wasn't ready to confront the detective just yet, and reversed into a three point turn in preparation to make his way back down the road—

He skidded to a halt when he saw several more men arrive and begin manhandling the detective.

What to do, help, or run—

Not knowing their intentions, he had little interest in sticking around—

As sudden as thunder, an unbelievably blinding shaft of sunlight stabbed out of nowhere, so intensely bright it overloaded his retinas. Startled by the inexplicable loss of sight, he released an involuntary yelp, and a prayer. 'Jesus!'

As vision ebbed back, he saw a burning disk, no wider than a dinner plate, crossing the bonnet of his vehicle, lifting swaths of blistering paint. The alarming effect reminding him of how destructive young kids used to scorch holes in books with a magnifying glass, and of how the poor woman looked when Josey rescued her from the road.

For Shannon, one thing was very certain, he wasn't driving anywhere, not in whatever the hell was going on outside in the open. His decision was helped along by the abrupt appearance of men who seemed intent on pulling him from his vehicle, and ushering him toward an entrance that he hadn't noticed.

They took him past the parked cars and into what appeared to be a manmade passageway. At the end of the dimly lit corridor it opened up to a massive cavern. Shannon knew an archaeological dig when he saw one, but the scene before him was like something out of an Indiana Jones movie.

People were burrowing into the walls like termites, perched upon bamboo platforms, their attention drawn away from their work by his arrival. He wasn't the only centre of attention; Josey was emerging from a tunnel to his left in the company of the men who had seized him.

The two groups came together, encircling the Australians so that they were left with no chance of wandering. At first there was a lot of excited chatter, which was impossible for the foreigners to interpret, but then the subterranean room became very quiet. Somehow, the speechless staring faces were more disconcerting than the raucous chatter.

Beyond their encirclement, people stood solemnly in groups watching and wondering who the two westerners were, and why they were here, some gaining a better view atop mounds of shale. The men in the circle, muttered among themselves curiously, occasionally looking about as if waiting for something to happen.

Josey really needed to distance himself from Shannon, but under the circumstances was forced to suffer the situation. It was anybody's guess as to whether or not his uninvited friend understood the danger they were in, his opposition to Verg's idea that something like this could happen was possibly far too entrenched for him to make the connection. He also wondered if the locals had come to any conclusion about what was happening. One thing seemed certain; leaving this underground haven right now would mean certain death. Thinking ahead though, he wondered if travelling at night might be safe, and a way out of their predicament. Another possibility was the monsoon may offer protection, but he wasn't feeling real keen to put either of these notions to the test - unless he had to.

'What're you doing here, Shannon?' he finally asked his ring-in friend.

'I'm asking myself the same thing, have you got any idea what we just saw out there?'

'Ask your favourite scientist when we find him.'

He knew what he meant. 'You're trying to scare me.'

'Is it working?'

The reporter panned his head. 'He's here isn't he.'

It was a reasonable question, one he would also ask when he got the chance, but he knew Shannon's interest was self-serving. Josey looked at him hard. 'Let's get one thing straight, I'm not here to facilitate your story – you're on your own.'

The unnerving gawps were making Shannon nervous. 'Why the hell are they staring at us?'

Josey found he's concern tiresome. 'They don't mean us any harm, calm down.'

'Maybe they're blaming us for the woman you found.'

Deep down there was delight in knowing Shannon had gotten himself into this mess by himself. A week ago he would have been willing to align with the journo in debunking Verg's hair brained theories, his claim that the next hole could open up away from the poles had been hard to take seriously. But now he thought if that's not what just happened, he'd be surprised.

On top of that, Davenport's sudden departure from Australia prompted Josey to believe the Australian SciCore manager was also here in China because of it. Even before finding the injured woman on the road; Josey had conditioned himself to expect something bad was happening in Tibet. It was impossible – and probably ill advised – to dispel the fear it was connected with Verg's reason for being here. He hadn't stopped wondering though; there must be other people involved, the theories of just one man seemed far too singular, surely other scientists must be coming to the same conclusions about the ozone loss.

Looking into the bemused faces of those closest, he couldn't help feeling sorry for the tragedy that was ravaging their country. A fearful thought beset him; what if this was happening to the whole world right now, to his family back home. With no communication, there was no way of knowing, and no way of allaying the fear.

A buzz of excitement arose from somewhere in the grotto, causing the circle of men to break ranks and spread out. One of the men did an about face and began creating a pathway between the onlookers. As he receded from sight, the assemblage reformed, nullifying the pathway he had created.

Shannon looked at Josey for a possible explanation. 'What the hell's happening?'

'Not sure.'

Not sure didn't quite calm him. 'I get the sense you know something.'

In less than thirty seconds the pathway reopened. Between the banks of excited people, a most exquisite woman walked toward them flanked by the man who had presumably left to fetch her.

'Who's this then?'

Before Josey could respond to Shannon, the woman was right in front of them, even more beautiful up close. She held out her hand in greeting. 'Detective Josey, I have been expecting you.'

When his hand met hers, he recognised they were roughened by the work of an archaeologist. He discerned that he had come to the right place, the place where he would find Professor Verg – and the archaeologist that Zan had sent the scientist on a quest to find, their prior meeting being the only way she could have known his name, and the fact he was a detective – unless of course the authorities had been tracking them ever since they arrived in China. He pushed that thought aside and concluded that Verg and the archaeologist must have spoken to each other about the threats, and the detective hired to get to the bottom of it.

Josey wasn't wrong about the archaeological dig being Aaron's destination, but hope of seeing him faded when told the professor had left to go to another location. Lui Jie, who was clearly the matriarch of the dig, was unable to tell him where that was.

Shannon's mouth was fixed open, confused about why the detective was so familiar with the woman. 'You *know* her?' he asked Josey incredulously. His broad brimmed hat was bumped high, lifted by the deep furrows that had formed on his forehead.

CHAPTER SIXTEEN
Belinda on the Case

SciCore in Australia lay in deep conflict over what was happening in and around the great Himalayan Mountains. The board of directors were still reeling over Professor Aaron Verg's leaked ozone claims. Now, thanks to Jack Pearson at head office in America, they were reeling for a much more damning reason.

His extraordinarily bad news about Tibet, which he emphatically demanded be kept internal, was overshadowing the perception Verg didn't know what he was talking about, a hard pill for the Australians to swallow. At least the media at large knew nothing–yet.

What the Climate Activists would do if they were to hear of the Tibetan story was anybody's guess. On one hand they may be forced to applaud Verg for his prediction. On the other, they would very likely claim the events at Kailash proves man is responsible for destroying the planet, and without any help from nature.

Presumably, nothing would change their minds about the cause. Their disruption, which was spreading rapidly around the world, would undoubtedly continue.

SciCore chiefs believed it was only a matter of time before the company was finally dragged through the muddy waters of conspiracy.

So far, Sleeman had no idea that Terry Bourke's Science reporter was in Tibet. But once again, thanks to Pearson, he knew the detective assigned to Verg was in China trying to find the runaway scientist. Something they perhaps ought to have been doing themselves, which was not necessarily Sleeman's sentiment – more damning evidence of his fear of media-discovery.

Earlier, it wasn't only their diametric opposition to Verg's views that encouraged their decision to avoid the media; it was more about what reaction they would receive given the lack of proof their scientist had, not to mention the constant talk of natural depletion. Verg had been told to keep quiet about the politically unpopular concept so many times that they were sick of saying it.

Their other problem was, even though his views had been successfully kept under wraps—at least up until he talked about it with his students—SciCore already had growing opposition. Their primary enemies were those who believed SciCore was fiddling with the environment, which they originally *were* - and would again if Verg had his way.

Growing speculation that the science organisation was under increased attack from CorpCause, was spreading around the corridors as fast as a computer virus.

Ral Davenport's disappearance had by now been reported in the press, and the media release was considered to be the beginning of a heightened effort by the protester group to cause trouble. SciCore's biggest worry was that CorpCause were cloaked in even more secrecy than they themselves, making it difficult to infiltrate their ranks.

SciCore weren't the only ones worried, Belinda was beside herself, because she hadn't heard one word from anybody since learning Aaron was on his way to Tibet, and although she knew Josey was on Aaron's tail, she'd have been a lot happier if she knew they were already together. Not hearing from Josey since then was unusual in that he had promised to keep her posted. Adding to the feeling something was seriously wrong was the fact Maxine had received no word either.

Then there was the certain knowledge Boz Shannon had vacated the office at the same time as Josey, and hadn't been seen since.

She questioned Bourke, the magazine editor, about Shannon. He informed her that the reporter had gone to China on a hunch, a self-ordained assignment, which he had said very little about, but she suspected Bourke himself was being tight-lipped, so she pushed for more by threatening to resign if he didn't come clean. He stuck to his story and that was the end of it.

With all of what was happening, Belinda believed Shannon's secret departure to China was far too coincidental for words, and that the strange Buddhist monk's determination Aaron go to Tibet, must be somehow connected to it; further affirmed by Aaron taking the amulet with him.

Following her request that the editor elaborate on Shannon's excursion, and finally being told it was none of her business, she trundled straight off to the lion's head, Russel Sleeman, SciCore's managing director.

Sleeman was feeling sick. Booth had called him straight after phoning Jack Pearson, the American SciCore Director, advising him about the scientist's disappearance at the Hong Kong airport, and that there was no clue as to where he'd gone.

Ten hours later the news that an atmospheric event was taking place at the equator was dropped in Sleeman's lap, via a personal *Skype* from Pearson.

'We've got a goddamn problem, Russell', Pearson glumly reported from the tiny screen. 'Stratospheric Clouds have opened a vortex in the Himalayas. Just like Verg said they would.'

Sleeman changed colour, shocked and unable to give an immediate response. He had good reason to panic, because he was on record as having pushed Davenport into dispelling Verg's warnings. He was aware this wouldn't go down well with the *yanks*. He knew that ultimately the buck stops with Pearson, but the axe would unequivocally fall back on himself.

'My hands were tied,' he explained to his superior trying to smooth over the massive blunder. 'Politically, with the government breathing down our necks, Verg was a virtual powder-keg.'

'You can back-peddle your ass off, Russ,' Pearson told him, 'but you'll be wasting your breath with the press when they get the full story on this. And they will. Head Office here in Boston plan to back Verg to the hilt, and be seen doing it. I suggest you start doing the same.'

That conversation was an hour ago, and now, to

complete a bad day at the office, Sleeman had Verg's forever pining girlfriend, Belinda Baxter, sitting at his desk making demands for information.

Ordinarily he would have definitely given the woman her marching orders, but that option evaporated in the wake of Pearson's Skype session from Boston.

Sleeman had the usual scowl on his face. Perhaps, *this time,* for good reason, one of his top scientists was missing; the other had done a runner in Hong Kong. He wasn't to know how much his visitor already knew until she said, 'I know the American's lost Aaron on the way to Boston. What I want to know is how and where do they think he's gone.' She already knew that too of course, having received the information from Josey via Maxine. It was all about finding out what *Sleeman* knew.

'I'm not sure how you got that, but I'm sorry to have to say, it seems you know as much as I do.'

She couldn't tell if he was lying, but wasn't about to suggest she knew more than he did until she was ready.

'I'm guessing that ever since you lost Aaron in Hong Kong, you haven't been able to locate him. Am I right?'

'You're telling the story.'

'I also know that Detective Josey is tailing the professor.'

'How do you know that?'

'Because I asked him to.'

'I suppose now you're going to tell me where he is. What game are you playing Ms Baxter?'

'It's called; I'll tell you what I know, if you tell me what *you* know.'

He took a slow breath. 'Go on.'

'Has Pearson mentioned Tibet recently by any chance?'

Belinda asked deliberately baiting him.

He looked at her as though she may have been hacking into his computer. 'What gives you that idea?'

'Something a little birdie told me.'

'You're guessing.'

'Cut the crap, director. I happen to *know* Aaron was heading for Tibet. And I know exactly where in Tibet.' She knew that outside of Aaron, Josey and herself, no one knew about the archaeologist and the discovery at Mount Kailash.

She'd rattled him, but he wasn't about to let her get away with it. 'Well I guess you don't need me then.'

'Actually, you need *me*.'

'And why in hell would I need you?'

'Because whatever it is you're hiding up there, it's about to be blown wide open.'

Sleeman put on his best poker-face. 'You're clutching at straws. I'm a wake-up to you journalist types.'

'Do you mean journalist like *Boz Shannon*.'

He knew quite well who Boz Shannon was, the science reporter from EASI, who's mere mention managed to place him on edge. 'What's that supposed to mean?'

'It means he's also following Aaron.' She knew this wasn't exactly a fact, but it was a reasonable hunch.

'I'll have Bourke's balls if he is.'

'Go ahead, call him, but first hear me out.' She watched him stew.

'Go on.'

'Something bad has happened up there and you don't want the world to know about it.'

'Still guessing.'

'I'm also guessing you wouldn't mind keeping the reins

on Terry Bourke.'

This hit a nerve. 'I'm listening.'

'It's time to set your own terms, if you get my drift.'

He had no idea what she meant, but said, 'And I suppose you're going to help me with that.'

'Bingo.'

'If you don't mind me saying, you're sounding a tad too helpful. What's in it for you?'

'I come with you to China. To find Aaron and see that he is all right.'

'Not a chance in hell. I can't clear that.'

She studied him; then explained why he should find a way. 'Look at the big picture, Russell. May I call you Russell?'

'Call me anything you like, just get on with it.'

She smiled. 'Right, so we both know something serious is happening up there, which is probably why there's no communication. So, for the time being, whatever story Shannon is putting together in his head, is locked down, hopefully. When that story is finally released, you need to know you have some say in how it goes down.'

Belinda was unable to pick the look on Sleeman's face. He was either considering what she was saying, or about to blow his top.

She went on. 'Terry and I are like that,' she told him with her fingers crossed for him to see. 'I can swing it with him to make sure you get to put in your two-bobs-worth. It may interest you to know I'm the one who prevented Shannon from releasing the university leak to the Herald.' She waited for his response.

He was blinking profusely.

'I just want your help to get into Tibet,' she said almost

pleading.

'How do you suppose I do that?'

'Like I said, you invite me to go with you.'

'Who says I'm going?'

She hardened. 'I'm not stupid, Russ.'

'So I see, but you're also not going anywhere, not with me.'

She stood from his desk and walked away, turning at the door to tell him, 'We'll see about that, after you've given some careful consideration to what I've told you. '

Two hours later, Belinda sat in the departure lounge at Kingsford Smith Airport, waiting for her flight to Nepal.

'You don't take *no* for an answer do you,' Sleeman said as he sat down beside her with his tail firmly between his legs.

Without looking at him she made sure he knew his place. 'Look at it this way Russ, at least I can help you keep a lid on the story, but that's okay, you can thank me later.'

Stifled rage certified that all *objections* to her presence had been involuntarily, and annoyingly, terminated.

CHAPTER SEVENTEEN
Arrival at Ground Zero

As they rode in a buggy across the tarmac at Nepal international, Jack Pearson asked Ral Davenport, 'How the hell did we miss this?'

A SciCore Eurocopter fidgeted impatiently up ahead, waiting to transport them to the trouble zone.

'We had to hear this from the goddamned University of Shanghai,' Pearson went on. 'What were you guys doing down there, sleeping?'

Davenport appeared downtrodden. 'Professor Huang had a geographical advantage,' he whined.

'I wouldn't be using that as an excuse if I were you.'

'I hear you, but Verg's predictions smacked of guess work. His Satellites weren't delivering.'

'The one over China sure as hell did. It's your data Ral, and you guys dropped the ball.'

'I admit it. At least I got up here as soon as I got the call from Huang, and so far we've managed to keep it under wraps.'

Keeping the vortex under wraps was what everyone wanted, but internal openness was paramount from here on out. It was the only thing they had going for them.

Pearson's first question for Davenport had been to ask how he found out about the hole, and why he hadn't shared the information with his counterparts. Although it was Verg's satellite over China that picked up the alarm, its data was being fed to Australia as well, which means they should have registered it at the same time as China.

Once again Davenport agreed they'd messed up. 'Verg's prediction had me rattled. I started to freak out about it. Then, after the attack on him, and the threat on me, I just needed to look into his claims. I thought the best way to do that was outside of Australia. I came to China to meet with company executives to ask if anyone knew of Verg's predictions. Professor Huang rang me at my hotel minutes after I arrived. You could've knocked me over with a feather when he admitted he knew all about the predictions, and had been watching the data.'

'Why was a university professor allowed access to Verg's SciSats in the first place?'

'I'm not sure. He also called Yu Chow minutes after the first injury was reported to see if he knew about the data. He didn't, no one at SciCore knew about it. Coincidently I was at SciCore when Huang rang there.'

Pearson creased his brow. In his opinion the Australian and the Chinese company-heads were completely out of step with each other. As director of the Chinese branch of the company, Yu Chow should have been on top of what was happening. Of course the American director had to concede his own people knew nothing about the

Australian's being offside with their key scientist. 'Where's Verg at this point?' he tested.

Davenport groaned in response. 'According to the authorities he's at some Archaeological site on Mount Kailash.'

The worry on the American's brow intensified.

'Don't ask,' Davenport answered with disappointment, 'I have no idea why.'

'Is the site near where we're going?'

Recognising why he was asking he said, 'It is.'

Pearson huffed. 'Then we need to talk to him, find out if he knows what to do about this.'

The *down-under* branch of SciCore had been seriously inflamed by their incompetent wavering of protocols. Protocols that clearly state any new discoveries must be shared globally and immediately, albeit internally. Pearson wasn't convinced they didn't know about the vortex opening before he did. It was clear Verg had warned them, and that Davenport was the only one who took it half-seriously. At least, as Davenport said, in spite of the widespread devastation on the Tibetan high-grounds, so far the ozone disaster had been kept quiet, largely thanks to China's adherence to concealment. With reports of growing numbers of victims pouring in, that situation had the potential to change quickly.

'Welcome aboard gentleman,' the chopper pilot shouted over the motors as his passengers climbed in and headed for seats at the rear.

Two seats were already occupied. Pearson gave Sleeman a cold glance ahead of fixing his eyes on the woman sitting beside him. 'Who's this?' he asked bluntly.

Sleeman went to answer on her behalf, but Ral jumped in. 'Belinda Baxter, she's a close friend of Professor Verg's.'

That didn't impress Pearson. 'What she doing here?'

Not one to calmly accept rudeness, Belinda immediately saw red. She pointed to the ring on her left hand and answered with icy confidence. 'Maybe I'm just worried my fiancé is lying dead in the snow someplace.'

'We invited her,' Davenport quickly added.

Pearson looked a little put out by her presence, yet not so beyond embarrassed that he couldn't immediately apologise. 'Forgive me; I sincerely hope we find him.' He held on her face knowingly. 'Have we met?'

Belinda gave him the slack he needed. 'We have, in Boston, when you and Aaron first met.'

'Right, right.' Pearson pivoted and settled in, mulling over his shortfall in not remembering her. It came to him in a light bulb moment, and he turned to let her know so with a smile, which she gave back in understanding.

Davenport took up the seat beside him, turned off his mike and lent in close to say, 'I should have told you she was joining us, sorry.'

'Don't be – I would have invited her myself if I'd thought of it.' He turned to face her again. 'Forgive my ignorance, Belinda – we've all been under a heap of pressure, no less you. I'm very sorry.'

The noise of the engines winding towards lift-off along with an announcement from the pilot prevented a verbal response, but her forgiving smile said it all.

'Seat belts and headgear guys!' the pilot was saying, his Chinese accent laced with a twang, possibly intended to parody the American.

Once everyone completed checking that they were fastened in and that their helmets were fitted, Pearson couldn't resist pointing out his disappointment. 'The US should have had eyes on this, months ago guys.'

'We were trying to make that happen,' Sleeman said weighing in. 'It was difficult. We weren't ready to show the results. Not without proof. Verg didn't have any.'

Belinda gave Sleeman a look that suggested he pull his head in.

The helicopter lifted off and headed in the direction of Golmud, where a train would be waiting to take them sixteen thousand feet up into the Tibetan mountains. They were booked in as VIPs, the only passengers.

'Folks, my name is Tong Zhou,' the pilot's transmitted voice announced loud and clear in the headsets. 'Aboard the train, when you get above seven thousand feet, you will need radiation suits from Xining on.' He pointed to parcels held fast to the floor by straps, 'Those babies go with you when you leave the chopper. One size fits all.'

Pearson looked out the window as they swept away, worry lines etching deeper. 'Belinda, would you happen to know what Aaron is doing up there in Kailash - with the Archaeologists?'

He wouldn't believe it if I told him, she thought. 'I can't wait to ask him that myself.'

'Nobody has a clue,' Davenport quickly added on her behalf, immediately aware the answer was inanely inadequate coming from a Sci-Core staffer.

Pearson sat in silence, presumably digesting what he'd been told. His next question suggested his mind had switched to another topic entirely. 'How many assets do we have on the snow?'

'SciCore sent a contingent up by train twenty four hours ago,' Davenport advised. 'Three snow cats - two twenty seaters - a five seater, and a sixty seater over-snow bus, along with fifty protected skiers.'

Pearson understood he was referring to skiers protected by Radiation Suits. 'Not enough. We've already got god-knows how many injured people spread over a thousand square miles.'

'Not all on snow,' Davenport reminded him.

'Most, right! We need every over-snow the country can muster. This is a goddamned political bloodbath.'

'I'll get Yu Chow to talk to Beijing,' Ral promised.

'No time. We need vehicles up there *now*.'

CHAPTER EIGHTEEN
Abduction and confinement

Things had settled down inside the cavern. A lot had changed since their first encounter with the matriarch of the archaeological dig. Even Shannon was beginning to believe they had no need to fear her. And that she seemed at complete ease at their presence.

The two southern visitors were well provided for during their wait; given a private area where they could sleep and eat alone if they preferred to do so. But, it felt like imprisonment, especially for Josey, his search for Verg had been dealt a massive blow. The matriarch understood his disappointment, and told them that she too felt the same way about the professor's unannounced departure from the cavern, and that she was unable to explain why he had left so suddenly - without telling anyone he was going. With the atmospheric upheaval not showing any sign of letting up, they were forced to make the best of a bad situation, just like all the others trapped in the cave. Josey was wondering if this was the location of Lui Jie's discovery, but dare not ask – particularly in front of the reporter, he had to assume that wherever it was, it would be a secret.

Surprisingly, the matriarch took the visitors through many tunnels that led to dugouts of varying sizes. They were shown what they were allowed to see. There was male and female sleeping quarters, which were lined with dorm-like bunks that sat side by side against the shale walls. They had places for the workers to read and relax; a kitchen area with a massive table at its centre, providing enough room for all, big enough that the inhabitants of this underground world might potentially eat together.

The burrow-like passageways were all without power, necessitating the use of portable battery powered lamps. Lui Jie pointed out that a person could not get lost so long as they understood each tunnel was numbered sequentially. The numbers ran clockwise from the central cavern and since all tunnels were dead-ends; one need only return the way they came.

Comforting in such a claustrophobic environment!

'To avoid disappointment, I must tell you not to enter tunnel fourteen, you will only be met with a locked door.'

They took their eyes to where she had pointed; tunnel 14 was the only dugout that had a lift arrangement as well as a ramp. They later learnt the lift was especially built for the old archaeologist who had died at the hand of the radiation, Mr Leung.

This has to be where the discovery resides, Josey thought. It was becoming increasingly difficult to exclude Shannon from what he didn't deserve to know, perhaps impossible Josey decided.

Having shown her guests all they needed to see in order to navigate their way around, she led them back to the main hall to continue their talk.

'Did Professor Verg give any indication as to why he came to see you?' Josey asked guardedly.

They arrived at a small table setting that was recessed into the solid rock floor. She asked them to be seated and gestured to a woman nearby to bring refreshments.

The woman scurried away and disappeared into tunnel-12, which was now known to be the way to the kitchen.

Lui Jie was taking her time answering, almost as if she was deciding how much should be said to the detective and his brash companion, a newspaper reporter from Australia no less.

Josey assured the matriarch that both their lips were sealed beyond finding Professor Verg, and that her discoveries were out of bounds. He would later make it clear to Shannon that if he printed one word deemed to be confidential; he may get himself into a lot of trouble with the Chinese authorities.

Josey repeated his promise to Lui Jie that the main reason for coming to China was to find the Professor for his client, Belinda Baxter.

The mention of her name brightened the archaeologist. 'The professor spoke very highly of Miss Baxter'

Returning with three cups that were giving off steam, the lady who had ran off to the kitchen placed them on the table, bowed and left.

'Please, have your warm drink,' Lui Jie offered with an open palm. 'It is milk tea; you may find that it is a little salty for your taste. After we have had our tea, I have something of pressing importance to tell you.' She brought her lips to the rim of her cup and sipped - deep in thought.

Josey and Shannon exchanged a glance and took her advice, anxious to drain their cups and get onto hearing what their beautiful host was so keen to tell.

'Long before the professor arrived,' she finally began, 'a local religious man, who I had never seen before, came to this place and told me that Professor Verg from Australia would come here to see what I have found.'

'Would that be an elderly Monk who calls himself *Zan*?'

She Looked at Josey in amazement. 'You are an acquaintance?'

Shannon was ready to ask, *who the hell is Zan*?

But Josey was already answering her. 'Not personally, but the professor told me Zan encouraged him to come to China and meet with you, that you both had a commonality.' Josey knew of course from Belinda about the attack on Lui Jie, and that the archaeologist's work had an intuitive parallel with the professor.

'Is there something wrong detective?'

'I'm not sure if I'd be prying to ask.'

'Ask what?'

'About your abduction.'

She glanced from Josey to Shannon and recognised that many things might be being kept from the reporter, who appeared very confused.

Shannon picked up on her observation. 'Would you like me to leave?' he asked with a dejected edge to his voice.

'No. I am happy to talk about it to you both. I have a reason for doing so.'

Josey was no clearer than Shannon about what she

meant. 'Of course,' he told her. 'Can I ask then, was your attempted abduction before or after Zan came here?'

She smiled wryly. 'I assure you Mr Josey, you have no need to act as detective on my behalf. The Chinese police would not be impressed if you did so.'

'I understand - it's just that when people who know each other have threats against them, there are often shared aims.'

'We are a long way from Australia; I suspect my abduction is quite separate from your investigation. Many enemies in China do not agree with my work.' She held up her hand. 'Please don't ask me to explain. I must be very careful not to upset the police.'

Josey wanted to say she was wrong in thinking there was no connection, his nose told him so.

'Please don't get me wrong detective. I would be very happy to help you with your Australian investigation, if only I could.'

He changed the subject. 'The Monk; may I ask what else he said to you when he came here?'

She thought for a moment – about whether to answer. 'He told me that when the professor saw for himself the things that I have unearthed, he would discover a secret in them.'

'What was the secret?' Shannon asked out of turn.

His question gained a glare from Josey, who then asked their host, 'Did Zan know the secret?'

She lowered her eyes to the table. 'No. actually I found him to be a very cryptic character - he came and went from here like a ghost.'

Shannon's ears pricked. He wasn't feeling certain he could keep his promise not to publish what he was hearing.

Josey wanted to ask Lui Jie to explain what she meant by *like a ghost*, but decided to wait until he could speak with her alone; especially about the Observer thing. He couldn't help wondering if Aaron or Zan had mentioned the secret organisation to her. He was truly wishing the probing reporter hadn't been privy to her comments so far.

'I am afraid I cannot shed more light than this.'

Shannon had already latched onto her *Ghost* phrase and stored it to memory.

She became restless; clearly with more pressing things on her mind, and with eyes on the detective, appeared to be harbouring a great burden. Gently bowing her head, she warned, 'Please, I ask most respectfully that you forgive me for what I must now do.' Turning to gain the attention of two men that had been standing nearby, she beckoned them to approach. They complied and paused next to the table, as if waiting for an instruction. Rising to her feet and stepping out of the recess she added, 'The authorities have insisted you be scrutinised. It is as a result of your coming here when all other tourists have been prevented. The attack on me has inadvertently placed you among those suspected of being my would-be abductors. Until government officials from Beijing can be contacted, and arrive to question you, I am bound to make sure you do not leave.'

A loud clap of thunder rumbled into the cavern. She looked up at the ceiling in consideration. 'I doubt that will be possible anyway. I implore you to go calmly with these men.'

The two burley Chinese fellows moved in to tend to the

dubious captives, even as she was saying, 'You have my assurance that you will not be harmed in any way, and kept comfortable in your personal quarters.'

She bowed gracefully and left.

Shannon eyed Josey uneasily as they negotiated the high step-up to join their chaperones. 'You were saying?'

One of the men gestured for them to follow.

Josey noticed Shannon was stressing. 'Stop worrying, its protocol.'

'You don't see a *problem* with this?'

'My only problem is not being able to follow Verg.'

'You say that like you know where he is.' He glanced at the ceiling. His disappointment morphed to a smirk. 'Oh well, like she said, we can't leave anyway.'

'Forget the *we*, Shannon.'

Light and sound filtered in from the storm raging at the surface, prompting Josey to join Shannon in his study of the solid rock above their heads; six thousand metres of Mount Kailash, the roof of their prison – and their only protector.

CHAPTER NINETEEN
Snooping

S hannon dutifully followed the kerosene-lamp's glow as it traced across the walls of the rocky passage ahead. He was on his own in tunnel 14, at the end of which was the solid timber door that Lui Jie had mentioned.

He released a massive padlock using an equally large key that he had gotten from the kitchen, the type once used to lock up seventeenth century criminals in their cells. Having been warned about the locked door, he'd watched out for anyone leaving the tunnel carrying a key and simply took notice of where they went. Twice he'd seen the key taken to tunnel 12, the kitchen.

The heavy door groaned ajar on oil-less hinges, the sound echoing into the blackness of a small dugout at the other side of it.

The light preceded him as he entered, the motion of the torch sending eerie shadows flowing across craggy walls and tables laden with skeletal bones.

At the edge of the light were three mummified forms, held together with clay and wire, seemingly nestled atop the rock where they were found, and surprisingly, fully clothed.

He took the lamp closer, immediately recognising that this was what he presumed Lui Jie wouldn't want them to see—

'Shannon! What the shit are you doing?'

He swung the light onto Josey, who was standing in the open doorway, aghast.

Unrepentant, Shannon beckoned him in. 'You've got to see this,' he said as he turned his back on the detective to lay eyes once again on the figures.

'Are you out of your mind?' Josey asked in an anxious whisper.

Shannon pointed at the mummifications, encouraging Josey to move past the lamp to see for himself.

He edged beyond the lamp's glare and saw the ancient figures adorned in the flickering light – he didn't need to be an archaeologist to appreciate what he was seeing.

'This is the big secret my friend,' Shannon surmised as he removed a tiny camera from his pocket. 'How old do you think they are?'

'Don't even think about using that thing,' Josey demanded referring to the camera.

'You're kidding—'

'He is not kidding, Mr Shannon—'

They turned sharply to the sound of Lui Jie's patient yet demanding voice. She was alone, which surprised them.

'Do as she says, put the camera away.'

Glancing at the key in Shannon's hand she said, 'I

knew you would be the one not to resist.' She walked in and stood with her back turned on them, studying the primeval mummies, as if considering a further response. After a moment she took her eyes away and walked toward the door. 'I will take that back from you now.'

He handed her the key as she walked past. She was clearly on edge. Long grotesque shadows from the lamp she held out in front preceded them into the tunnel, the way ahead momentarily taken over by Shannon's light as she turned her back and locked the wooden door, securing the ancient prisoners in their tomb.

They followed the dance of the flickering lights as she led the way through the burrow, finally electing to deal with Shannon's question about the age of the mummies.

'I brought Professor Verg here to show him what I had found; just as you have decided to do at your own discretion.'

Guilt reigned supreme, more so for Josey in letting Shannon out of his sight.

She looked back at them and saw it. 'As you know, the professor had been told about my discovery by the monk, and subsequently requested seeing it. Obviously, I could not refuse. However, when he saw for himself, he found nothing suggesting the ancient mummies harboured any secret other than the fact they are forty thousand years old, more than thirty thousand years older than most Egyptian mummies, which of course he fully appreciated out of respect for my discovery.'

Shannon couldn't hold his tongue. 'Sorry, did you just say *forty* thousand?'

Josey wasn't completely inept on the subject, but thought, trust Shannon to be cheeky and open his big mouth – he seemed to forget he was here uninvited. But, seeing as how Lui Jie didn't seem put out, he asked the question himself. 'I thought mummification only dated back to the Egyptians.'

'And that is perfectly true, it was an art known not to exist before that. The mummies that you have taken upon yourselves to come and see today, were mummified naturally, trapped suddenly within the mud and rock. Please, let me finish my story.'

Josey noticed Shannon was thinking about asking another question and silently presented him with a *don't do it* expression.

'Professor Verg then asked if I had found anything else. It was as though he was hoping I had. I told him yes, and that I would show it to him if he wished.'

'And what was it?' Shannon asked.

'A sheath, with something very strange to me, wrapped inside. When I leant into the shadows beneath the mummies and brought it into the light, Professor Verg was watching from over my shoulder. I was sitting on a stool, with the object on my lap as I unfolded it.

'I heard no response from him at first. I thought that he was being very quiet for some reason. I looked back at him and could not believe the expression on his face. Beads of sweat had formed on his brow. He asked if I had opened it. I told him yes, and that I did not know the meaning of what was inside. Only, that Zan had said, he, the professor, would understand. Yet, the prospect of actually seeing it frightened him.'

Shannon needed to speed her story along. 'What was in the sheath?' he asked again.

'A granite tablet,' she told him patiently. 'Which has

the same carbon age as the remains, but the professor, he already knew what the object looked like before I showed it to him.'

'How do you mean, *he knew?*' Shannon appeared to be taking over the questioning, but Lui Jie seemed not to mind.

Josey was really battling with the story's mystical connotations, and was wishing Shannon would shut up and stop acting so fascinated.

'When I began to unravel the perfectly preserved material, the professor placed his hand on mine and told me to wait. He then described exactly what was inside. He said he had seen its contents in a dream.'

Shannon couldn't erase a frown that had become permanently etched into his brow; he knew nothing of the *dreams*.

'The object that I had previously revealed was exactly as the professor then described. Covered in a thin layer of dust, was a circular tablet of black granite, disturbed only by my fingers from the first time I'd touched it. I removed the artefact and handed it to him. He ran his hands over it and could not believe the level of skill, and the unbelievable detail of the embossed symbols that adorned its surface.'

Lui Jie turned to the men and asked, 'Do either of you gentlemen know of the Dharma Chakra Wheel?'

'The word dharma is familiar,' Josey mused.

Brainiac Shannon knew. 'It's an extremely ancient symbol belonging to the Buddhists.'

Lui Jie's estimation of the newspaper reporter rose. 'The shapes etched into the stone had a very strong resemblance to the Dharma Wheel, but in a lot of ways it was very different also; this was something I had never seen before. Around seventeen centimetres across, it had a raised hemispherical shape at its centre, covered in pure gold, which could then be turned freely within a perfectly carved groove.

'Like all Dharma Wheels, there were eight spokes, in this case, four of them radiated from the dome at the centre in the form of parasols, another of our very old Buddhist symbols, which I'm sure Mr Shannon will have seen.'

Shannon was clearly feeling better about his newfound inclusion. 'Of course, yes.'

So far nothing she was saying particularly jelled with Josey, it was extremely hard to visualise the object she was describing.

She picked up on it. 'The remaining four spokes will perhaps awaken your mind, Detective,' she suggested, 'as they did mine - at the end of each spoke, protruding outwards from the disk, themselves having many radiating spokes, were Buddhist representations of the *sun.*'

Wow – coincidence, Josey wondered? The look he was getting from Shannon confirmed he too was seeing a connection between the object being described and what was now happening in Tibet. The hemisphere, the base of which could be likened to the equator, and the symbols for the sun, were all too suggestive - especially for Josey. 'Did the professor make any sort of comment about the object?'

'He did not, but I suspect it meant something to him.'

Josey wondered why Verg hadn't mentioned this particular dream, when his other dreams were just as fanciful. Forever the pragmatic, he needed to push all this mystical stuff into the background. He needed to concentrate on where Aaron Verg might be, and look for anything in what Lui Jie was saying that might include a clue, perhaps some reality about why he left so suddenly and without telling anyone he was going. 'Might we be permitted to see the tablet, Lui Jie?'

That was my next question, Shannon thought.

'I am afraid you cannot, the professor took the artefact with him when he left.'

He stole it? Josey wondered with alarm, this might not sit well with the authorities, and might place Shannon and him in as much trouble as Aaron.

Josey's bigger worry was that if Verg was anywhere in the open, somehow blindly driven by some sort of instruction written into the surface of the tablet, it was hard to imagine he wouldn't be subjecting himself to deadly doses of radiation. Josey sincerely hoped this wasn't Professor Verg's fate, because he now felt that the last person on Earth who deserved being taken down by this environmental disaster was the professor, a disaster that he warned would happen.

Had the secret of the granite tablet from thousands of years ago emerged independently in one of Verg's dreams, or had the Buddhist monk planted it in his mind?

CHAPTER TWENTY
Word from Verg

In the muted white of a Himalayan night, a relentless howling wind slapped its icy tongue against the outer skin of a trapped twenty seater snow-cat, rocking it as easily as a child's toy. The machine's motor purred softly beneath the dominant scream of the blizzard, providing much needed warmth. The cone-like beams of the headlights struggled through the storm's ferocity only as far as allowed, beyond which it was impossible to see anything other than a pale white limbo.

'It's a complete bloody whiteout,' Skipper John noted aloud.

He had brought the machine to a halt, considering it far too dangerous to proceed over snow that was known to have many fissures dotted around like abandoned mines. Inside this temperate cocoon with him were five other rescuers and the worst of the injured from the Village of Yu'yon.

Just like the Pan Himalayan trains, the cats were sealed against the mountain's frigid environment, but travel by night remained essential. During the day, occupants were required to wear radiation suits inside and out, but because the suits were in short supply they were reserved for the rescue team only, which meant all other passengers had to travel by night.

With the communication satellite down, the skipper had spent the last half hour trying to raise someone on the CB-radio, *anyone*. He'd tried the train station, the hospital, and every other cat on the mountain; plus all personnel that were hooked into the private system that triangulated signals between *the cat, a low orbit satellite, and a ground-based dish*. He finally decided to give it a rest and see if anyone was trying to reach *him*. Success came a few minutes later. The radio suddenly went wild with disturbance, interspersed with parts of words:

'John . . . are you receiving? . . . *Ca - - - ere me - - any sit - - - on - - - pro-f - - - sor - - - got bout fif - - - suff - - - rad - - - bur - - - an - - - ed hel - - - righ - - - I'm—*'

Amongst the gibberish, the Skipper believed he had recognised the word, *professor?*

He recalled to-mind that all personnel had been briefed about a visiting Australian, a professor by the name of Aaron Verg, a man SciCore were very anxious to locate. Perhaps someone had, but heavy static had washed away any chance of knowing who that was.

Prior to the intermittent problem with the satellite, Intel from head office suggested Verg had been heading for Mount Kailash, to an Archaeological site there.

'Skipper John here,' he said into the now silent machine . . . 'have you any news of Professor Verg?'

The dashboard radio exploded with crackle once more, as if attempting to deliver an answer; *nothing intelligible*.

'John Daniels here', the skipper continued. 'SciCore mobile relief force – can you please repeat your message . . . I say again, please repeat your message. . .'

He left the line open for the next half hour, but received nothing more than continuous noise.

Not far away, the Pan Himalayan was pulling into Lhasa station with the promised extra over-snows, along with its four VIP passengers and a handful of professional skiers. The new equipment had been waiting at Golmud when the SciCore contingent arrived there. Even Pearson was impressed by the organisational skills of Yu Chow, China's managing director of SciCore.

Further to his prowess he had preordained that this particular train should arrive at night, allowing the occupants to safely exit wearing only thermal snow gear.

Radiation Suits had been worn during the daylight hours, but were now bundled in boxes brought along by carriers that had come from the nearby hospital, where the SciCore contingent were to be bedded down, a place where they could discuss their next move. Pearson, Sleeman and Davenport were assigned shared accommodation. Belinda was given an area to herself.

The hospital was beneath ground, train tracks a dead giveaway that the tunnel which marked the end of the Himalayan line, was chosen as the rather clever location. With an additional layer of snow atop, it was believed personnel and patients would be safe from daytime's radiation. Warmth from a standby locomotive's diesel engine was fed through an insulated duct. Silos housed a vast supply of fuel that fed the trains and the cats, and now the hospital.

The tunnel ate into the hillside the length of the Pan-Himalayan train, ending in a dead-end. Three tracks with a ten foot shoulder each side equated to a total space forty feet across. Patients were laid out on stretchers placed across each track, the area between them creating isles for helpers to move between the injured. The last train to Lhasa remained at the station to house suited personnel and supplies.

New to the tunnel hospital were cavities that had been dug into the walls on both sides. These were similarly equipped with stretchers and bunks. Various lengths of cloth were hung across the openings for privacy. Some dugouts were not much bigger than the width of a single bed. Others were large enough to hold a small table with chairs. Each makeshift room was reinforced with Bamboo walls and ceilings

SciCore's director, Yu Chow, remained in charge of operations, both for the movement of supplies and the running of the hospital. A short stocky little man, he had a pleasant face. Presently though, it was creased with worry.

Belinda traversed the isles, anxious to see for herself the patients who had been injured, leaving the men to their conference with the director, which took place in one of the dugouts equipped with a table.

There was no shortage of light, electricity was pre-existing. Electricians had tapped power cables into ceiling lights. The cables hung down to junction boxes from which medical equipment was attached. Belinda counted fifty stretchers carrying victims with varying amounts of damage to their skin. Damage to organs could only be guessed upon until scans were performed, a task that would take time.

In one of the larger dugouts, a massive MRI machine had been set up, along with medicines, bandages etcetera. Most patients followed Belinda with their eyes as she passed by, but very few of the busy people attending to the injured had time to even look her way.

One man on a stretcher appeared to be dead, confirmed moments later when a woman who was taking his pulse, shone a torch into his eyes, and then covered his face with his blanket.

Belinda shuddered at the thought Aaron or Josey might be lying on one of these stretches; not to mention the very real possibility the Tibetan disaster could already be spreading to the rest of the world, a fear Josey had shared days earlier.

CHAPTER TWENTY ONE
Hope in the Tunnel Hospital

Underpinning all this sickness and misery was the memory of the endless warnings her fiancé had so openly given. Belinda shed a tear when she thought about how it might all have been avoided; if only Aaron's warning had been listened to. The needlessness was sickening.

It was especially upsetting to learn Yu Chow had not learnt of Aaron's prediction until after it became a reality. So far she hadn't had a chance to talk to him about that, but promised herself she would—

A big commotion began at the mouth of the tunnel. Several of the helpers with less pressing patients to deal with, hurried toward whatever was happening.

The sound of people shouting encouraged the urgency.

Curious, but careful to keep out of the way of helpers running between the tracks, Belinda flowed with them. As she neared the entrance it became clear more victims were arriving in rescue vehicles.

People in blinding white snowsuits appeared in pairs, carrying patient-laden stretchers.

She stepped back into a recess in the wall as bearers began to rush by, looking for space on the tracks to put down their stretchers. By the time the last of them had passed, she had counted fifteen.

She saw Pearson and the others poke their heads out to see what was going on. Feeling helpless, she made her way back toward them. The activity along the wall was intense. Stretchers were being repositioned to make room for the arrivals.

She came to an impasse, blocked by stretcher bearers and helpers alike. Pressing her back to the wall to stay clear made it impossible to turn away from the carnage. The latest injuries looked worse this time. Her heart was pounding. At any moment she was afraid she would see her fiancé lying on one of the stretchers. It became too much.

She closed her eyes to shut it out.

The blackness amplified the sounds. Distressed voices became more poignant, pain more extreme. She opened her eyes again - startled to find a man standing right in front, looking at her.

Caucasian.

'Are you all right?' he asked.

American.

She felt silly for some reason. 'I'm fine. Just a little overwhelmed I guess.'

'Understandable. Who're you with?'

Odd question, then she realised he meant which organisation. She pointed to her cohorts, watching from their dugout. 'I'm with SciCore . . . I mean, I don't work for them; I'm here at their invitation. I'm trying to find my fiancé.' She was gushing, still in shock at finding the man standing so close. Of course he didn't have a lot of choice; there wasn't much room to do otherwise. She didn't miss noticing he was a little handsome, about forty, and tall.

'Chinese?' he asked.

'Do I speak Chinese?'

'No, your fiancé, is he local, or—?'

'Oh, sorry, no, he's Australian.'

'*Australian*.' he repeated, as though that might mean something.

That scared her. 'Why, have you—'

He cut her off. 'That wouldn't be Professor Aaron Verg would it?'

She felt hopeful and alarmed both at the same time. 'Have you seen him? Is he all right?'

'Don't get your hopes up, but I maybe got a message in the cat – pretty sure someone was trying to pick him up on the CB.' He held out his gloved hand and said, 'I'm Skipper-John by the way.'

'Belinda.'

Skipper John's colloquial name suggests he's a fixture, she thought.

Ending the hand shake he gave a muted smile. 'Got the call while we were stuck in a white-out - about forty five minutes back toward Kailash. Weather was playing havoc with reception, but thought I heard the caller say the word *professor*. My ears pricked, because Professor Verg's on our list to seek and locate.'

'Supposedly he's at some archaeological site,' she

prompted hopefully, thinking that's what he was leading up to. She could have gone into what she knows about the archaeologist, but expressed more interest in his knowledge of the location.

'Mount Kailash is where the dig is,' he told her, 'so maybe that's where he is. It's about thirty miles to the west-*a here*,'

Belinda felt a wave of hope and faith flood in. 'Can *you* take me there?' It was a cheeky question but worth a shot.

The snow-cat skipper responded hesitantly. 'Sorry, I need to be assigned.'

Disappointed, she asked, 'Are you able to say if he was there?'

'I'm really sorry, no. Most of the message was completely garbled—'

'Is everything all right here, John?' Yu Chow interrupted. He had broken away from the other men to come and see what was happening.

'A development of sorts, Yu Chow,' John told him in a calm professional voice. 'I was just saying to Belinda here, I may've picked up a communication with Professor Verg on the CB, possibly at Kailash – I wasn't too far from there.'

'Oh, that is very good news,' the director responded ahead of a supportive smile directed at Belinda. 'This must make you very happy?'

She wasn't smiling. 'Not really. We still don't know if he's all right.'

Yu Chow looked at Skipper John and mustered a serious face. 'I suggest you take Ms Baxter to the location as soon as it is possible.'

'Slight problem,' John began to explain. 'I'm locked into three assignments ahead of Kailash, not due to go out there for another four hours.'

'Fortunately, six more cats have arrived with personnel,' Yu Chow revealed. 'Consider yourself reassigned. Take Ms Baxter to see her fiancé.'

'Right, done.'

Yu Chow said to Belinda, 'I will go with you; I must speak with Professor Verg myself.'

The ominous look on his face prompted Belinda to ask, 'What's wrong?'

His expression didn't change, seemingly at odds with his answer. 'I do not think there is anything to worry about. It is just that the authorities, they have asked me to speak with another that you know.'

'You're scaring me.'

'An Australian that I believe you are well acquainted with, a detective.'

'Mr Josey.'

'Yes. I am sure that once I talk with the archaeologist out there, all will be explained.'

'Yu Chow, don't get me wrong; I appreciate China has its own ways, but I've had all of the evasiveness I can take. Just tell me what's going on. Please.'

'All right, I will tell you. A few nights ago, there was an attack on the archaeologist.'

Belinda's eyes widened. 'Yes I know - why are you being hesitant?'

As surprised as he was that the Australian woman knew of the attack he let it slide. 'Because I am afraid your fiancé is a suspect.'

Her cheeks filled out and she said, 'That's absurd.'

'I wish I didn't have to tell you that you're detective is also a suspect.'

'You have got to be kidding me.' She considered the bad news carefully and saw the upside, 'I assure you they've got it wrong. I was in Australia with the professor and Mr Josey when we got the news about the attack on Lui Jie; I guess that lets them off the hook.'

He still looked worried. 'Not necessarily. Without any communication we cannot say if the authorities have reached there to interrogate him.'

'You're scaring me again; they do know why I hired the detective, right?'

Skipper John was at a disadvantage. He gestured over his shoulder and asked the director, 'Should I make myself scarce?'

'No, John,' Yu Chow answered quickly. 'Make your machine ready to go. Provide as many seats free as you can.'

The skipper gave a citizen's salute and took his leave as instructed.

Yu Chow reiterated Chinese protocol to help Belinda understand. 'Once an official request has been made, it must be followed through, even if the outcome is already known.' He went on to assure her the government knew everything there is to know about the three Australians.

'What do you mean *three?*'

'There is an Australian reporter being held at Kailash also, I imagined you might know about him too.'

Belinda figured out straight away that he was talking about Shannon, and was totally piqued at hearing he had found his way into Tibet, even though she had guessed it when trying to persuade Sleeman to help her get into

China.

'Do they know each other?' he asked her.

'They *know each other*,' she echoed looking peeved, 'that's the best I can tell you.'

'Are you okay?' he asked with sincerity.

'I'm sorry,' she apologised with a mute smile. 'It's been a very taxing week.'

'For us all,' he agreed.

She looked back at Pearson and the others, who were still watching. 'Will you get any trouble from them with my leaving?'

He looked over his shoulder at the foreign SciCore leaders and promised, 'Not while we are in China.'

CHAPTER TWENTY TWO
Journey to Mount Kailash

Deep down, Belinda really couldn't have thanked Yu Chow enough for his help. An hour later they were well on their way to Mount Kailash, pushing a path through the relentless blizzard. Visibility had improved since the whiteout that the skipper and his crew had experienced earlier. Snowfall had eased, but then the wind had picked up, sweeping snow close to the ground in a blur that resembled a plague of locusts speeding through the cat's headlights. The lights were good for about fifteen meters; after which blackness took over. Although the going was slow, there was comfort in the fact sunrise was five hours away, giving plenty of time to make it to the dig site under the cover of darkness. However, there wouldn't be enough time to return to base before dawn. The upside was that the cavern would protect them equally as well as Lhasa's train tunnel. It was this fact that underpinned Belinda's confidence in finding Aaron alive and well.

All up, there were only five people on the twenty seater cat, allowing room for potential victims to be transported back to the hospital. Belinda sat up front with Skipper-John and the director. Only two other men, medics from a special rescue force, sat behind them. Usually there would be five-or-six in the rescue team, but Yu Chow's directive was to free-up as many seats as possible.

The cabin was warm, a cosy cocoon that could easily be likened to an interplanetary vehicle on some frozen planet. The sound of the wind, filtering through the walls of the cat, resembled the slapping brushes of a carwash, combined with the howl of a thousand sirens.

Leaving the other SciCore executives behind gained minimal objection. Pearson said he felt more comfortable remaining at the hospital where he could oversee operations and monitor the injured. Sleeman and Davenport indicated they were happy to give up their seats for potential victims that might need to be brought back. Yu Chow suspected all three were suffering a degree of trepidation over the sheer idea of traversing mountains well known for having claimed many lives. Not to mention the new menace that was now an unprecedented norm for the Himalayas.

Belinda was talkative throughout the journey, speaking knowingly about the circumstances that brought the professor to Kailash.

Yu Chow knew the full story already, but she wanted the others to hear it. Hear about how Aaron had not only predicted the Antarctic holes, but the Tibetan vortex as well. How he was hounded by demonstrators for suggesting the ozone depletion might be largely natural.

None of the men offered their own opinions.

She told them he never once denied mankind was contributing, but this point had been ignored, especially by Shannon. She didn't pull punches when talking about her least favourite journalist. And she didn't pull punches with the Australian SciCore executives either, who seemed to have been comfortable with their heads in the sand.

The director could have been forgiven for thinking Belinda was grouping him in with his Australian SciCore counterparts, and felt compelled to bolster the Chinese Intel. 'You should know,' he advised her, 'your fiancé came to Tibet because Professor Huang, from the University of Beijing, advised him when the vortex had opened up. Coincidentally the archaeologist we are about to meet at Kailash, is Huang's niece.'

The connection between Lue Jie and Professor Huang, both of whom she knew of from Aaron's meeting with the monk, was news to Belinda, but she thought coincidence was a bit of a stretch. She wasn't convinced Huang was the catalyst for Aaron's change of plans in Hong Kong, taking the amulet with him when he left Australia strongly suggested Tibet had been his destination all along – *Oh God, I dare not mention Zan.* She could see Skipper-John was trying to join the dots. She realised she may be getting in a little too deep, and definitely had no intention of bringing up Zan.

One of the doctors couldn't refrain from asking, 'What's the connection between your fiancé and the archaeologist?'

Yu Chow glanced at him in the mirror. 'I think Doctor Bojing should perhaps wait to meet the professor before asking anymore questions.'

Belinda truthfully believed it would be better if they waited, and opted to say, 'Yu Chow is probably right. It's a long story. Let's just wait till we see him.'

The men could tell the woman was holding something back. Clearly there was much more to the story than was being told. John and his colleagues were decidedly intrigued by the Professor Verg story, but found the whole thing a little strange.

It wasn't hard to see the Australian woman was just as *afraid* as she was *excited* – afraid for the safety of her fiancé.

They weren't to know that the worry about Aaron was mixed with the feeling of responsibility for Josey, for hiring him and placing him in the face of danger.

CHAPTER TWENTY THREE
Josey works over the case

Josey and Shannon had been left with plenty of time to think about the ancient tablet, and about their fate if the worst came to the worst with the Chinese authorities. With computers and mobile phones out of commission, Josey could have guessed Shannon would be spending his time developing a newspaper story in his head, along with a few old fashioned hand written notes - he wouldn't have been wrong.

Josey did what he always did – went over the facts, also in his head.

What do we already know?

He once again cast his mind all the way back to Verg's first visit to the Sydney office. The story about Zan was nothing short of fanciful, or at the very least misunderstood.

Who meets someone on an off-chance, and then goes on to act like the meeting was expected - even planned, the latter most likely. If Zan *was* at the scene of Aaron's motorcycle accident, he must have then followed the scientist to the city. So, on the day, with no one going anywhere due to the traffic snarl, he sees Verg approach the shop, ducks in unseen, knows by the state of him that the first place he'll go is the bathroom, waits and makes his acquaintance. Perhaps seeing Aaron home safely was his original intention.

Josey had to admit though, the events that preceded the coffee shop, are a little harder to explain. There are the dreams; dreams about Zan; incidents that Verg had dreamt before meeting the man, not to mention, why was the monk even at the scene of the biker attack.

He had to have met him somewhere before. What other explanation is there?

Thanks to old man Verg's friend the clergyman, Father Mitchell Bennett, giving testament to having seen the monk at the hospital, and then Lui Jie's affirmation, Zan's existence is indisputable.

But, who is he? Josey wasn't about to subscribe to the observer-thing.

Even Lui Jie couldn't properly describe who the monk is, but then, given he is a fellow countryman; his sudden approach out of nowhere would have been less daunting for her. He didn't really think she believed the monk was a ghost. His predictions and talk of secrets being exposed were obviously enough to exclude him as a suspect in her attempted abduction – at least, in *her* mind.

Actually, the more he thought about it, *were Zan's predictions any more surprising than Verg's?*

It was reasonable to accept he'd somehow found out about Lui Jie's discovery, but what about the secret that's supposedly embedded in the stone tablet? According to Aaron, the monk had alluded to knowing what the secret was, but how – and why did Aaron need to figure out what it was for himself?

What Josey knew about antiquities would fit on a dinner napkin, and he was well aware of his deficiency.

Shannon on the other hand was only too eager to share his encyclopaedia of knowledge. 'There is one thing I know about Chinese symbols,' he offered just hours after hearing Lui Jie's description of the stone tablet, 'there's a practise that dates back thousands of years, where they communicate with the dead using a special cauldron called a *Ding*; a sort of rotund urn, which they place in the burial tomb. I'm not sure if this still happens, but parts of the body are put inside. They're offerings that allow the living to communicate with the dead via the cauldron. Symbols inscribed around the object's perimeter speak of the individual's present and past lives on Earth, and the afterlife - sort of, *messages* in and out of heaven.' Shannon was doing well until he added, 'Of course it's all bullshit.'

If he was to be honest, Josey thought it sounded like mumbo-jumbo too, but responded with, 'One thing I've learnt about bullshit, it's only bullshit if it doesn't suit your purpose.'

'Come on Josey, you don't believe this crap about the tablet do you?'

Josey felt that for all intents and purposes, the story that the tablet harboured a secret was starting to sound like something out of a Von Däniken novel. He had no interest in opening that conversation, or in listening to Shannon go on about it. None of this was helping him figure out where Verg had gone, or why he had unofficially left on foot?

The answer came to him right at that moment. 'Verg's figured out it's a map,' he said aloud, as much to himself as to his mandatory companion.

'A map to where?'

'Who knows, like you said, the tablet might carry a message about a particular location that interests him, showing him the distance is less than what could be travelled on foot before sun rise.'

'Fair enough, but can I point out you don't have the tablet, if following is your big plan.'

Josey cast his mind back to Lui Jie's description of the artefact, and had to concede the thing was hard to visualise from her narrative, and certainly wasn't enough to work out where Verg had gone – or why.

'I have something that might help you, Detective.'

They turned to her voice, gradually becoming used to the fact her footsteps were as light and silent as a feather. Once again, the matriarch was standing right behind them. For how long, they had no clue. She walked into their quarters and sat on a stool beside Josey; she had a cell phone in her hand and it was displaying a photograph.

In spite of not being able to visualise the tablet from her description, Josey instantly recognised it. 'The granite tablet,' he said with raised spirits, yet at the same time trying to understand why she hadn't shown it before.

'I hesitated letting you see this,' she said on noticing the keen expression on his face. 'I was afraid you might try to follow.'

He looked at her apologetically. 'Lui Jie, if this stone is

capable of showing me where the professor has gone, your fear is well founded.'

'Just as I thought,' she said kindly.

'Whose phone is this?' Shannon asked.

It's a good question, Josey thought. 'Is the phone the Professor's?'

'No, this phone is mine; the professor took his with him.' She reached into her pocket and brought out a second cell phone that Josey immediately recognised as his. 'I wanted to put this picture onto your phone, but do not know how. If you are able to transfer it, you may take your phone with you when you go.'

Go; go where? Shannon thought suspiciously. 'You're letting us leave?'

She held on the reporter without an answer then shifted her focus to Josey. 'I know it's not as good as having the artefact, but it is most definitely better than nothing.'

Josey knew this meant he was the only one being allowed to leave. 'Can you show me how the picture will help me find the professor?'

Shannon sensed his participation was about to come to an abrupt end.

'I am afraid the picture alone will not help you,' she told Josey, aware he would be frustrated. 'I will explain.' She pointed to an area of the picture that showed a shallow recess in the middle of the tablet. 'When I first saw this circular shape, I wondered if something was missing from it.'

'And I think I know what it might be,' Josey said surprising her.

Shannon shared her astonishment. 'You do?'

She put two and two together, realising how the

detective knew. 'You are familiar with the amulet,' she reasoned.

'I am,' but he stopped himself from going on about Zan and the amulet in front of Shannon, he could see he was about to start asking questions.

However, he had no control over what Lui Jie was prepared to reveal. 'The professor worked out that the amulet fitted comfortably into the tablet, but could not fathom what its purpose was – or if he did, he wasn't prepared to say so in my presence. After he left without informing anyone, I started to believe he had worked it out – as it seems you have, Detective.'

She drew attention to a symbol and said, 'This is a representation of a Buddhist temple, which you will never be able to find on your own. As I believe this is where Professor Verg has gone, it is up to you to do whatever you must, I am in all good conscience, unable to stop you, but what I *am* able to do is provide you with a guide.'

'You have my undying gratitude Lui Jie,' he told her with all sincerity.

'I hope your gratitude is not soured by disaster. Your task to protect the professor is a responsibility not to be envied.' Her glance to Shannon was clearly passing the advice to him.

She told Josey, 'Your guide is a man called Da Wang Lu; he has offered to assist you; he is travelling tonight to see his family, and must pass the monastery on his way. He wants to leave at sunset, which will give him many hours of darkness to reach his home. Although he has a very speedy snow-bike, should you be slowed by the conditions in the first hour, I strongly suggest you both return to the safety of the cave.'

Shannon's sense of exclusion was now a reality, *skidoos only carry two people*.

Josey assumed Lui must have been pondering over whether or not to defy the authorities in letting him follow the professor. 'I hope this will not get you into any trouble.'

'It will not.' She handed him his phone. 'It is up to you whether you take the picture with you, whilst it can hardly take the place of the real thing in helping to find your friend, it may assist you in some other way – I can not say.'

'Well, thank you again, Lui, and thank you for allowing me to have my phone back.'

'Yes, thank you,' the anxious reporter added flippantly. 'Can I have my phone too?'

'Not just yet,' she told him politely, clearly worried he may want to use the camera.

Josey was set to disappoint him too. 'No offence Shannon, but this's where you and I go our separate ways,'

'Fine, leave me here to the mercy of the Chinese,' he moaned in his usual manner.

Although not indifferent to Shannon's disappointment, Lui did ignore him, warning Josey, 'Battery life is very limited in sub-zero temperatures, but I have had your phone fully charged. Keep it within your layers of clothing, close to the warmth of your body. You will feel if communication is restored. I am certain many people are already trying to reach you.'

Josey was ushered away to be provisioned with extra clothing and food enough for himself, the professor and the guide.

Shannon's final words for him were laced with sarcasm. 'If you don't mind me saying, leaving a fellow countryman behind isn't very Australian'

Josey felt he had a point, but so too did Lui Jie, responsibility for the professor's safety was enough of a burden. Shannon would be a hell of a lot safer staying in the cave.

The dejected reporter didn't see it that way, he found a place to sulk about being left to deal with the authorities, which was now made all the more difficult by the fact two of their detainees had decided to leave before the mandatory interrogation. And in spite of Lui Jie's claim she would not be in trouble with the authorities when they arrived, he had very strong doubts.

CHAPTER TWENTY FOUR
A plan to rescue the Australians

Inside Mount Kailash, those who could sleep did so. Both entry points to the cave were crudely sealed with bamboo barricades, which were more to do with keeping people in, than radiation out. The fact no one inside had been affected during the previous daylight hours, it was considered to be safe inside the cavern. It wasn't known if this was totally true.

Skipper John and the others approached the site with only an hour left before sunrise. As expected, they were held up by the relentless storm, and now with no time left to make it back to Lhasa.

Five miles out from the site, the snow had given way to bare earth and easing rain, but the wind persisted and continued to do so until the skipper brought the machine to a stop near the main entrance to the dig-site.

Two night-watchmen draped in wet weather skins met them outside the barricade. Cautious at first, the men relaxed when they saw Yu Chow step out from the over-snow. Exiting the machine, Belinda was alarmed at noticing one of the men who had approached the director seemed emotionally upset. She wasn't able to understand what was being said, but something was obviously wrong. Yu Chow looked so distressed; she was worried something bad had happened to Aaron. It was mostly fear of the answer that held her back from asking.

Skipper John and the medics with their bags of medicines and instruments, came out and stood at her side, leaning into the wind. 'What are they saying?' she shouted above the howl of the storm, assuming one of them might have a handle on the language.

It was John that listened for a moment and told her, 'There's been a death.'

'Oh my-god, who?'

He motioned for her to wait while he continued to listen, before telling her. 'One of the archaeologists by the sounds, a local woman injured too.'

Everyone was being buffeted about and anxious to get inside, a cue for the skipper to get things moving. 'Yu Chow,' John interrupted. 'We need to move.'

The director broke away from the dubious welcoming party and waved the visitors toward the entrance. 'Yes, yes, come, I will escort you in.'

The bamboo structure was lifted away by guards, and the troop followed Yu Chow into the dimly lit cavern. Belinda's heart lifted a little, bolstered by the hope she would soon be together with her fiancé.

It was 5am when Lui Jie was awoken. The time was of little consequence once told that Yu Chow had arrived with two medics and the woman called Belinda Baxter.

She hurriedly dressed and made her way to the area they called *The Temple*. Unlike most other areas, its walls had been decorated in colours associated with the Buddhist Monks; bright reds and gold.

Introductions were reasonably stilted. Lui Jie had a lot of issues to deal with, not the least being the death of her mentor - and the critically injured woman found on the roadway.

Learning that the woman had been found by Detective Josey, and that he'd played a major part in saving her life, Belinda felt heart warmed, but the telling of the story brought tears to the Matriarch's eyes.

Assuming she was crying over the loss of her mentor, it was impossible to resist giving her a hug, in spite of not knowing if the gesture was appropriate. Belinda told her, 'I'm so sorry for your loss, Lui Jie.'

Buried in the arms of this stranger, the matriarch spoke as she sobbed. 'Mr Leung was a great man. He was like a father to me.' And then gently easing the Australian to arm's length, she was effectively calmed at the sight of the visitor's genuine empathy.

But Belinda was aching to ask about Aaron, taking this moment to scan the visible area in the hope she would suddenly see him. When her eyes returned onto their host, the grieving woman had drawn her eyes away.

'Lui, what is it?'

The arrival of the professor's fiancée was unexpected for her, and now presented a challenge. Lui Jie needed to be careful about explaining to Yu Chow the absence of the two Australians and the part she played in it. Restoring eye contact with Belinda, she told her, 'The professor has left. I'm sorry; I know how much you were looking forward to seeing him.'

Belinda's heart took an immediate dive. 'My God, not again,' she breathed. 'And the detective?'

'Detective Josey has also gone. He is continuing his task to find your fiancé.'

Yu Chow looked rattled. 'You were instructed to keep these people here.'

Although the director's tone seemed designed to install undue stress on the Archaeologist, Belinda saw a defiant strength in her, and believed that by ignoring him, she appeared more concerned that the men had put themselves in harm's way by leaving the cavern.

'Where is the reporter?' Yu Chow asked in an attempt at drawing attention back to himself.

'Welcome to the party,' Shannon's voice cut in like a knife. Heads turned. His crinkled clothes indicated he had come directly from where ever he'd been sleeping.

Belinda told her compatriots from the cat, 'This's the Journalist I told you about, gentlemen.'

Looks on faces told Shannon good-things might not have been said about him during their journey. He gave his usual smug, devil-may-care grin.

Yu Chow had no interest in whatever was going on between Belinda and the Journalist. His main concern was redeeming himself with the matriarch. 'Lui Jie, we need to deal with your people as quickly as possible.' He gestured to the two medicos. 'Please take these men to the injured woman.' Looking at Shannon, Chow asked, 'Now, Mr Shannon, what can you tell us about the professor and the detective leaving?'

'Not a lot I'm afraid.' Shannon was flicking his eyes around, avoiding resolute eye contact with the director.

Although puzzled, Belinda understood he was trying to tell her something in private and told Yu Chow she needed to pay-a-visit, requesting that Shannon show her where to go.

On reaching the latrine for ladies, and on looking back to see the director wasn't watching, Shannon told her. 'I think maybe you should have a talk with the woman, she'll be able to shed some light on where they've gone.'

She looked at him quizzically. *Was this the new and improved helpful Boz Shannon?*

'The archaeologist found an object,' he explained moulding the air with his hands as if in a game of charades, 'it was a carved stone disk that your fiancé was keenly interested in, us too, except at first she wouldn't show it to us, or to be more exact, couldn't—'

'Shannon, you're not making any sense,' she told him in frustration.

'Ask the matriarch.'

Returning from delivering the medicos to the burn victim, Lui Jie saw the two Australians in a huddle and joined them. More than anybody, she understood how important it was to locate the professor without letting the authorities know where that was. She also understood Belinda was the one person who had the most to lose if something happened to him. She caught a glimpse of Yu Chow heading over, and excusing herself from Shannon she marched away with Belinda in tow.

Shannon went to follow, but Chow grabbed him firmly by the arm on arrival. 'Let the women talk. I must speak with you in private.'

Shannon swallowed a nervous lump in his throat, relinquishing his resolve to walk away.

CHAPTER TWENTY FIVE
A way to the ruins

Liu Jie took Belinda to the base of *Tunnel 14*, to the dugout where the ancient mummies lay at rest in their everlasting embrace.

'I believe you have a right to see what brought your fiancé to Tibet,' she told her.

Moving to the first mummy, Lui touched it with reverence, marvelling at its hunched posture, she spoke with immense pride and wonder. 'This one is a female,' she explained. What we know about her is that she travelled here from what is now Tanzania. We cannot say why, but we know from other discoveries that she travelled through Egypt, Iraq and Afghanistan.'

She shifted to the second mummy on the right, which was somewhat entangled with the first. Once again she touched the remains. 'And, as extraordinary as it is to believe, they are thousands of years older than any other mummies ever found.'

Belinda was so astounded, not only by the obvious significance of the find, but by the fact her fiancé was for some reason ordained to become privy to it, and now she. Her questions and doubts were too overwhelming to muster an immediate response. Eventually, all she could think to say was, 'And your uncle's carbon dating proves this.'

'Oh, I see you know of my uncle.'

'Only recently.' Belinda focused on the remains. 'They seem to be in a huddle, like they are frightened.'

'Yes, it must have been something very sudden that has taken them. Their *embrace*, indicates they were together when they died, and living in the same time. Except for the supports that have carefully been added, their poses are exactly as found when I released them.' Taking a moment to study the face of her guest, the matriarch recognised Belinda was knowingly focused on the smallest of the mummies. 'This is their small child,' she confirmed.

Although nodding acknowledgement, Belinda seemed unsettled.

'Is there something that you do not understand?'

'No, it's not that, Shannon mentioned an object that you found with the mummies, can you tell me about that?'

Lui studied her guest with interest, recognising an involvement with the professor beyond that of fiancée.

'I'm trying to figure the connection between the mummies and the thing that was found.'

The surprise on Lui Jie's face made Belinda realise she

may be pushing too hard, but she needed to know if it had something to do with the secret Zan had spoken of. 'Did Aaron have anything to say about it?'

She gently exhaled and said, 'He was fascinated, but said that it meant nothing to him – at least that is what he told me.'

'You didn't believe him?'

The matriarch could see the concern in Belinda's eyes. 'Truthfully, I am a little disappointed he was not able to shed more light on what he saw. However, I do believe the tablet has enticed him to go to another place.'

'Lui Jie!' The raised voice was that of Yu Chow calling her from the mouth of the dig, preferring not to enter the dark passageway.

'Yes, I am coming', her voice echoed back along the tunnel. 'We should go,' she whispered to Belinda while gesturing toward the doorway.

Belinda led the way out as requested.

'There is a very ancient ruin, twenty miles north of where we are,' Lui told her in a low voice as she began closing the door, 'an abandoned Buddhist Monastery, this is where I have told Detective Josey I believe Aaron has gone.'

With heightened hope, Belinda waited for her chaperone to secure the door.

'No Monks have lived there for centuries.'

'And this is the place you think the tablet has taken him to. Do you know why?'

She turned the key on the door. 'I do not. However, there is no other such place, for perhaps a hundred miles.'

'Lui Jie,' Chow's voice persisted in the gloom. 'We need to talk.'

'Yes, we are coming.'

Belinda had been fully expecting Chow's urgency would be about making it *clear no one was to leave until the authorities arrived*. She couldn't have been more right.

After settling down for milk tea with Lui Jie, the two Australians and Skipper John, it quickly became clear that Yu Chow had become even more concerned than ever; perhaps fear had unsettled him again, having thought about the army finding the detainees missing upon arrival. He claimed he was equally fearful of the perils that may befall them if they embarked on the same dangerous journey as their friends. 'We are in enough trouble with Beijing already,' he tried to reason with everyone. 'Trust me; you do not want the Red Army after you.'

A chill loped through Belinda's veins. 'Why the army, surely this is a police matter?'

'Under normal circumstances, yes,' Yu Chow admitted. 'But, I think you would agree recent events are anything but normal. While we are faced with such peril, the Chinese police are not permitted to enter the danger zone. All investigations are being conducted by law enforcements that become available during extraordinary circumstances. It could be any one of a half dozen authorities.'

'If not the PLA,' Shannon warned in his usual knowledgeable manner, 'it could be the PAP, or the PLASF, or the Paramilitary forces, or even the feared Public Security Forces.'

Chow gave him a disapproving glance, raising the reporter's regret for opening his mouth.

Lui Jie saw Belinda's worry and weighed back in,

focusing on the director. 'I think we need have no fear of The Red Army, or any other authority. Perhaps Yu Chow, you should take audience with the Buddha, he may calm your concerns. We are very well equipped here,' she reminded him, 'with much food, water, and shelter. Do not feel your responsibilities will be lessened by your compassion.'

He recovered with, 'What would you have me do?'

'I will go with these people to where I believe the Australians have gone,' she answered. 'Already the professor has shown great concern for *our* safety; now let us show him the same courtesy. Perhaps one of your doctors can stay to help our resident doctor. I have seen for myself that our patients are stable and not in a critical state. We can also take Tian, our guide for the local area. Do not be concerned about Mr Leung; we have placed his remains beneath the snow, where he can lay at rest until the next rescue vehicle arrives.'

Yu Chow wasn't impressed with being reprimanded, but he had to concede the wind had been taken from his sails. With Beijing's backing, he had the power to stop the archaeologist forcibly if he so chose. Instead, he opted to give her an explanation, and a plan of his own. 'We must hope that the two men have made it safely to the ruins that Lui Jie has told us about, because already the sun has risen. But *you* must wait for nightfall.'

Skipper John took that to mean the trip was on. He looked at his watch. 'We've got six hours to kill.'

'Yes,' the director told him. 'But John, if the Australians are found, I must insist you bring them back here to face the authorities. Mr Shannon and I will wait for their arrival and explain the situation. One Australian detainee is better than none.'

Shannon wasn't happy about being the one excluded, yet again. As much as it pained Belinda, she took it on herself to promise him a scoop as soon as they got back with the professor.

'He may not be here when you return of course,' Yu Chow pointed out. 'The authorities may arrive well before that, and they may want to take him back to Gulmud straight away.' He placed a firm hand on Shannon's shoulder. 'I am not without influence my friend. You will be fine.'

Shannon looked anything but convinced. 'I hope I'm not the only one who ends up in the clink.'

The word *clink* brought a frown to the director's face, but his interest wasn't enough to make him ask what it meant.

While waiting for their departure, Belinda and Lui Jie spoke privately in her quarters, covering such matters as the extraordinary discovery of the ancient mummies, and of their associations with the professor and Zan – a series of validations. She was delighted to learn that the illusive little man *really had* visited the Archaeologist to predict Aaron's arrival, the visit and the prediction providing further credence to the monk's existence.

CHAPTER TWENTY SIX
Verg's vigil in the snow

For two hours and forty five minutes he trudged through pelting monsoon rains, never ceasing to mull over his prediction of a disaster in the upper atmosphere, no longer just a prediction. The threat to mankind pervaded his thoughts, pushing aside a more personal hazard, the real possibility he might soon perish on the mountain at the hand of the radiation.

Deep indentations marked Professor Verg's footsteps, only to be quickly erased by the blizzard. Blinding snow had replaced torrential rain, both far more extreme than usual, yet welcome friends right now, providing protection from the ever present solar wind and its resulting creation, magnetic storms.

His mind drifted back to the young faces at the university, hanging on his every word. He hoped those words still resonated, and that they and the rest of the world were free of this unprecedented event.

He rested from his gruelling walk and reached for the amulet, which now hung from a twine around his neck, brought it close to his face and inspected the four embossed parasols that were equally spaced around the circumference of the stone. He'd fastened the disk using the small eyelet positioned atop one of the parasols, assuming it to be the top of the disk, and therefore representing north.

Removing the stone tablet from his backpack, he sat it flat in the snow. The amulet from around his neck, he lowered toward the tablet's centre, whereupon he inserted it into the matching recess, it clicked home. This was the third time that he had stopped to make a calculation.

The temple ruins, represented by a Dharma Chakra wheel to the left of the eyelet, lay in a nor-westerly direction on the amulet. The position of the ruins was marked by a small anticlockwise Swastika, a symbol that swept back into antiquity, way before the Nazi's claimed it as their own.

Earlier, Aaron had huddled in the snow for half an hour at less than a half mile from the dig, afraid to venture further until he had worked out how the compass worked. The point of reference became obvious once he identified it, the archaeological site was symbolised by three skulls, his point of departure.

And now, six hours into his journey, although the compass on his wrist watch wasn't capable of telling him where the Temple was, he checked it anyway to see how closely it agreed with its ancient counterpart. It wasn't that far off.

He was pleased that he was still on track to reach the Buddhist temple; the time left however, was not so pleasing – fifteen minutes to the ruins – ten minutes till sunup.

He needed to hurry. Looking over his shoulder to the east, he saw a splattering of light filtering through a thick blanket of snow.

Exhausted, he drew deep from that place where mind overpowers matter, and found the strength to quicken his pace, albeit with a niggling doubt.

Why the hell have I been chosen to do this?

The thought had followed him ever since arriving in China. To travel half way around the globe on the say-so of one man, smacked of being a little crazy. This was a question he'd asked himself many times. If he thought he hadn't answered it, would he have made this journey?

Maybe the answer is what I want it to be.

His *doubts* were caught in a revolving door, the Yin and Yang of what was real, and what wasn't. His father had called Zan an Angel; Fantastic Neurological flashes from the mind of a deeply religious man whose dying—?

Abruptly, blinding sunlight stabbed into the snow nearby, and incredibly, created a bubbling puddle of steaming water. Conditioned by the badly burnt people that he'd already seen, and not to mention his very own prophecy, he knew that what he was seeing before his own eyes was no menial event. If there was any doubt the sun had become lethal, there was no such doubt about the melted snow left by the orb's indifferent blast from the heavens; so too the stone walls of the ruins, his destination, now suddenly towering skyward, a pale stone-ghost masked behind a curtain of windswept snow, the crumbling walls offering dubious shelter.

He ran toward them on unwilling legs, the sticky snow

causing him to stumble and fall face down.

Inches away, protruding from the snow like a stone cold marble statue, a man's face, transformed by searing heat - and the frigid hibernation that followed - never to awaken.

There was no time to ponder the man's fate; melting snow was morphing into rain all around, exploding into puffs of steam.

The victim had very obviously been struck by the radiation; that would be the professor's own fate if he didn't get a move on. He struggled to his feet and once again pushed through the pain. Streams formed with each step, tiny splashes lifting like crowns, a moment ago not possible.

Just another fifteen feet to go before the temple would wrap its massive walls around him. Little comfort as he was soon about to learn. As he made it through the stone archway that seemed destined to stand perpetually over the decaying wooden door, he was once again attacked from above; the roof had long since surrendered to time; the gaping hole sanctioning the arrival of lethal radiation. He jammed himself into a recess in the hope of avoiding a direct dose. The reprieve was effective yet brief; rotting timbers giving way at his feet. A resounding crunch reverberated in his ears as he landed on something brittle, twelve feet below—

CHAPTER TWENTY SEVEN
The mystery of the Temple

When his senses returned, he became aware that only a few moments had passed. He knew this was true, because ground-snow was still falling from the hole he had created, having followed him into the underground passageway where he landed.

He assessed his surroundings as best he could in the dim light, windowless stone walls indicating he was within a manmade subterranean sector.

Safe – for the time being.

Except for a faint glow filtering in from above, there was no other light; the passageway faded into blackness in both directions. Having fully expected he might find tunnels beneath the abandoned ruins, he had made certain to equip himself with a torch, which he *borrowed* from the archaeologists.

Included in his backpack, were some tins of sardines, fruits, nuts, and the screw-top container from the same shop in Lhasa that Josey had visited, carrying a litre of water. And, some stolen produce from the kitchen at the dig.

He rummaged through his rations and took the torch from his bag, only to discover it wasn't working. Annoyed for not testing it before setting out, he gave it a solid slap. The sudden jolt brought it to life; it flickered, and then settled, finally painting away the gloom.

'Oh, shit!'

Surrounding him was a carpet of skulls with ancient smiles. Some were mercilessly smashed, having served to soften his fall; – *intact for who knows how long, till now.*

He couldn't dispel a deep guilt over their belated defacing.

Collecting himself, he got up and carefully stood clear of the grinning skulls, and made an executive decision to head to the right for no particular reason, *baseless plans are only as good as the outcome.*

He'd taken just a dozen steps before a noise in the opposite direction modified his decision.

Noises in abandoned buildings usually don't just happen. Perhaps it was a further collapse of the aging structure.

Sooner or later the once mighty temple would lay flat beneath the snow. He convinced himself the sound was caused by a falling rock or timber, but in the absence of a proper reason to continue in the direction he was going, he decided to go the opposite way, towards the sound. Checking the compass on his wristwatch he noted the change would lead him to the west. He set out, following the light of his torch.

Far enough into the tunnel to have visually receded

from where he began, to the maximum the torch could reach, about a hundred feet, he noted he hadn't seen a single doorway.

So far - no fear of being lost.

The noise he heard had been faint, like a dull thud. He needed to pause occasionally, restrain breathing, and listen.

He walked on for some distance without the noise being repeated. Then, it came again. Ahead, just inside the cessation of the torchlight, dark vertical shapes appeared, interrupting the repetitive texture of the stone walls. On closer inspection they turned out to be the adjacent entrances to a corridor crossing at right angles.

At the junction, he panned the torch left and right, establishing that the new passageway once again went beyond the strength of the light, in both directions.

No point in procrastinating about which way to go.

He opted to continue clockwise, to the right, *north*. This being the first turn, he needed to begin marking a trail. He utilised small strewn rocks that had been scattered around over time, forming them into right-angles on the cobbled floor, rounding the corner to point back to where he started.

A few short steps into the right-hand passage, he heard the thud – twice, again from behind.

Someone else is down here. Perhaps seeking refuge?

He stepped back to where the passageways crossed, adjusted the line of stones to mark the new direction, *south*, and followed the sound, which was repeating every few seconds now, louder with each step. The rhythm of the massive stone blocks that formed the walls were giving him a measurable sense of distance, each one roughly a five foot span.

Counting the blocks allowed him to estimate how far he'd travelled; this crude method of measurement told him he had traversed close in proximity to a city block. The sight of a doorway stopped him in his tracks.

He hesitated for a moment before moving to stand in front of it. Gripping the medallion that hung from around his neck, his fingers danced across it as though interpreting braille.

He moved closer, centring the torchlight. It wasn't the door's sheet metal structure, with rivet like dome-heads lining its edge, or even that it stood in stark contrast to the temple's predominance of stone and wood that held him in wonder; it was the embossed symbol that marked the middle of its face.

He lifted the medallion and cupped it in his palm to study the ancient detail, seeking confirmation. There was no disputing it; the *symbol on the amulet* matched the *symbol on the door*, except that the one on the door was concave. Even before he inserted the stone medallion he could see that it would fit perfectly, just like it had with the Tablet.

Once in place, the amulet acted like a key. When he turned it, the vault like barricade hissed open with such suddenness and shrill tone, it startled him. He removed the amulet as the door began receding into the stone wall, into a cavity, ending snug against the smooth rock surface of the Jam.

The blackness inside seemed unaffected by the invading light from Verg's torch. It was as if the space beyond was without walls, or so distant that all ambiance failed to reach them. He swung the torch left and right, along the passageways where he stood, and welcomed the solidity they offered compared to the cold emptiness of the black limbo beckoning in front of him. If not for the matching symbol marking the door, he would never have allowed himself to be drawn into this unknown void.

Points of light appeared inside – *faint* – growing in size and intensity – yet, no radiance reached an edge of the intense blackness.

The floor, which seemed to be non-existent, except for the stars that sparkled there, was inviting him to take a leap of faith, to *step inside*.

He accepted, *afraid,* yet with an esoteric belief that somewhere inside this room of stars lay the answer to all his doubts.

The moment he took one step into this abstruse realm, gravity dispersed. He stopped, amazed by the sensation of floating in space. He didn't tumble or loose footing; rather, he continued to move forward without moving his feet.

He drew a deep belated breath; he hadn't done so in quite a long while.

Perceptibly, his passage into this eternal cosmos was bringing him no closer to the trillions of stars that had quickly accrued, bar one, which had grown first as a distant cloud of dust; void of detail.

Closer, its pale light became the image of a *very recent event*. His mind leaped to that incredible, indelible memory – Mount Kailash, and the rocky grotto encased inside the cavernous archaeological site, and to the ancient figures left lying in their final resting place, the poses, undeniably that of the ancient mummies found by Lui Jie.

Aware of a sudden drop in temperature, he turned and saw that the stars had vanished. They had been displaced by a splattering of windswept snow. Sleet drifted in on a draft and settled its icy crystals on the thick furs that blanketed the shadowy trio.

Am I really seeing this?

Although developing a strong desire to leave, he doubted any deliberate attempt to move would achieve this wish. As impossible as this scene was, he was driven to investigate, to re-evaluate what he was actually seeing, three people huddled together in a desperate embrace, a baby between two adults, just like the mummies in the Cavern – not mummies, solid and real this time.

Are they dead? Is this how they died?

They remained motionless, not responding to his presence. He crouched, and cautiously prodded the figure closest - *still no response*. In the dim flickering light of a flame burning nearby, he realised they had indeed frozen to death, *but when, the air is cold enough to kill, but not to preserve tissue.*

The stench was not that of the dead; but that of *the unbathed living, dead no more than a few minutes*. He reached out and dared to touch the man's face – it was warm—

He pulled away as though touched by acid.

Aaron, do not be afraid.

The voice came from the darkness all around; he didn't know where to face it.

What you see before you is not of this time, and yet all of time can be a single instant relative to where you are as an Observer. You're special insights, are fusing past and present at this moment; sanctioning the ability to look upon the one who precedes you. Like him, you lay frozen in the snow where you fell at the hand of another, and yet here with me now; do not be alarmed, I will not allow you to die. Accept what I am saying without fear, gaze upon the family before you, and understand.

Peering deep into the darkness, expecting to find the source of the voice, he couldn't see anything, but he knew it was the monk.

He forced himself to dispel disbelief.

These people are as they were, forty thousand years ago.

Staring back at the remains, he wondered if *his* body too is frozen in the snow, just as the monk has told him.

A knot formed in his stomach, he heard his own voice asking, *can I believe any of this is real, and not just in my mind? – One final dream before I die?*

You are not dying, but you are dreaming, yet, while dreams fade – realities persist, even in the face of absurdity. What was once absurd is now fully understood. What is still considered absurd will one day also be understood. What you can imagine, must be possible. Your strange thoughts about the unobserved universe are therefore likely to be true.

You are in the perfect place to be the receptor of broad thinking. Into this realm, Astronomy, Astrophysics, Cosmology, Gravity, Space and Time will be the workplace of your mind.

'You will advance so fast that by the year twenty forty four, you will break open the final frontier of space, expose the truth

about the universe, and explain the link between naked singularities and black holes, and perhaps creation itself. You will see that creation is encompassed in all these things, united as one simple existence, an eternity of collapse and re-creation. You will learn that knowing all these things will pose even more mind bending questions, such as what are we doing here? Are we merely observers, or do we have an even greater purpose? As you come closer to answering all these questions, you will ask yourself, does the physical universe have need of us and vice versa, or do we exist together, mandatorily, in an eternity of creation and collapse.

But by then, your time on Earth will be done. In time, with the help of the ancient stones; the secret that is imbedded within them, will deliver the knowledge you will need to begin your quest. When you awaken, you will not immediately recall everything that I have told you. But you will fulfil the challenges ahead as promised – you will not be alone so long as you are mindful of someone who is close to you . . .

CHAPTER TWENTY EIGHT
Lost in the Ruin

He opened his eyes, wiping away the vision, and the fading memory of it.

'Verg, can you hear me?'

The detective was hovering above - melting through like a cold flame, drifting somewhere between the stars and the storm.

'Are you all right, Buddy?'

His voice seemed real - different to those spoken in a dream. The chill on the professor's skin was like a million ice needles – *real*. He became increasingly aware that he was lying on his back, surrounded by skulls – exactly where he had landed when he fell.

'Verg, its Josey. Are you hurt?'

Josey wasn't floating; he was clutching a rope that had been suspended from the splintered floor above.

The dream, although vague, still annexed Aaron's mind. He raised his head and glanced around at the dark passageway, sensing the familiarity.

'Can you try and move?' Josey suggested from the end of the rope, preferring not to settle and contribute to the carnage caused by Verg's fall.

The thought prompted Aaron to see if he could get to his feet. Pain shot into his hip. He suffered through it, propping onto an elbow, sitting with legs out straight, rolling to the side and lifting a knee. With hands flat amongst the broken smiles, he shifted from a crouch, finally lifting into a bent stance. He staggered, sending bleached skulls skipping away.

'Mr Josey, is everything all right?' It was Josey's guide calling from above.

'Yes, thank you for your help, Da Wang,' he told him. 'Safe travels to see your family.'

Aaron wasn't listening, he was fixated on the corridor, the one he thought he had already gone down - the one seen in his *dream*. It was only partly lit by the torch at his feet, and somehow looked different. He recalled getting the torch out of his bag after the fall. Logic told him he must have gained a glimpse of the corridor as he fell, which became subconsciously embedded in his mind, bringing on yet another hallucinatory dream.

Josey was almost to the bottom of the rope when he looked down and noticed Verg pointing the torch into the dark passageway. 'Don't even think about going down there, Verg. You'll get lost.'

Aaron's eyes remained fixed on the blackness beyond the strength of the light. 'What the hell do you think you're doing here, Detective,' he demanded without looking at him.

'Might ask you the same question.'

'Shhhhh! Did you hear that?'

Thump. Thump. Thump.

Josey heard it this time.

This was the same sound that had taken Aaron's attention in the dream.

Coming from the room with the symbol on the door?

The urge to relive the dream—if that's what it was—was too great. He set out, following the light of his torch.

Josey swore and released from the rope, reluctantly sinking his boots onto the scattered skulls, stepping double time to get away from them and catch up. He couldn't comprehend the young scientist's complete lack of hesitation, advancing into the darkness as though familiar with what lay ahead. His considerable pace didn't miss a beat as he turned into a passageway to the left, ignoring the right.

Josey followed, trusting his guide wouldn't fall into a pit, or take too many more turns.

Thankfully, less than two minutes later he came to a sudden stop at a deep recess in the wall. Josey wasn't disappointed to discover a heavy metal door blocking access. He was on the verge of insisting on going no further anyway. 'Why do I get the feeling you've been down here before?'

'Because I have.' Aaron had his torch trained on the middle of the door, on a shape he immediately recognised.

Before Josey had a chance to respond, the professor had removed the amulet from around his neck and inserted it into the matching concave replica. He gave the key a sharp clockwise turn without pondering which way to rotate it. The door hissed like a pressure cooker, sliding open to reveal god-knows-what.

Josey's analytical mind began to search for rationality. *How did Verg know to come here—and why?*

He decided the professor must have searched the subterranean passageways when he first arrived, having fallen on his way out. Then, believing he had dreamt about the door was enticed to return after hearing the mysterious thumping. Josey had to admit that the thumping, which he had heard himself, was a solid mystery. But that aside, *what was Verg hoping to find inside this dark room?*

Did he enter the first time he came here?

Once again the professor proceeded without trepidation, taking the light with him at an alarming rate. Josey followed for fear of being left in complete darkness. 'Wait, what's in here?'

'You wouldn't believe me if I told you,' the professor said without breaking his stride.

Josey wished he had his own torch, which still sat uselessly atop the rotting timbers in his backpack at the place where he had entered. Without it he was forced to rely on keeping Verg in sight, a task made difficult by the inadequacy of the torch-beam to establish any sign of an object, or an opposing wall.

To his horror, the professor, and the light, dissolved into the oppressive darkness. He called out for him to stop, but the plea was ignored, or unheard.

Josey was alone and disorientated, uncertain whether or not to follow, or perhaps try and find the door they had entered through. The black took on a solidity that seemed bent on closing in, crushing him, preventing him from ever leaving.

He called out again and again, but got no answer.

CHAPTER TWENTY NINE
Failure to reach the Temple

Travelling by day and suited against the radiation, the over-snow with Skipper John at the controls, carried the spontaneous rescue team toward the ruins.

If their friends on foot had not yet reached the site, they would be faced with the double threat of either dying in the blizzard, or perishing in the resulting radiation if the present storm suddenly cleared. There seemed little chance of the blizzard subsiding though, and given the extent of the whiteout, there was little chance of seeing a fissure before it was too late.

Belinda kept her eyes on the window anyway, sitting in silence beside the skipper. To John's right sat Tian, a tall bony looking man who would be their guide until they reached the ruins. Doctor Bingwen sat beside Lui Jie on a second row of seats, the cat was equipped with a further four rows of seats behind that, which would become useful only if able to transport Un-suited people at night.

Lui Jie had expressed her disappointment she may not be back in time to accompany Mr Leung's remains to the capital of Beijing, where they were to be held in state at the invitation of the president; until such time as a government funeral could be arranged. It was assumed that this wouldn't be till after the crises had passed. The possibility the disaster might already be the new norm; she pushed it from her mind.

John joined Belinda in her careful observation of the white nothingness ahead of them. There was a need to do so, because the radar had become less than efficient due to the ferocity of the storm.

The storm was nothing compared to what was about to happen in the next second—

—A shaft of sunlight the width of a bus stabbed out of the heavens and began tracing its hellish beam across the snow in front of them, turning snow to steam.

'Oh my God – John what the hell is that?'—

The distraction took the skipper's attention away for only a second, just long enough for the cat to suddenly spear deep into an unseen trench—

The big machine shuddered to a halt.

Unceremoniously thrown forward, the occupants were left with no time to brace for the impact.

John was recovering from having struck his head on the dashboard, trying to focus back on the phenomenon that had taken his attention. It was no longer possible to see out of the windscreen, snow had packed hard against it, which thankfully hadn't fractured.

Still stunned, Belinda and the others were trying to get back to their feet, which wasn't easy given the floor was now angled at forty five degrees toward the front, where most of them had ended up.

Still in a daze, they took hold of whatever they could to keep upright.

Belinda leant back against the windscreen having picked herself up from where John had lain bleeding from a knock to the head. 'Are you all right?' she asked him.

Before he could answer, the ambience within the cabin began to glow white hot. Swamped in this internal whiteout John struggled to his feet. His head swam from the knock, sending him hard against where Belinda was propped, whereupon he gripped her by the arms and pulled her savagely toward him as if to release her from a magnet. They fell and became momentarily sandwiched face to face on the floor before John rolled her clear.

Spreadeagled on their backs they reluctantly squinted into the blinding blaze, the source of the light beyond the windscreen; the deadly column of sunlight, eating away at the snow like a laser, instantly creating a pond of boiling water that bubbled fiercely against the glass.

Belinda's voice trembled, 'Are we going to die, John?'

He looked back into the whitewashed faces of his passengers and saw they too were asking the same question.

He was incapable of finding his voice.

His fearful expression convinced them that they were all in a *deathly serious* place.

CHAPTER THIRTY
Two discoveries

Josey wasn't sure how long he had been standing in the same spot, surrounded by darkness and immersed in a dank cold that was beginning to infiltrate his snow-gear. He couldn't see the steam leaving his mouth, but could feel its warmth live and die for the one-second it took to brush across his frozen face. It began to occur to him he might die in this place. He wondered what story would be given to his family in Australia.

I am very sorry Mrs Josey, your husband is missing somewhere in Tibet; I'm afraid his remains might never be found.

'Damn you Verg!' he suddenly shouted—'Are you still alive in here!'

No answer - not even an echo?

Something colder than the air itself touched the side of his face - something wet. He felt another - and another. He removed a glove and held out his palm to catch whatever it was to investigate it, *coming from above*. He did something he hadn't yet thought to do, he looked up. A pale light revealed snow was falling - *from the roof,* a roof that was becoming brighter by the second, progressively exposing the room's massive height.

Its swirling—

The light intensified, and so too his understanding of what he was looking at . . . *It's the goddamned sky.*

The realisation swept over him in a wave of fear; the roof was long gone, and the clouds were clearing. He was standing at the base of a shaft that appeared to reach the height of a twenty story building, and he was faced with the very real possibility unfiltered radiation may threaten to align and bathe the floor, which he could now clearly see. He reasoned, the room's curvature accounted for the absence of echo. Scanning the entire base of the wall, he first saw that the sliding door that he had entered through stood a hundred feet away, thankfully, still open.

Did Verg go back out without saying a word? He clearly must have heard me calling.

Then, he saw there was a second door directly opposite – *closed.*

Maybe Verg left through there - it had shut after him and that's why he couldn't hear me.

A slight sting on his face and right hand encouraged him to inspect the cause. He once again removed his glove. His right palm was covered in red blotches - *burns?* He decided it was time to get back to the passage. He started toward the open doorway, but was stopped in his tracks by a blast of lethal sunlight splashing across the stone floor in front of him, across his only means of escape. The sun's slightly oblique angle allowed him temporary refuge, *for how long?* He couldn't be sure . . .

'Josey . . . Is that you down there—?'

He peered into the glare. The caller protruded from the rim of the shaft, the blazing sun at his back. He called to identify himself. 'It's Shannon!'

'What th' hell?'

'Don't ask . . . It's a long story! . . . Have you found Verg?'

Josey was able to make out that Shannon was wearing a radiation suit, and wanted to know if he had more with him. He didn't get a chance to ask.

'You better get out of there my friend; while you still can!' Shannon was well aware Josey was only dressed in snow-gear.

Josey wasn't about to argue; in the few seconds it would take to reach the door, how much harm could he come to? The door began to rumble closed; the decision was made for him. He ran through the light of the sun. Unlike nuclear fallout, the sun's unhindered rays could be felt, beginning to visibly etch into his snowsuit. The only escape lay ahead via an ever decreasing gap.

In the final few feet, he dove at the narrow opening in the hope he wouldn't be crushed.

The heavy door clipped the toe of his shoe as he passed into the relative safety of the merciful darkness of the corridor.

He lay on his side, panting, certain the door's journey would not have relented; not in the way an elevator door at the Mall would upon sensing human contact.

He was pleased to be in the pitch black, away from the hell that reined inside the shaft. He wasn't afraid of not being able to find his way out; the distance to the-one-

and-only turn was clear in his mind's eye, but what then?

Would Shannon have brought any spare suits? Was anyone else with him? If not, why was he on his own, and how had he found the location of the ruins? And what about the professor; what grizzly fate might he have met?

He shelved his thoughts and began making his way out, palming the wall, picturing his location. His pace was much slower than before, back when he'd been following his dubious guide. He didn't want to miss the turn.

When his palm found air instead of stone, he knew he had reached the corridor that would lead him to where he came in, to the skulls scattered on the floor, to the gaping hole and the rope that would take him to the outside. What new threats awaited there?

He was pondering this question when a blinding light coming from the passageway ahead, stabbed into his dilated pupils. He squinted in an attempt to regain vision.

'Josey, I thought I'd lost you.'

As his eyes adjusted, the blinding light, which was no more than a handheld torch, gradually became acceptable to look toward. Although unable to see beyond the glare, the voice was clearly Verg's, but he wasn't alone.

CHAPTER THIRTY ONE
Trapped

There were low murmurings coming from Verg's direction.

'Who's that with you?'

'People who urgently need help.' He swung his torch, revealing a dozen souls - men, women, and one child. They appeared to be Tibetan tourists.

The sight was shocking, reminding Josey of the poor woman he'd found on the way to the dig site. These people were suffering from burns, some more severe than others. 'Where did you find them?' he asked. 'I mean, where the hell did you get to?'

'Sorry, I went through a door thinking you were right behind me. I was following the sound we heard and found one of the men thumping the floor with a length of timber. They were disorientated as far as I could tell. I tried going back, but for some reason the amulet no longer matched the key. I called out, but when you didn't answer I moved on – There wasn't much choice.'

An old man separated from the cluster of injured people and brushed past the professor, turning to face him with eyes fixed on the amulet. He had one of his own, which he removed from the inside pocket of a thick animal skin jacket. He was gesturing, as though he was trying to explain something about the two objects.

'I think he's trying to show you why they were trapped,' Josey offered.

The man was talking excitedly, arousing interest from his stricken comrades.

Recalling that Belinda mentioned the professor had visited China before; Josey thought he might understand some of the language. 'Any idea what he's saying?'

'Not a clue, but he's clearly intrigued I have one similar. I'm intrigued myself.'

'I wouldn't get too excited, obviously the amulets are many, a path to a safe house for travellers - and a key to enter.'

Verg had a different take on it. 'No, look, they're different.'

Josey saw his point; the duplicate that the man was wearing didn't have the embossed eye. 'Maybe they're all different.'

'Maybe.' He was tempted to tell Josey about his vision of the mummies, but decided to keep it to himself.

The injured party watched on and wondered what the westerners were discussing. They had hope in their eyes; perhaps hope that they would somehow be rescued by these two foreigners.

Josey told Verg, 'Hey, I know this'll excite you, your friend Shannon's up top.'

Verg looked like he might be stewing over the idea of Shannon being referred to as his friend, and the fact the slimy reporter may end up being some sort of liberator.

Without warning, one of the injured men collapsed onto the stone floor, vomiting where he lay. Verg swung the torch. The beam graphically brought to light a mass of bleeding sores that had erupted across the poor fellow's entire face. Horrified by the distressing sight, he told Josey, 'If Shannon has transport up there; we need to get these people to it.'

'It might not be so easy,'

'Why's that?'

Josey was surprised he didn't understand. 'The snow,' he reminded him.

Verg's eyes widened. 'What about the snow?'

'The acid – you didn't feel that in the shaft?'

Blank . . . 'What shaft?'

'Bloody hell Verg, you sound like you never even went in there. The snow was acid, look.' He showed him the red marks on his hand, received when he cupped the falling snowflakes.

The professor began helping the stricken man to his feet, effectively ending the discussion, and seemingly avoiding any interest in what Josey was showing him.

Josey couldn't have guessed what was running through the professor's mind at that moment, but the expression on his face suggested, that after falling onto the skulls, he may have suffered one of his episodes. It was impossible to know, or even imagine, that this could be the reason Verg knew the way to the door, but once he had gone in ahead, he must have made his way across the floor so fast, that he'd done so during a lapse in the snowfall. He let it go, opting to join in on helping the injured make their way back along the corridor, toward the carpet of skulls, and the way out.

When they reached the collapsed entry point, the injured—judging by their disquiet—indicated they had not seen the ancient remains before, suggesting there was at least one other way in; and out, which they hadn't been able to find—

'Don't come up!' It was Shannon again, calling from above. 'It's not safe!'

Verg shone the torch onto the injured. 'We have sick people down here!'

The reporter grimaced when he laid eyes on the extent of the injuries. 'Jesus.'

The sound of Verg's voice had established the scientist was with the detective.

Josey asked Shannon if anyone else was with him, but he confirmed he was alone.

Before he could be interrogated further he dashed away. 'Pretty sure I have first-aid equipment with me,' he called back. 'I'll check it out!'

He was gone before they could respond.

It was possibly the only immediate course of action anyway, but Josey was still keen to ask if there were extra radiation suits.

Shannon was about to find out the hard way, just how much they would be needed.

CHAPTER THIRTY TWO
Shannon has bad news

He stepped from the confines of the ruins just at the moment direct sunlight found its way to the ground. Right before his eyes he saw the snow begin to boil, and he felt the heat penetrate his radiation suit.

The cat was fifteen feet away – too far. He saw a blister rise on the material of his right sleeve. This sent him charging back into the cover of the monastery.

He came to the top of the gaping hole, introducing a dusting of potentially lethal snow over those scattering below. He slid down the rope, his gloved hands barely touching it, bringing with him even more unwanted white powder. While showing his compatriots the damage to his suit, he gave them the bad news. 'We're not going anywhere from this place'

Even the Tibetans understood his meaning, and those fit enough to do so, began dragging the injured further into the protection of the passageway. The besieged group huddled together and pondered their plight - well away from the collection of ancient skulls and the gaping hole above.

Shannon noted that every chance they got, the professor and the detective deliberately locked heads in private conversations, indicating his presence was not being well received, or included. He guessed they were discussing how he'd found his way to Kailash on his own – *if only Verg knew what he knew, he wouldn't feel so smug.*

The immediate danger outside the ruins abruptly abated, to the point where quick trips became possible. Five of the fittest among the injured were clad in radiation suits that had been located in the storage lockers of the cat. The seriously injured were assisted aboard the heated vehicle one at a time, alternately sharing the last remaining suit to traverse the short distance through the snow storm. Josey, the professor, and four of the least affected, stayed below the monastery to prevent overloading the vehicle, which had been moved into the shadow of a free standing wall outside the main structure.

With nothing to do but wait, Shannon's concerns that his counterparts had suspicions about his arriving at the ruins alone, rose to the fore when asked by Verg to explain it in detail.

He told them the reason he'd decided to take his chances to reach the professor, was because he wanted to warn him his own people were out for his scalp.

'What the hell are you talking about?'

'They think you're responsible for jamming the communication satellites.'

'Is this another one of your bullshit stories, Shannon?' Verg asked with a rising blush.

'Believe me, you'll find out I'm telling the truth soon enough.'

Josey stepped in to calm things down. 'Aaron, let him talk.'

Shannon's story began with what he said transpired back at the railway station, when he and Yu Chow arrived there after being picked up from the archaeology site by one of the rescue cats. He'd shared the ride with a few of the sick and injured, along with the body of Chen, the old matriarch. While we were waiting for the train, 'Pearson called an urgent meeting at the makeshift hospital, basically trying to minimise damage to himself and the company . . .'

*

During the meeting, and against Pearson's wishes, the Australian reporter is permitted to stay and listen to what is being said, but has been relieved of his phone, note book, pen, and a small pocket recorder and camera, items that were returned to him by Lui Jie back at the dig.

All of the rooms where they might have sat for their meeting have been seconded for patients in need of specialised equipment. Where they now sit, surrounded by train tracks and stretchers, affords them a most surreal setting; their voices blending with the sounds of agony.

'Yu Chow,' Pearson says, 'I'm trusting this is not going to be a problem in Beijing.'

'I cannot give you that assurance, Mr Pearson.'

'You're saying you have no influence with these guys?'

'Influencing the ministry of environment must be weighed up very carefully. I have no idea how they will react when we are able to talk with them.'

'I thought you said they serve as China's nuclear safety agency; and this surely is a safety issue.'

'Begging your pardon Mr Pearson, but - this is *not* a nuclear attack as such.'

'You know what I mean,' he clarifies with annoyance.

Shannon barely manages to stifle a grin.

'We don't even know how many injured we're dealing with,' Pearson pushes. 'And unless we get some sort of dialogue going with the authorities and get the satellites sorted, we might never know.'

A man whose been loosely referred to as the station master, vacates the stool he was sitting on and moves away from the meeting. They watch him walk to the mouth of the tunnel and stand there, silhouetted against the grey wall of windswept sleet. He stands for a moment as if listening, then paces back to announce, 'The train is coming.'

Shannon's face drops to somewhere near his boots, raising a hint of enjoyment on Chow's face. 'Well Mr Shannon, it looks like this is your ticket out of here.'

'I'm going with the train also,' Pearson says, 'I'll be more use in Beijing.'

Chow stares at him blankly. 'You are most welcome of course. I do not think any of us can be of much help here.' He turns to the Australian scientist. 'And you, Mr Davenport?'

'I'll be staying; I have friends out on that mountain.'

His decision worries Chow, telling him, 'It would be very dangerous for you to involve yourself; I think that you should consider returning to Beijing also.'

'I'll be staying here until I know my friends are safe.'

Yu Chow didn't argue.

In the fifteen minutes it takes for the train to pull into the station their three most pressing issues are theorised over—

The hole in the ozone.
The resulting radiation.
And the collapse of the communication satellite . . .

CHAPTER THIRTY THREE
Things change

The usual activity commences as soon as the train comes to a complete standstill. There is a moment of airlocks hissing open, followed by a flurry of suited people alighting with various forms of cargo.

One man in particular who is luggage free, darts in and out between the human traffic looking for someone. He stops one of the porters and speaks to him. A moment later, presumably armed with information, he continues along the platform.

Pearson and the others are oblivious when the anxious man comes to the window and sees them sitting at the table. It isn't until he is standing at Yu Chow's elbow and talks to him in Chinese that they become aware of his presence. His demeanour is far less than relaxed.

Yu Chow's expression confirms that the man is giving him some sort of news, and probably not good news. At the conclusion of the man's guttural delivery, Yu Chow responds with a deep sigh, stands and takes him over to the soup as though it might be a magic potion to relieve stress. The look on Chow's face as he returns to the table is anything but stress-free.

Pearson asks, 'What was that all about?'

They can see how worried he is about answering as he sits and appears to gather his thoughts, finally saying, 'He comes with information about the satellites.'

Looks go around the table like those of a small gang of nervous meerkats.

'And?' Davenport asks.

'It has been discovered that no less than five of our communication satellites are being jammed.'

Pearson looks ready to explode, 'By what?'

Yu Chow expels a breath from narrowly parted lips, and gazing intently at the Australian, tells him, 'Not by what - by whom.'

Davenport can't help squirming a little. 'Why are you looking at *me*?'

Pearson is now eying him too. Everyone is.

'Because our messenger friend here has come to us from the Chinese National Space Administration, and informs me that a rogue satellite, two days ago, was manoeuvred into position, and has deliberately brought about this jamming.' He looks from one bewildered face to the other, ending his study on Davenport. 'I am afraid I must tell you it is an Australian satellite—'

'Say-what?' Neilson's reaction sounds vicious enough that if he had a gun he'd put a bullet into somebody.

Chow provides unexpected support for the Australian. 'Director Pearson, don't be too quick to, how you say – point the finger.'

'I'll point more than my goddamned finger.'

'We might consider pointing at *Australia*, because the satellite is a SciSat; one of Professor Verg's.'

Pearson's mouth springs open; gobsmacked. His cheeks take on a tinge of red as a highway of veins rise above his temples. *'A SciSat?'* he repeats incredulously.

Yu Chow's eyes lock on Davenport again, expressing a certain sort of sympathy. 'I'm sorry to have to bring you this news.'

The American springs to his feet, catapulting his chair across the room. 'Jesus Davenport; how the hell has your guy pulled this off, and why?'

'Oh I see, now he's *my* guy.'

'Don't be a smart ass.'

The messenger from the National Space Administration, who had appeared not to be listening, jerks his head around and looks ready to intervene.

Yu Chow notices the man's demeanour and jumps in to calm the brash American down. 'We must keep our heads, Mr Pearson, please.' He glances at the man and gives a nod, assuring him the situation is under control, after which the fellow cautiously returns to eating his soup.

Pearson lowers his voice and focuses on Shannon. 'Not a word of this, you - or I'll have your guts for garters.'

'I do not think you need worry,' Yu Chow says having picked up on the sentiment, 'I doubt the reporter will be reporting anything, given it would put him in much more trouble than he already is.'

Shannon understands what he means, and he can't say he isn't worried. It is well known the Chinese authorities have little patience for foreign journalists, especially those that are considered to be actively introducing mischief into their country.

Five minutes go by without anyone uttering a word.

One by one they file away from the table and begin moving aimlessly around the room. Pearson stands by the window watching the activity on the platform. The station master tells them he has work to do and leaves the group to themselves. Davenport finally puts on his head gear and leaves as well, making no mention of where he is going.

'I'm off to the latrine,' Shannon tells Chow.

'Of course, when you return we will board the train.'

'Whatever,' Shannon mumbles under his breath as he walks away.

Upon his return, he finds his Chinese custodian gone, and Pearson still staring out the window, now puffing away on a cigarette.

Against the white glare, Shannon imagines the big American resembles an angry fire breathing dragon. The reporter gets no acknowledgement when he sidles up, but it doesn't prevent his attempt at starting a conversation. 'Well, this's fun?'

Pearson sucks on his inflamed tobacco, replenishing his calming cloud of nicotine, expelling it as he speaks. 'I'll tell you one thing boy-o; damned if I'm going down with Verg over this.'

Shannon pauses to think; then says, 'How do you suppose he did it; bring a satellite half way around the world to knock out five GPS satellites?'

'He's a goddamned scientist - how the hell would I know.'

Shannon isn't about to give up. 'I have to say, I'm

surprised satellites can be even jammed.'

Pearson turns, takes another drag and blows the smoke into the reporter's face. 'Like I said; I'm not a scientist.'

Doing his best to cough away the cloud that has infiltrated his lungs, Shannon decides there isn't much point in continuing, he can't use the information anyway, not if it pans out the way he expects.

He's about to walk away when Pearson picks up the thread of the conversation. 'Actually, it wouldn't be all that hard,' he volunteers, 'the right software on a laptop - and bingo.'

After he turns back to what's going on outside, Shannon holds on the bastard's stone-faced profile, *he knows I can't do a damn thing with this.*

Pearson rotates his entire body to deliver a final warning. 'All of which means, I don't want to see you anywhere near a computer.'

'Computers are useless right now, dumbass,' Shannon says almost inaudibly.

This produces a threatening frown, 'What'd you say?'

'Nothing,' he says like Mr Innocence.

With uncertain acceptance, Pearson returns to his smoking and his study of the activity on the platform.

Glancing around the almost empty room, Shannon asks, 'Where's my gaoler gone off to?'

Pearson remains statuesque.

There are a few people coming and going in radiation suits, and a couple of men who have taken up the one and only table, but it is the small window at the far end that begins to take Shannon's interest. Framed in it, is one of the all-terrains - at a standstill in the blizzard. The cat's door swings open and a man gets out and walks away, leaving it empty.

Without saying a word, Shannon leaves Pearson to sulk on his own, and to get a closer look at the abandoned over-snow through the window.

In spite of the carpeting blizzard, the driver's fading footsteps are still visible, leading into the tunnel hospital. Shannon waits in thought, but not for long.

Quickly deciding to take his chances, he leaves the station house and makes his way around to the vehicle, finding it still running. Standing beside the machine dressed in a radiation suit, he can easily be taken for the driver. He climbs the short ladder that leads to the cabin and brazenly gets in.

One look at the dashboard brings him close to changing his mind, but he tells himself it can't be that hard to work out how the machine runs, he'd picked up enough clues watching Yu Chow at the controls during their trip from Kailash.

The throttle is where you'd expect; the steering is dead centre on the dashboard with a joystick on each side to work the gears.

Navigation will be the tricky part, but once again he feels confident he has picked up enough tricks from his gaoler to make do. He has no idea of the exact location where Verg and the detective have gone, but he does know his way back to the dig; and he has a fair recollection of what's been worked out from the tablet. His hope is to solicit help from someone, but hasn't the vaguest clue who that might be.

If all else fails, with the cause of the communication blackout known, the GPS will probably be back in business within the hour, in which case he can simply place a call to Josey and tell him what he knows. When he divulges to Verg that his own people are his biggest enemy, he feels certain he'll be brought back into the loop with open arms, and maybe even directed to the temple.

He gives the throttle a pump and checks outside to see if anyone is paying any attention.

The few people he can see through the storm, are paying him no heed. Confidence boosted, he shoves the tiny joystick forward with his left hand and supplies the gas needed to set the machine in motion. It responds with ease, smoothly driven forward by the automatic gearbox. He turns the wheel to bring about the necessary hairpin turn and makes his exit away from the station . . .

CHAPTER THIRTY FOUR
Collapse

Massive ancient timbers cracked like thunder, followed by a rumble that brought Shannon's story to a resounding halt. Even at fifteen feet from the collapse, the mountain of snow that had sank through the ceiling, came close to burying those closest to it. The gaping hole had exposed them to swirling clouds of lethal radiation. A scramble to recede deeper into cover began in earnest, the able bodied aiding the injured.

'We'll pick up on this later, Shannon.'

The journalist dismissed Verg's less than trusting comment with, 'There's nothing more to pick up on.'

'So you say.'

A man urgently called out in his local language.

The three Australians swivelled their heads in his direction, but saw no obvious reason for what sounded like an urgent alert.

A woman standing nearby saw their confusion and

spoke in English. 'He has found a trapdoor.'

Pleased to have located an interpreter Verg said to her, 'I'm Aaron – and *your* name?'

'I am Alix.'

The man called out again.

'What's he saying?'

'He says we can go under, away from the danger.'

With no further prompting needed, they made their way across to where their guy waited – above a wooden hatch in the stone floor. Verg moved in to take hold of one of the metal rings that constituted the door's two handles.

Alix tugged at Josey's sleeve to gain his attention, and indicated the Australians should permit the local men to help with the lifting.

Together they heaved with a mighty effort, and the reluctant timbers cracked away from the stone an inch or two. Others moved in, and with deft fingers placed precariously under the door's splintered rim, they strained against stubborn hinges that had lain at rest for probable centuries. The air that escaped was moist and smelt of ancient mould—

Another rumble signalled a further smothering of snow, delivering the gathered skulls to their final resting place.

With the trapdoor leaning against its hinges in the open position, Josey shone his torch in. The illuminated floor of the chamber seemed to be plain earth and not much further down than about nine feet. A solid bamboo ladder presented a steep climb in.

One of the men who had helped with the door, elected to lead, aided by the flashlight. His passage was aided by additional light from glow sticks that Shannon had located in the cat.

With everyone settled and the trapdoor swung closed, the besieged party took timeout to adapt to their barren surroundings, and to come to grips with their dire predicament. Food had also been brought in from the cat and handed out; some of the locals hadn't eaten for days.

Alix spent her time telling the Australians about what had happened to the dozen people in her company, and how they had been taken by surprise by the radiation. Inversely, the foreigners explained who they were, and went some of the way in clarifying the cause of the disaster. The Tibetans were often emotionally affected by what they were being told, and openly showed their respect for the visitors from overseas, but this was all about to change dramatically.

'What the hell are you doing here?' Verg asked out of the blue as he pressed a fist into the reporter's shoulder.

'There's gratitude, I put my life on the line and this is what I get.'

'Tell me something I can believe,' he pushed out giving him another shove.

'Hey, ease up.'

Josey noted the disquiet on the faces of the tourists and intervened. 'Mate, I think you should do as he says and ease up, you're upsetting the people.'

To his credit, he backed off immediately. 'Sorry,' he told Josey as he put some distance between himself and Shannon.

Josey followed him. 'I know you guys have a history, but we all need to be on our best behaviour here.'

'Fine,' he said as he found a place to sit and cool off.

Shannon caught Josey's eye as he was moving over to join them, the detective's negative expression stopping him in his tracks. He reconsidered his approach, leaving the two men to enter into yet another private huddle.

Josey saw there was an immense responsibility hanging heavily over Professor Verg's head. He decided to take his own advice and for the time being, shelve any misgivings. There were a lot of questions as to why Shannon had arrived at the site on his own; and he understood why Verg would be brimming about it. Looking as tired as a man can get, the professor had closed his eyes, so Josey let him get some rest. Questions and answers could wait.

The subterranean room had little comforts, and keeping warm relied solely on snuggling close to each other. The allotted radiation suits were being worn over snow suits for extra warmth while sleeping, or when not moving about, which was most of the time. Both the radiation suits and the snowsuits were shared to cover the shortfall. Shannon pretty much kept his radiation suit on the whole time; he'd been elected to venture out every half hour to check if they could make it across to the cat, minus the key to start it. On one of his reconnaissance trips he found a man dead near the entry point to the ruins, the fellow had blindly left the confines of the over snow, apparently he could either have been unaware of the danger, or he was worried about his wife, who was under the ruins with the others and relatively uninjured.

Their vigil below the ruins continued without knowing how long they would be stuck there. They also had no way of knowing if the satellites were back on line, not that it would have done them much good, because all the mobile phone batteries were dead, and there was no way of charging them. Ordinarily they could have plugged into the cat's USB, but the cable connector was missing. The CB had been tried on several occasions by Verg; he'd gone out once an hour to check for himself; in spite of Shannon assuring him he had been trying every half hour.

Not knowing if the radiation would subside, or if someone might come with another over-snow to take them to the railway hospital, thoughts invariably turned to the possibility they might not be found in time. Soon, food and medicine would become their biggest problem.

Going over the question of how Shannon managed to find his way to the ruins on his own, and his explanation of how he got hold of the cat, Josey fully understood the discomfort the professor was feeling, and why it was eating at him, his suspicions were similar to his own. Verg was so put out by the reporter's freedom to come and go from the cat, that hardly an hour trapped in their new abode passed without him asking Josey if he trusted him. The first time he'd answered the question he'd said, 'From what Belinda has told me - I get your concern.'

Verg stuck to his conviction. 'He's hiding something.'

Not that he was prepared to say it for fear of starting another fight, but Josey had been thinking the same thing. He had to remind himself that Shannon had arrived with a warning, and that it stood to reason he could have gone further afield to escape the Chinese authorities. But then, perhaps he came to the ruins because he believed he stood a better chance in the company of his own countrymen, especially as he knew they too were wanted men.

Verg shot to his feet unexpectedly and marched across to Shannon, his body language clearly laced with rage. Before Josey had a chance to stop him, Verg had lifted the reporter from where he sat and slammed him against the stone wall. 'What have you got inside your stinking jacket there, Shannon?'

The Tibetans tightened their ranks, fearful the foreigners might have turned into mad murderers. Josey's insights allowed for a much more tempered approach, yet with equal alarm.

The professor's behaviour was completely out of line, and dangerous. Several of the younger men appeared to be readying themselves in case they needed to defend the others. Josey was attempting to break up the altercation, but an elbow to the face put him on his back.

'Leave it be, Detective.'

The distraction allowed Shannon to break free and head for the ladder. Verg wasn't done and meant to take chase but Josey brought him to ground with a grade-A tackle before he'd managed two steps. Struggling to get free, he rapidly realised the detective had a grasp as strong as a bear trap. 'Ask him what he has hidden inside his jacket,' Aaron pleaded while being held down.

The defiant escapee had reached the bottom rung of the ladder and was beginning to climb—

'Shannon,' Josey shouted angrily. 'Stay put,'

Alix was doing her utmost not to pass her panic onto her frightened friends, who had huddled together to create safety in numbers.

At the top of the ladder, Shannon was straining against the hatch to try and open it.

'Get your bloody tail back down here Shannon,' Josey

recommended, 'I swear if I have to come up there—'

There was little choice; he couldn't move the hatch on his own anyway.

Tended closely against Verg's ear, Josey gave him a recommendation too. 'Will you behave if I let you go?'

'Yes, get the hell off me.'

Embarrassed by defeat, he followed Josey to the base of the ladder to confront the disgruntled reporter.

Dusting himself off Aaron said to Josey, 'Open his jacket; you'll see he's got something hidden.'

Shannon held his arms clear in submission. 'I was going to tell you,' he said feebly. He tilted his head toward his pocket.

Josey reached in and knew exactly what it was before he even retrieved it; the missing USB cable connector. 'Where's your phone?'

'In the other pocket.'

'Get it out.' Verg told him through gritted teeth.

Shannon sheepishly reached in and retrieved the cell, but got no further than the edge of his lapel before Josey snatched it from him and turned it on; the screen lit up. He checked the mute button and found it activated. Mixed reactions emerged from the tourists, including an edge of relief that they now had a means of communication. In spite of having some idea the man with the charged phone had been behaving deceitfully, like the foreigners they felt his deceit was his fear of going into a Chinese Gaol. In addition, Josey and Aaron felt his being here was a half-cocked plan to travel down the mountain with his countrymen to achieve an escape.

Shannon's explanation was more about delivering his warning to Verg that the authorities were after him, but to his disappointment Aaron refused to buy into worrying about that.

In the absence of a provable scenario, Josey shunted all traces of doubt from his mind so that he could concentrate on more important matters.

'You're a bloody low-life, Shannon,' Verg told him.

'All right,' Josey demanded, 'Let's hold the agro and get to the bottom of this.' He eyed Shannon doggedly. 'You have some explaining to do, so get on with it.'

Caught out, his eyes darted nervously; reluctantly realising the detective was right. He was about to abide, when the resurrected phone silently vibrated in Josey's hand. He held the illuminated interface for Verg to see before putting it to his own ear. 'Hello?'

'Josey, thank-god,' crackled the relieved voice. 'It's Belinda—are you with Shannon, is Aaron with you?'

'Yes, we're all here - safe, but we have other people with us - some injured.'

'That makes the call bitter sweet, I'm sorry to hear people are injured. We have a doctor on-board, hopefully he'll be able to help – I've been trying to reach you since the satellite came good. I've quite a story to tell.'

'I think we both have, but your news the satellite's back may top ours.'

Verg was impatiently reaching out to take the phone.

'—hang on, someone wants to talk to you,' he said handing the cell across.

Eager to hear his fiancée's voice, Aaron took the phone smartly and stepped away for a little privacy. 'Bel, are you okay?' He heard her breathe a sigh of relief.

'I am now; with what's been happening up here I've been beside myself with worry.'

'How did you—?'

She cut him off. 'Aaron, love - I know you have a million questions; join the club. I'm sure Shannon can answer one of them. Has he told you he took off and left all of us stranded here in the middle of nowhere?'

The professor's eyes cut onto Shannon, carrying a clear hint as to what he was being told.

Shannon quite rightly squirmed.

'I think we're about to hear it from the man himself – are you sure you're all right?' he asked jumping past further explanation.

She hesitated, raising worry. Then finally she said, 'We are, if you don't consider our cat is stuck in the snow. We need help.'

'Who's with you?'

'I'm with four others, including the cat skipper and a guide. The skipper needs you to come with Shannon's cat to pull us out. We've called Lhasa, but he says the temple is closer.'

Aaron saw the quizzical expression on Josey's face and told him, 'Belinda's in trouble. Get shithead to fire up the cat; don't let him go out on his own.' He focussed back on the call. 'Sweetheart, we'll be on our way to you as soon as we sort out Shannon.'

Her voice lowered, taking on a confidential tone. 'You'd better warn him he's in a lot of trouble with the Chinese; one of them is with us.'

Aaron was too elated to overly concern himself about the extent of Shannon's behaviour, or who the Chinese on board might be; his concentration was on getting to Belinda as soon as possible. 'It's annoyingly ironic that we now need his help, but he won't be travelling alone.'

'I suppose we can thank the little bastard for finding you . . . Put him on actually, the skipper wants to give him the coordinates. Maybe he's worked them out already; otherwise he'd never have found the ruins.'

On that note they ended the conversation.

Belinda's presence in Tibet was a double edged sword for Aaron; he was both glad and sad that she had followed him, into what was fast becoming a hell on Earth.

What Aaron didn't know at this point, was the hell that Belinda had already gone through; along with all the other people on Skipper John's all-terrain cat.

CHAPTER THIRTY FIVE
Communication

In spite of the trouble Belinda was in, there was an accumulative air of relief following her unexpected phone call, the only one still worried was Shannon. He apologised, begged and pleaded with the detective to help him explain his actions to the authorities. Josey pointed out that he had little influence and in fact could provide little to no support for the way the reporter had handled the situation. Further, he wasn't really interested in taking up valuable time talking to Shannon when he needed to be thinking about how to appease the Chinese himself, not to mention set his mind to solving the case, which was hopefully about to take a leap in the right direction, now that he could talk to Maxine in Australia. The call to Max had to be put on hold in order to conduct Belinda's rescue. He didn't want to call from the cat for obvious reasons, but he was able to charge up his phone – there were four other phones sucking in power during the trip, including Alix's and one other of the Tibetan's.

They lost time waiting for the right weather in which to reach the cat, they would have lost more time if not for the benefit of donning radiation suits. Once on the move, Shannon told them the journey would take an hour if all went well. There was little conversation with him, Josey and the professor had said all they wanted to say.

Josey spent the time thinking. A lot had happened since the beginning of the case, but nothing that advanced it beyond the hunch he had before leaving Australia. He didn't have any proof about the person he suspected of trying to kill his friend's fiancé, but he did have a clue about why. He also knew that person wasn't responsible for the attempted abduction of the archaeologist, because logistically it would have been impossible. But even more inexplicable than some of these aspects of the case, was the professor himself. Why had he come here on the whim of a mysterious and elusive monk?

And where was the Monk now - the guy who seemed to have all the answers?

Thirty minutes into the journey a blizzard set in, which halved the speed of the cat. With sufficient charge in his mobile, he decided not to wait in contacting Max. He went to the rear of the vehicle and kept his voice low. She had so many questions he hardly had time to get to his own, but he did, including the most obvious one – *was the rest of the world being hit by the radiation*?

'What radiation?' she'd asked, which answered the question – but at the expense of terrifying her. He told her to keep the news to herself; other than mentioning it to Carl, who he knew could be trusted not to repeat it. Josey had more than one reason for not wanting her to speak to his family about it, but knew it was wrong not to.

He gave Max the abridged version of how Verg had been on the money about the vortex and moved on. Primarily he wanted to know what she had found out about SciCore, and about the biker.

'The biker's name is Joseph Sheppard,' she told him.

'One of the demonstrators?'

'Yes, and you'll be pleased to know you were right, he's connected to Davenport's son, Lester.'

'The boss's son – as we thought. So Sheppard writes the threatening letter, and his association with bikes explains the smell of oil on the paper, but not much about the motive.'

'It might when I tell you the son *works* for Sheppard, and Sheppard runs a company that invests heavily in SciCore.'

'How heavily?'

'It amounts to two thirds of their annual budget; they call themselves, Flock Investments, which is kind of cute in a weird way.'

'How do Flock Investments make their money?'

'As far as I can work out they're purely investors with no production arm.'

'Well we need to know what they get out of the SciCore investment and if they have other affiliates. If so, what do those affiliates do? I'm keen to know if any of them work in manufacture.'

'So far I only have the name of *Flock's* accountants, which is about as useful as knowing the true identity of Santa clause I guess.'

'No, that's a good start. Get Carl to delve deeper.

Become a would-be client asking for references, and if they won't give out names, ask for the type of work they do.'

'Carl will be pleased to hear you're all right, Chief, he's been calling every other day.'

'It's nice to know people care.'

'Shut up you idiot,' she laughed.

'Do me a favour and let my girls know I'm all right. Try not to scare them. Tell them I'll be in touch soon.'

'Will do, and say hello to Belinda for me. Stay safe, okay.'

'We'll be fine - try not to worry. The case is building, but don't ask me how this will all end - I have no idea. Do this quickly, Max, if the satellite can be taken out once, it can be taken out again.'

'Done.'

'Bye.'

'Bye Boss.'

Josey came forward and sat with Verg, two seats back from where Shannon sat at the controls. He glanced across at the professor, who had finally moved his eyes away from the way ahead and closed them; there wasn't much to see anyway. He didn't look particularly comfortable, but at least he was getting some rest, or so Josey thought.

Sensing he was being watched, the young man spoke with his eyelids shut. 'What are you looking at?'

Josey felt compelled to speak with equal bluntness. 'Maxine has identified the bloke who attacked you.'

He lifted his head and opened his eyes with observable interest. 'Really, who?'

Josey filled him in on all that Max had told him,

including about Sheppard's company.

He'd never heard of Sheppard and knew nothing about the investments. He wasn't really sure how the information helped the detective's case. Josey could, but for now he was keeping that under wraps.

Although he'd told Max he had no idea how Verg's mission to Tibet tied in with the case, he promised himself he wouldn't keep the questions at odds with each other. Somehow it was all connected, but how? He needed to try again to get inside Verg's head; inside what Josey believed was a confused mind. He ventured forward as respectfully as he could. 'Can I ask you something, Aaron?'

'Should I be worried?'

His favourite catch phrase.

He sounded a mite cryptic, but Josey ignored it. 'When you jumped ship in Hong Kong, was it because of the vortex?'

'It was, and now you'll ask me how I knew.'

'I will.'

'Did Lui Jie mention her uncle to you?'

'She did, the professor from the Shanghai University. Correct me if I'm wrong, but he's the guy the monk says validated the carbon dating of the remains.'

He gave confirmation with a light nod. 'Huang called me while we were on hold in Hong Kong; said who he was, and that he had been following my work for months. He knew about my prediction. It prompted him to do some research of his own, but was unable to support my findings. He put that shortfall aside the moment he heard the vortex had opened.'

With this one piece of information from Verg, a whole

bunch of answers to questions fell into Josey's lap, but it also raised others. 'You know, I have it in my head that you were coming to Tibet all along; am I right?'

'Because of the Amulet,' he acknowledged insightfully.

'Exactly, what changed your mind about it?'

He scoffed, 'I wish I knew. But, when Huang rang me in Hong Kong I started to feel the monk had his finger on the pulse from the very start.'

'I hear you; and on that score, does it strike you as being far too coincidental; the monk first links you to an archaeologist in Tibet, whose uncle then calls you out of the blue at the very moment the vortex opens, diverting you from Boston to go there? As far as I recall, your prediction made no mention of it happening in Tibet, or anywhere else in China?'

'A word of advice, Detective; don't let the monk get under your skin, or next you'll find yourself being invited to join the Observers.'

Josey smirked, pleased the professor could manage a sense of humour in such a dire situation, and delighted the state of affairs seemed to have erased his stutter some time back. He was also pleased Verg appeared not to be buying into the mystical stuff. The scientist's next comment proved it.

'Belinda's told me you don't subscribe to superstition, so I gather you feel the discovery about the biker is leading to some sort of conclusion to the case.'

'It is, and it's clear the attack on the archaeologist is connected somehow.'

He pivoted his head with both eyes open this time. 'What possible evidence points to that? Why would you suspect this Shepherd character has come all the way to

China—?'

'On the contrary, I know he hasn't.'

Verg settled back and shut his eyes.

Josey hoped it was only his *eyes* that were closed. 'Let's talk about you're satellite.'

He sensed a change of subject. 'Are you telling me there's a connection there too?'

'There is, but let me ask you first, seeing as how you designed it, I thought you might understand why they're blaming you for what happened to their communication satellite.'

'Believe me, I haven't a clue. I can't wait to ask.'

Josey thought for a moment, considering how much Verg should be told, given there were answers yet to surface. He decided he couldn't be caught out mentioning Sheppard's connection to investments, because it almost automatically meant some of the money would have found its way into the development of Verg's satellites. There was no harm in talking about his boss's son though; he had a right to know Lester Davenport was an employee of Verg's attacker.

To say Verg was surprised was an understatement.

What Josey also couldn't talk about just yet was the benefits *Flock* received from their investments with SciCore, because his hunch was telling him it involved manufacturing, the details of which were still being investigated by Carl Norris.

'Do you mind if we talk about Zan's mission? I'll have a lot more to tell you about Flock later.'

'Zan's *mission*?'

'What would *you* call it?'

'To be honest I haven't labelled it. I thought you didn't

subscribe.'

'I don't, but the connections and coincidences are way too compelling to ignore; the vortex for one connects you to everything that is happening, right back to the biker attack and your meeting with the monk in the coffee shop.'

'It took you a while to believe that happened.'

'I was waiting for proof.'

Verg recognised where that proof came from. 'The archaeologist, right?'

'No, it was the talk you had with the priest that convinced me, but Lui Jie presented solid confirmation, even if she did call him a ghost.'

'She called him *that*?'

Josey smiled at how relaxed Verg sounded. Normal. '*Like* a ghost was the way she put it.'

'I can identify.'

'So getting back to the mysterious mission, what's your take on it now?'

'Now?'

'Now that you've done exactly what he asked you to do, come here on a wing and a prayer sort of thing.'

'He wasn't wrong.'

Josey couldn't deny the enigmatic Zan was right in one sense, but wanted to know why it was so important for the professor to come and see the archaeological find. He so far couldn't see a connection between that and the atmospheric disruption, other than the obvious connections between the events and the people in them – not to mention Verg's prediction. And with the latest claim that the young scientist is somehow responsible for jamming the satellites, one has to at least consider that his involvement in it might be seen to be true by others. Although Zan sounds like a fantasy, the Chinese woman backing up his story puts paid to the monk not being real. And with Davenport rushing to China; did he also get a warning about an impending disaster?

Josey didn't want their chat to come off sounding like an interrogation, but had to ask, 'Are you going to accept his invitation to become one of the Observers?'

Aaron reached beneath his jacket and revealed he was wearing the amulet like it was now his favourite charm, even though he had resolutely refused to accept it originally. 'I don't pretend to fully understand this thing, or what it means to be an Observer, but it sure as hell opened a door in a Buddhist Temple, and dare I say – my mind.' He tucked it back beneath his jacket and became reflective. 'Maybe we're all observers, have you considered that?'

Josey just looked at him without a response.

'I mean, that's what we do isn't it? *Observe*. I'm sure you've heard the conundrum; if there was no one to look at the moon, would it really be there?'

Josey noticed the professor had brought his bag with him, and he knew why. 'May I see the tablet?'

He reached into his backpack. 'I was wondering when you'd get to that.' He brought it out and placed it onto his lap.

Josey was seeing it for the first time for real; the picture didn't do it justice, the object was magnificent in detail. To prove Lui Jie had given him the picture, he brought it up on the screen of his phone.

Verg raised his eyebrows. 'You're a dark horse. And what do *you* make of it?'

'I know that together with the tablet it's a map to the ruins.'

Verg studied the tablet as though in the next few moments a fuller answer might come to him.

'I can tell by your face you think it's more.'

He removed the amulet from around his neck and released it from the leather twine. 'I doubt you've worked out it does this.' He positioned the amulet on the backside of the tablet and gave it a gentle push; it clicked into place. Handing it over to Josey he said, 'Come on detective; let's see what you can figure out.'

Josey tried to refuse the offer, but Verg forced him to keep hold of it. 'It's a mystery – you like mysteries I'm told.'

Josey tilted his head, uncertain he should even be touching the thing. He noticed Shannon twisting in his seat, trying to see what they were doing, but the seatback was preventing him from doing so. 'We've got a curious reporter spying on us,' he pointed out.

Verg lowered his voice to almost a whisper and told Josey to turn the tablet over.

He did so as carefully as one might turn a baby. He was now looking at the flat bottom of the gold hemisphere, the four parasols and the four suns.

Verg explained, 'As soon as I clicked the amulet into place, the position of the parasols shifted in relation to the suns. Take a look at Lui Jie's photograph; you'll see I'm right.'

Josey brought the picture back to the screen on his phone and immediately could see that the parasols had lined up with the suns. 'So what does this tell you?'

'As soon as I saw how the two fitted together, I realized

the base of the hemisphere might represent the equator.'

Josey privately patted himself on the back for coming to the same conclusion when he was with Shannon in the grotto.

'At first I thought the star symbols were suns, but now I'm convinced they're satellites.' He was talking in a rapid whisper, excitedly.

Josey hadn't picked up on that one, but then presented an obvious question. 'How does a forty thousand year old stone mason, for want of a better description, know about the Earth - let alone satellites?'

Aaron ran a finger down the left side of the tablet and explained his theory further. 'Assume this star symbol in the west is my Australian satellite.' He slid his finger down the right side. 'And this, in the east, if you look close, it's a mirror of the right side.'

'And?'

'Watch what happens when I rotate the amulet.'

The disk turned as smoothly as a modern day bearing, amazing in itself, but it was what had happened to the stone surface. He tapped his finger on a section that was now smooth and featureless. 'See, the star symbol to the east has *vanished*.'

Touching the stone and expecting to feel the edges of where the symbol once was, he felt nothing but smooth granite; suddenly understanding Verg's point. 'It's the missing *satellite*.'

Aaron raised his brow. 'Or, loss of communication.'

'How is this tablet even possible?'

Aaron shrugged, 'You tell me. But I'm guessing none of the other amulets do what this does—'

'We're here,' Shannon announced to his passengers.

Verg took the tablet from Josey and placed it back in his bag. He anxiously moved to the front of the vehicle, plainly looking forward to being reunited with his fiancée. As they pulled in next to the incapacitated cat, they immediately noticed there must be more to Belinda's story than she relayed over the phone. There was a swath of blistered paintwork running diagonally across its roof. The same type of damage had been subjected to what they could see of its nose, now buried behind what appeared to be a massive lump of solid ice.

They all understood the cause

The door of Skipper John's stricken cat opened and Belinda stepped out into the rescue team's headlights. Her face resembled a tiny bright mask nestled inside the rim of her royal blue hood, steam from her breath shining like a rising cloud.

They watched her plough her way through the snow to reach their door, which when opened heralded a cold blast from outside as she rode it in, into the warmth of lover-Verg's arms.

She comfortably moved on to Josey, who seemed to be getting an embrace with equal passion.

Shannon had no knowledge of the detective's history with her, but was clearly assessing whether or not there might be one.

CHAPTER THIRTY SIX
Starburst

Little time was spent discussing the horror that beset Skipper John and his passengers, and even less time entering into the link between Yu Chow's presence and Shannon's link to it.

Injuries were minimal and thankfully none were due to radiation exposure. The topic of conversation became the task at hand, getting John's cat released from the snow and ice.

With the two big snowmobiles hooked together by a length of chain, the rescue cat driven by Yu Chow, skated across the loose powder snow fighting for grip. At the same time, Skipper John poured on the power in reverse to relieve the load. With three almighty efforts the stranded machine was dragged backward, freed from its stranglehold, jumping out of its containment with a joyous roar from man and machine.

The glare that Shannon was getting from the SciCore

director cemented the suspicions that there had been an altercation between them.

Most believed that the animosity was a consequence of Shannon's absconding of the cat. It was also assumed that there would be more to that story, including how Shannon had managed to reach the ruins unaided.

And, as expected, Shannon's miraculous mastering of the catamaran wasn't quite true.

Back in Lhasa, Yu Chow had spotted him through the window of the station's waiting room, trying to escape in the vacated machine.

The reporter was then forced to accompany Chow on a rescue mission to pull Skipper John and the others out of the snow drift.

Then, while everyone else was working on digging John's all terrain free, Shannon absconded with the other, offering no chance of pursuing him. The trip from Lhasa to the stranded cat had given him time to study the controls, and the basis of how the coordinates worked.

When Shannon escaped from the crash site with the cat, Skipper John had already set the coordinates for the ruin, providing Shannon with an easy task.

In reaching the ruins this time, to ensure Shannon made no further escapes, Chow mandatorily invited the reporter to accompany him in the first cat, not wanting him out of his sight. The others spent the time it took back to the ruins catching up and formulating plans to pick up the stranded tourists. Little to no time was given to the rest of Verg's mission, which clearly wasn't finished; and not open for discussion. He and Josey had that in common.

The Australians were expecting a joint gruelling from Yu Chow as soon as they were settled into the lower level of the Buddhist ruins, but his priority shifted to moving among the locals to get some sense of their injuries, and to talk to them about his plans to get the injured to the hospital in Lhasa. Lui Jie was at his side the whole time, assuring her fellow Tibetans that the authorities were aware of their plight and that they would soon be safe. She also spent quite a bit of time exchanging information with Alix, the volunteer translator.

Any doubt that the SciCore director was livid with the Australians became quickly dispelled once he was done with dealing with the locals. He moved them clear of the tourists and quietly laid down the law. 'I cannot express my disappointment more; you have all placed me into a very difficult position. Although it may not seem so, I am in worse trouble than you. I only ask that in future you do as I say, and stay put until the authorities arrive.'

Josey's phone rang, triggering Yu Chow's eyes to fall on him disapprovingly.

It was Maxine calling.

Regardless of Chow's reprimand, Josey pointed at the buzzing phone and told the director, 'Sorry, I need to take this.' Not waiting for permission, or perhaps a refusal, he walked out of earshot with his back turned. 'Go ahead, Max.'

'You were on the money, chief, Flock Investments are into manufacturing in a big way; under a different name. The subsidiary company is called Davrow, and they make circuit boards among other electronic devices.' The line went quiet at her end. 'I can hear you working this through,' she told her boss.

'And I'll bet you know what I'm thinking.'

'Would it be *Dav* equals Davenport?'

'You tell me; does it?'

'It does. Ral Davenport is on the board of directors.'

Josey turned and found Belinda looking at him from out of ear shot. The look on her face seemed to be suggesting she knew what was being said about her fiancé's boss, about her ex-lover, a man she trusted.

'Is the company based in Australia?'

'It is, but like most companies they get quite a lot of shipments from China.'

'No surprise there I suppose, but we need to know where those shipments come from.'

'I've had no luck with that; they're coming via New Zealand.'

'Get Carl on a plane, it shouldn't be too hard to check the importations.'

'Hang on; your wife wants to talk to you.'

'Then I better,' he joked.

'Yes, you better,' Rebecca answered.

'Sweetheart, you got me. How are you?'

'How are *you* is more to the point. I couldn't believe what Maxine told me, Aaron was right all along about the equator.'

The phone cut out for a moment.

'You there, *Bec*?'

'Yes I'm here.'

'I'd better speak to Max before this line goes all together.'

'Keep safe *you.*'

'You too, and love to Molly - bye'

Maxine came on the line.

'Do this as quickly as you can, Max, we could lose communication again at any time. Excellent work by the way.'

'Stop it, I'm blushing.'

'That'll be the day—'

'What'll be the day?' The voice was Belinda's, standing right behind him. 'Good news?' she enquired; 'you look pleased—'

Shouting from the tourists brought an abrupt end to their brief banter.

'What now,' Josey said rhetorically as he and Belinda headed back to join the others.

As they grouped together with Chow and their Australian counterparts, several able-bodied people were anxiously climbing the ladder to the level above, conversing loudly, unintelligibly.

'What's going on?' Josey asked Alix as she came over.

She had an answer, but not one that made a lot of sense. 'A man has seen a bright light in the night sky, and says the sky itself is like a cosmic show.'

'Maybe they've brought in a chopper,' Belinda offered.

Josey, Shannon and the professor were already heading off to investigate.

'Wait!' Yu Chow shouted angrily, he wasn't happy about letting them out of his sight.

They ignored him, meeting up with Skipper John, who was a couple of rungs ahead of them on the climb.

'Could it be a chopper, John?' Josey reiterated.

'No way, the winds are too unpredictable.'

At the entrance, a second ladder had been fashioned from loose timbers, allowing for an easier climb to the outside. Two things hit them as soon as they emerged, the wind had dropped, and the clarity of the sky was astounding, they could see the stars for the first time since the blizzard began, massive clusters of sparkling diamonds that are rarely seen so clearly, and often not at all from the heart of cities – but the man who announced the spectacle was right, this was a cosmic show, one star stood out like a beacon. At twice the luminance of a full moon, its light was bathing all the upturned faces in a pale blue glow. People were astonished, most of whom watched in silent wonder.

'Do you know what this is?' Josey asked the one man who might have the answer.'

The professor's answer was enigmatic. 'I think it's part of the reason I'm here.'

Josey turned away from the light and looked at him then. He started to say something, but a man nearby who had begun shouting, sounded to be demanding attention. When they turned they saw he was an elderly gentleman whose eyes were firmly fixed on the amulet around the professor's neck.

Here we go again, Josey thought.

The curious man moved closer and began reaching out as if to touch it. He quavered in shock when Lui Jie intercepted him, holding him back as she spoke. They had no idea what she'd said to him, but his abiding response prompted her to relax her hold.

Noticing the professor seemed lost for words, unable to enquire about what had the man so animated; Josey stepped in. 'Lui Jie, can you tell us what the man's saying?'

Her answer was for Aaron. 'He wants to know if you are the one that they have been expecting.'

Verg looked at the man blankly for a moment. 'I can't deal with this,' they heard him say as he turned and walked back toward the temple.

The stunned faces drove Josey in pursuit. 'Hey, Verg – show a little manners, pal, these people have been nothing but polite to us.'

Josey thought it was the reprimand that got him to turn, but the anger in his face told him otherwise, and raised concern over what he might say next. He was staring at the sky, at the star, which was intensifying to the point where it became impossible to look straight at it.

Squinting into the glare, Josey sensed Verg squirming at his side. 'I ask again, what the hell is this?'

'You want to know what this is; it's my b-bloody satellite exploding.'

Josey faced him, but he was already recommencing his stride toward the ruins, even as Shannon was arriving with intrigue dominating his face. 'What was he saying to you?'

He held off answering while taking out his phone to try turning it on. He showed Shannon, who then checked his own phone, finding it too had no signal. He took a painful glance at the light and then back at Josey. 'You mean—'

There was no point in saying it; Verg's exploding satellite had resulted in the loss of communication, perhaps permanently this time.

'What'd he say?' Shannon again asked as Josey paced away hot on Verg's heels.

'Let me talk with him,' Belinda insisted as she shot past them, taking up the lead.

They saw her meet up with the professor at the entrance, patiently consoling him, seemingly with total understanding of his state of mind.

Josey thought, *if anyone's on a mission it's her,*

Remnants from the explosion were finally fading from view. Shannon sauntered up beside Josey and joined him in his inspection of the sky; the clouds were closing in, the stars, along with the spectacle of the exploding satellite were slowly hiding. With the return of darkness came the rising wind. Josey looked back and saw Lui Jie huddled together with the man who had been fascinated by the amulet.

Shannon picked up on it. 'What was the old guy on about?'

'It's a long story,' He told him as he headed for the entrance.

'Oh, come on – give me something,' he moaned.

The exploding satellite and the worsening weather had put everyone on edge. Verg had expressly requested that the old man be kept away from him. Not only was he stressed, but his stutter had returned. Yu Chow tried talking with him, but overtones of accusation about the explosion barred all success. Josey was interested in talking with him too – about the ancient tablet's predictions.

Using the weight of experience, Josey pushed these thoughts aside and concentrated on the hunch that had been manifesting since Maxine's call. Who exactly was involved with Flock Industries apart from Davenport?

What was Davenport's son's involvement other than his association with Joseph Shepherd, the failed assassin?

How is the attempted assasination on Verg and the failed abduction of Lui Jie connected to Flock Industries, and the manufacturing company Davrow? How much does Davenport actually know about his son's involvement with Joseph Shepherd? And now, on top of all this, how is any of this connected to the exploding satellite?

A lot of questions, but with one simple answer if his hunch was right. Now that communication with Australia was once again out, his hunch was all he had to work with – it was enough.

Earlier, Josey had taken Lui Jie aside and quizzed her on who the old man was; she'd told him, 'His name is Abbot Le Camus, a priest. He explained to me that the amulet holds a promise of a man who would come from the west, to save his people from what he called, *fire in the snow*.' Lui Jie kept her voice low as she asked Josey, 'What is *your* understanding of the amulet?'

He became hesitant. 'I can't claim to have a great understanding of it, but I'm told it represents a right-of-passage into a secret group of people that call themselves *The Observers*. I also know that Zan gave it to him, or at least tried at the start. He was pretty reluctant to take it, but something seems to have changed his mind.'

Lui Jie also seemed hesitant. 'In spite of this, his reluctance to accept his new status persists I think.'

'With respect, I must tell you that I come from a place where, in my life, practicalities reign supreme. It's hard for me.'

'You do not need to appologise, even I am constantly surprised at what life throws at me. I think that there are many things we do not know about our world, and the mystery of the universe in which we live. Do you not feel this too?'

Josey grinned. 'Lui, you've got me there.'

'A very prudent answer, Detective; let it not be said that you do not possess wisdom.'

He looked around at their predicament, trapped beneath the ruins of a Buddhist Temple, and wondered if she was right.

She smiled, 'I think we are all very tired. Tomorrow we will see things in a new light.' Bowing gently, she dismissed herself and found a place among the locals to settle down for the night.

Josey was running all these thoughts through his head as he tried to get some sleep. But, tomorrow's *new light* that Lui Jie spoke of didn't promise to be all that bright, as he and the other Australians would be heading back to Lhasa, and then onto Beijing for their mandatory interrogations. His mind drifted back to the old Buddhist priest, and wondered why he was so taken by the amulet Verg was wearing; was it really a sign? – when infact it was one of many. The old guy obviously recognised there was something different about it, just as Aaron had said, connecting it to the prophesy that he spoke of. Verg himself had shown that together, the amulet and the tablet appeared to be predicting the exploding satellite, perhaps the vortex too.

His last thought as he drifted off to sleep, was that the case and his hunch, needed to come to a head – and soon.

CHAPTER THIRTY SEVEN
Abduction

At first, Josey's dismal expectation for the following day seemed to be developing exactly as he thought it would.

He couldn't have been more wrong, it was about to get a whole lot worse.

Immediately after partaking of what little food there was, the SciCore director launched into explaining his plan for the Australians, and those among the Tibetans who required hospitalisation. Following a check of the weather, it was decided upon the advice from Skipper John that travel would have to wait till nightfall. All they could do is hope the conditions would be half as good as the night just past. The day was spent simply trying to keep warm; those who were able to partner-up did so.

The isolation gave Josey time to think, but it was to no avail, the more he thought about how and when to make accusations, the less a possible opportunity presented itself, that would all change very soon and more dramatically than he could have imagined.

Things began to change at the end of that second day; the weather once again forced them to spend another night in the freezing cold. Everyone awoke to the sound of Yu Chow shouting on top of his voice. He actually gave Josey a light kick, waking him. 'He's gone again! You people are in a lot of trouble.'

Josey knew who he was talking about as soon as his brain locked into gear.

Belinda stirred, lying beside where her fiancé had been sleeping, awakening to Chow's shouting, and to the cold empty space at her side.

'Relax,' Josey told the director, trying to reign in his panicked reaction, 'he might just be taking a break; have you had a look?'

'I am not stupid, Detective, of course I have looked and he is not up there. He is gone.'

Up there referred to an area set aside on the upper level for a makeshift latrine. Josey was about to go and have a look for himself when Belinda drew his attention.

'Cam - look.'

He turned and found her holding Aaron's back pack, which she'd partly opened, inviting him to peer inside. When he did so he saw that the edge of the tablet was protruding from beneath other items in the bag. Assuming the director was right in saying Aaron was nowhere to be seen meant that the professor was indeed gone, but not willingly, he would never have left the tablet behind. Josey covered the artefact and shook his head at Belinda, prompting her not to reveal its presence. 'We need to go after him,' he told the director.

'I'm sorry I cannot allow that.'

'I don't think you're in a position to make that call.'

'No Mr Josey, you are not in a position to disobey me.'

'Watch me,' he said as he swung his gaze onto Skipper John. 'What chance do we have of finding him?'

The skipper looked confident, but his position was problematic.

'Do not do this, John,' Yu Chow demanded.

He held on the director with steely determination, silently making his decision. Facing Josey he told him, 'Weather permitting, if he's out there I'll find him.'

Josey took Belinda's arm. 'Are you right to go?'

The weight of reason allowed her to ignore the director's disapproval too. 'Ready when you are.'

'Don't even think about leaving me here,' Shannon demanded.

Without making eye contact Belinda said, 'You're your own boss, do what you want.' As usual he was already suited up – ready to go.

Moving to object again, Yu Chow thought better of it when he noticed his actions were being frowned upon by the Tibetan's, their defiance somewhat encouraged by Alix's translation of what was going on, not to mention Lui Jie's disapproval of the director's tough stance.

Ascending the ladder, the irrepressible evacuees could hear Chow angrily reminding them of their grievous mistake. Lui Jie approached and respectfully gestured for him to be calm. 'Yu Chow, let them go to find their friend, do not fear the authorities, I will be here with you to explain the situation. I do not think you will be in any trouble. I will speak with my uncle to apply his influence in Beijing.'

He met her eyes sternly. 'I think you place too much trust in his success, and theirs.'

Having made it to the level above the trapdoor and the mound of snow that had buried the skulls, footprints became apparent; obviously some sort of struggle had occurred.

They made their way up the ladder that had replaced the rope, and out into a comparatively bright cloudy day with a light sprinkle of snow, confirming the need for protection. The wind too had subsided, all of which provided them with multiple footprints to follow.

'Even without these footprints he clearly didn't leave voluntarily,' Belinda revealed, 'there were valuable items in his bag that he'd never have left behind.'

John skipped over this information and concentrated on the task at hand, checking the compass on his watch. 'They're heading west, or close to it,' he said realising the compass couldn't be trusted. 'It's a place to start.'

Unfortunately, within fifteen feet the tell tail prints petered out. Without wavering John trod away in the direction of his cat. 'There's another way we can do this,' he said giving his companions alternate hope.

He looked to the north and noted a distant blizzard, but said nothing.

Having reached the twenty seater cat, they'd only just stepped up from the snow when the clouds thinned and filtered sun bathed the snowfields. With all occupants suited up against radiation, daytime travel was considered safe, at least while they were within the confines of John's cat, but the known shafts of sunlight were a definite worry. John needed to offer his occupants a choice. 'We're in deep shit if we get hit by sunlight. I need to know if you're okay continuing.'

Josey glanced at Belinda and recognised her resolve. 'We are if you are.'

Shannon was looking out at the glare coming off the snow and decided to slide along his seat to distance himself from the window.

Approaching in the distance was the snow storm that had been mentioned; both a curse and a possible blessing.

Turning to Belinda in the seat next to him, Shannon told her, 'Do I get a say in this?'

She looked anything but happy with being forced to share his personal space, and she expertly ignored him.

Josey wasn't quite so gracious. 'You can get out now if you'd like, Shannon.'

'I'm fine,' he said uncertainly, 'let's get this over with.'

'Then we're all agreed?' John asked.

The thought of Aaron being out on the snow gave Belinda a fearful chill. 'I'd like to get moving if that's all right, John.'

'Right, here we go.' The skipper poured on the power, commanding the big machine to claw forward. Noticing Belinda's anxious expression in the mirror he felt the urge to dispel her fears of not surviving the trip, or of never finding the professor. 'This looks more hopeless than it is folks; I'll be following a computer generated grid. It allows me to search a three mile ring around the temple without the risk of doubling back.'

Shannon scoffed, 'Good luck if that storm reaches us. We won't be able to see a damn thing I wouldn't have thought . . . What'll you do if you hit another fissure, no one will ever—'

'Shannon—shut it!' Belinda had clearly had about as

much as she could take of his whining.

'Keep calm people,' the skipper suggested, 'we *will* get through this, I promise. And we *will* find the professor.'

If they knew what had already taken place in one of the yet unchecked radar grids ahead, his promise of *finding the professor* might not have resonated so positively. But before that, the snow storm was promising to become a bigger problem than realised.

Within minutes they were in a complete whiteout, forcing the skipper to bring the big cat to yet another standstill. He turned to Verg's fiancée apologetically, 'I'm sorry; we shouldn't be stuck here too long.'

She managed a weak smile, 'Can anyone survive out in this?'

'He's in a snowsuit, there's a pretty good chance. The blizzard's his friend,' he assured her, 'far better than the alternative under the circumstances.'

Circumstances meant being caught in the sun without a radiation suit, which they'd established he couldn't have had – based on the number of suits left at the temple; another fact that confirmed he hadn't left voluntarily.

Josey noticed Shannon was wiping a thin layer of frost from his window, straining as though he'd thought he'd seen something. Any doubt evaporated when Shannon turned and they locked eyes.

The reporter's expression brought the detective across to sit at his side, but not before making sure Belinda was focused elsewhere. 'What is it?' he asked in a low voice.

'I'm not sure; I thought I saw movement.'

Josey leant past him and put his face close to the glass. Out in the blizzard, no more than ten feet from the cat, someone was lying face down with a good amount of blood staining the snow. The figure was either dead, or frozen into immobility, clearly not the reason for the movement Shannon thought he saw. For Belinda's sake Josey needed to broach the subject delicately. He joined the Skipper and quietly notified him.

She cottoned on immediately. 'Cameron; what's going on?'

His face was an open book, which sent her pacing to one of the windows. 'It's not him,' she said without time to make a proper assessment.

Although her conclusion was far too quick, Josey hoped it was true.

'It's not him,' she repeated in a whisper to herself.

He thought she might be avoiding acceptance, and caught John's eye, indicating they best get it over with and check. When the door hissed open and they both stepped out into the howling wind, Belinda made no attempt to follow. She didn't see them reach the inert body and roll it over; she knew what she'd seen and had no intention of watching.

They very quickly realised the man in the snow was Asian, and very dead. Turning toward the cat, Josey saw Belinda was at the window, her face cupped against the glass; he gave her the thumbs up to let her know it wasn't Aaron and hoped she understood his meaning. He looked back at the corpse in the snow and whispered under his breath, 'No disrespect intended.'

John searched the poor fellow's clothing for something that would identify the body; taking him aboard was not an option. He found some papers, which he would pass on to the authorities. 'I'll record the coordinates and put in a flagpole before we leave.'

On the way back to the cat, Josey bailed the skipper up. 'I get that it'd be dangerous carrying on right now,' he pleaded, 'but is there any way that we can?'

'I hear you, she's stressing out, right?'

'Big time.'

John sized Josey up and said, 'Well, there is one way.'

The *one way,* consisted of Josey sitting forward on the nose of the machine, giving the skipper signals, extra eyes on the snow, albeit restricted to a couple of dozen feet ahead. It wouldn't have even been safe to do so if not for the extensive cloud cover. Safe might have been overstating the situation; shafts of sunlight had a habit of suddenly spearing out of nowhere.

Belinda took Josey's place beside John at the controls, her eyes straining, flicking left to right, fearful Aaron might be lying in the snow like the other poor man and not be seen in time to pull-up.

The big cat hadn't moved more than a few yards when Josey's arm shot into the air with a closed fist, signalling John to stop. With the engine revs quietened, they could hear his muffled shouts. 'There, there - I see him.'

In the distance, a figure could be seen retracing faint footprints away from their position. As soon as John opened the door, Belinda pushed past him, leaping from the cat and trudging through the powder snow as fast as allowed.

'No wait,' John advised strongly.

'I think I can recognise my fiancé when I see him,' she protested without stopping. In spite of her guarantee, Aaron was barely visible through the sleet, but getting clearer with each agonisingly slow step. The gap between them finally closed, bringing them together in an unsteady embrace, the gentle impact releasing a splattering of loose snow from their suits. Aaron's snow gear did not have the benefit of a mask, and his face was showing signs of exposure to the intense cold.

Josey slid from the bonnet and met up with John at the open door.

'I don't know about you,' the skipper said to him, 'but I can't wait to hear what happened here. Do you think the dead guy in the snow is part of it?'

'Not the way you think.'

John was surprised by Josey's swift response. 'You sound sure.'

'I am.'

'Okay, would I be prying to ask—?'

'A little too soon maybe,'

Skipper John measured the comment with a slight fascination. 'Right, well – it might be a good idea to get these two lovebirds out of the cold . . . Hey you two!' he shouted. They broke from their embrace and turned to see him waving them back.

Hooking onto Aaron, Belinda started him toward the cat. 'Before you get bombarded by their questions, care to enlighten me on what happened?'

'To be honest it's a bit hazy.'

'There's a dead man in the snow, just the other side of the catamaran – do you know what happened to him?'

He ceased walking, trying to remember.

'Now what,' the skipper murmured rhetorically as they watched them in their stationary huddle.

It wasn't that hard for Josey to fathom what was happening. 'Judging by Verg's body language, the dead man is news to him.'

John considered the fading footprints that stretched across to the professor and his fiancée, and then those pockmarks that led away from the blood-soaked body. What had happened seemed clear to him. He looked at Josey quizzically.

'It's a long story,' was all he got, 'let's not jump to conclusions.'

John tilted his head uncertainly. 'If you say so,' he decided. He was becoming increasingly aware there was something out of the ordinary going on with the professor.

'Are you all right?' Josey asked guardedly as the couple arrived at the cat.

Belinda answered for him as she ushered her fiancé through the open door. 'He's fine!'

Aaron paused, his focus now locked on the dark blemish in the snow. 'Is that . . .?'

'Don't worry about him now,' Belinda answered before facing Josey, 'He doesn't remember all that's happened. Cam, we should get him inside and hear what he's got to say.'

They let Belinda lead the way before helping Verg negotiate the rungs of the ladder.

Returning to the warmth of the cat, Josey and the skipper exchanged a worrying glance.

The snowstorm was worsening by the minute; there was no way of determining how long they would be stuck. John kept the engine running, careful not to mention that the fuel tanks weren't infinite. He stayed on the radio, keeping his distance from the others to let them talk in private at the back. Shannon was made to feel he should stay with the skipper, leaving Belinda and Josey to hear the professor's story exclusively.

'I woke up during the night shivering,' Aaron told them in a subdued voice, 'I saw someone coming toward me carrying a blanket – I assumed it might be for me because I had the shakes. It was almost impossible to see down there, as you know. The next thing the blanket was thrown over me and I was hit over the head; I must have blacked out.' He focused on the frosted-up window reflectively. 'When I came round, I was l-lying in the snow, next to that poor bugger out there.'

Josey's investigative mind was racing. 'Getting you up the ladder unconscious, and then dragging you all the way out here, couldn't have been done by one man.'

'He's not the one who attacked me – the man out there is a t-tourists from the temple. The guy with the blanket was bigger - heavier set.'

'So the attacker somehow forces the tourist into help-ing,' Belinda surmised, 'and then, *kills him*?'

'That's my guess,' Josey agreed, 'which begs an even bigger question, why stop there?'

This brought a glare from Aaron. 'What are you trying to s-say?'

The last thing Josey wanted was to reintroduce the professor's stutter. 'I'm saying I think he tried.'

Aaron and Belinda locked eyes knowingly, and Josey picked up on it. He sensed Belinda was of a mind to believe Aaron may have had one of his episodes. Her expression seemed to suggest now was not the time to pursue the issue, not with everyone listening.

'Okay, let's leave it there,' Josey decided, 'I'll let you

guys get some private time.'

'Cam,' Belinda said amiably as he started moving away to join the others at the front . . . 'thank you.'

He returned her geniality, glanced at the professor and continued on his way.

As soon as he was out of ear shot she leant in close and whispered to Aaron, 'I know something's happened; tell me.'

His answer was straight to the point. 'The detective's right - I should be dead.'

Belinda looked dismissive. 'Thank-god you're not.'

'Maybe it's not God we should be thanking.'

She studied him for a moment and repeated, 'Just tell me.'

Aaron dropped his voice to a whisper. 'The monk was here, when I came round, just like before. I'll swear he took me away from this place, away from this *time* . . .'

Over the next half hour or so, each time Josey glanced across at the love birds, as the skipper had called them, they were huddled together in conversation. He could only guess at what was being said, but whatever it was, she was clearly listening to him absorbedly. The feeling that the professor was somehow Belinda's mission in life, once again swept over him. But, there was little time to ponder it, he had just one thing on his mind at that moment, and felt that when he revealed the truth of what was behind the attacks, it would upstage any mystical vestige the artefact might hold. He couldn't have known that the contest between the two concepts would be irrevocably drawn together more than he imagined.

At the conclusion of Aaron's exposition, Belinda

looked up and saw Josey studying them and gave him a reassuring smile, indicating all was well with her man. Returning his focus back on the terrane ahead, he sensed the skipper was steadfastly facing him and turned to meet his gaze. 'Something on your mind, John?'

'You do know if the police saw those prints in the snow out there, the professor would be arrested on the spot.'

With a nod he countered, 'He didn't kill that guy.'

'How can you be certain?'

'Because I know who did.'

'Who?' The look he got from Josey prompted John to add, 'Yeah-yeah, it's too early, you told me.'

Belinda and Aaron didn't notice Shannon approaching and couldn't be sure he hadn't heard Aaron saying to her, *'Perhaps even more mysterious; who on earth makes a prediction like this, millions of years ago—'*

'Forgive my interruption, can I get a shot?'

They looked up and saw him standing a meter away clutching his cell phone.

'A quick shot of you two with the stones?'

He got his answer when Verg wrapped the tablet into the cloth and placed it back into his pack.

Although feeling slightly rejected, Shannon managed to accept he'd already been blessed with a pretty good story anyway. 'Right, well - thanks I guess.'

Unapologetically, Aaron and Belinda held their silence until the reporter had completed his awkward return to his own seat.

He covertly positioned his camera on his lap and took his shot.

The blizzard raged on into the night, coercing the

cocooned occupants to succumb to sleep. The skipper slept upright in his usual chair, still wearing his headphones in case a radio message came in. Josey and Shannon had spread full length on their individual bench seats, while the professor lay with his head on Belinda's lap, on the seat where they had spent most of the day.

Only half asleep, Belinda's eyes shot open with a start when the gloomy interior lit up. Someone was outside shining a torch through a window. The circle of light panned slowly throughout the cabin - searching. She stirred Aaron to wake him just as the light swept across them. He saw it wavering away, and without a second thought leaped to his feet, slammed down the button that opens the door and jumped from the confines of the cabin, the ruckus raising the alarm.

The cold hit him like a million knives; there had been no time to don a jacket.

A soft glow spread as he heard Josey's demanding voice from behind, the detective's cell phone lit up in his hand. 'Professor, leave this to me.'

He saw the detective was already rugging up, and decided the advice was well founded, certified by a deep chill that convulsed through his body. This was a cold not to be argued with.

In the glow of Josey's cell phone torch, although limited, prints were clearly visible; leaving no doubt someone had been lurking around the vehicle.

The skipper emerged with a flare gun in one hand and a torch in the other, followed by Shannon with a further backup light from his phone. Their lights vacillated in the hope of pinpointing the intruder, eyes straining into the whiteout for signs of movement. The deafening roar of windswept snow slapping against their fur lined hoods made it difficult to hear anything else—

Shannon's light jerked away, accompanied by a faint cry. Josey and the skipper's only point of reference to the sound was Shannon's phone shining skyward out of the snow. Barely visible beside it, the reporter was lying where he'd fallen, clearly injured. Beyond where he lay, the faint hint of an assailant could be seen receding into the whiteout.

'John!' Josey shouted, 'keep the others inside and shut the door.'

Although offering no argument, he hesitated, worried about leaving the unarmed detective to attend to Shannon on his own. Crouched and focused on feeling for a pulse as he was, Josey would be left open to being attacked himself.

'Is he okay?' John asked as he approached the pair on his way to the cat,

'He's alive,' he confirmed as he withdrew his hand with blood on it.

John noticed Belinda and the professor watching from the open doorway, and continued on to do as Josey asked.

'Wait; you might need to give me a hand.'

Focussed on the task of dealing with Shannon, they almost missed seeing the illusive figure heading toward the door of the cat. Without a second thought, the skipper shot off a flare in the prowler's general direction. The flaming missile stabbed through the night without making its mark, instead exploding against the front of the cat in a bright firework. Pupils shrank to the glare, leaving their eyes to readjust to the lesser intensity of the flickering flames that quickly died in the melting snow. The grey of night returned, offering no sign of the skipper's target, but it was comforting to see Aaron standing on guard at the closed door. John turned off his phone and while putting it into his pocket asked, 'Did you see the guy, was it the one you suspect?' Intent on getting back to safety, Josey gave no answer, but John wasn't done asking. 'Is that a yes, no - too early to tell?'

'All in good time, skipper.'

He took the warning on the chin and set his mind to the task at hand, lifting Shannon's legs while Josey took the load from the front. Walking through deep snow and a howling wind made the going tough enough, but the extra burden of a man's weight presented an additional test of their strength.

From inside the cat, they saw Shannon's bearers pass through the headlights and around to reach the door. Gesturing to the console Aaron called for his fiancée to open up - 'the blue button,' he told her.

The door slid open as the rescuers arrived at the ladder. Aaron stepped down onto the bottom rung; meaning to take the load from Josey at the front, but the skipper had another job for him. 'In the tray,' he pushed out breathlessly, 'under the console, grab me another flare.'

Aaron rummaged in the dimly lit interior . . . 'Got it.'

He threw the cartridge to the skipper, who had readied himself by lowering Shannon's butt to the step. Two seconds later he had the flare loaded and sent on its way into the night sky. The illumination turned the whiteout into a blinding glare once again, enough to see the assailant wasn't close enough to be seen, which meant by all accounts he probably wasn't close enough to be a problem - he kept watch anyway as Josey and the professor lifted Shannon inside. John followed and quickly moved to the console to shut the door and kill the display lights, effectively plunging the interior into black.

They kept their heads low, spreading Shannon out on the floor, working in the dim glow filtering in from the headlights. He was partially conscious now and mumbling incoherently, shivering, not just from the cold.

'He's in shock,' Josey told the others.

John arrived with a small first aid box. 'I'm not sure what's in this,' he told them as he opened it, 'I've never had call to look.'

On closer inspection, Josey found the location of the wound. 'It's his neck and he's pumping out blood real fast.' Feeling around amongst the blood with his fingers he managed a sigh of relief. 'It's bad enough but if it'd been severed he'd be dead already'

The look he got from Belinda was admiration. She was thinking, *I know he's not our best friend, but the man just came close to death.*

Bubbling blood slowed as Josey applied pressure. 'He'll be all right so long as we don't let him bleed out, he's got two of these arteries, they supply the brain, explains why he's a bit out of it, but he'll need a tight bandage and a hospital sooner rather than later.' He glanced to the skipper and flicked his eyes to the weather outside. 'Can we make a move?'

'Risky, but hey.'

'Here, let me do that,' Belinda said as she relieved John of the bandage he was pulling from the first aid box. While working with Josey on Shannon's wound she caught the detective's eye and asked, 'Who's doing this to us?' Her question sounded rhetorical, but that changed when she noticed the skipper give Josey a bit of a look as he headed off to get the snowcat started. Then the glance *she* got from Cam brought her to a realisation. Her expression was both illuminate and annoyed at the same time. 'You know something don't you?'

He tried not to confirm she was right, but his blank silence caused him to fail dismally. 'Is there a pin in that box,' he asked as he completed strapping Shannon's neck with the bandage.

'You're being hesitant.' She pulled the box toward her and found a pin, but her mind didn't waver. 'Josey, who is it?'

The answer was clearly stuck in his throat.

The cat jolted as the skipper got the machine moving again; Shannon's eyes widening in reaction, not only at the sudden jerk forward, but also at the so-called safety pin that dithered unsteadily in Belinda's hand as it approached his neck, his expression only relaxing when she'd finished threading it through the material without stabbing him.

Shannon's antics went unnoticed by her as she rested her hand on Josey's sleeve. 'Is it someone I know?'

His expression didn't change. 'It's not someone you don't.'

Shannon's eyes were panning from one to the other like a tennis spectator.

Oblivious to the patient, Belinda kept her focus on trying to decipher why Josey was being so annoyingly cryptic.

Unavoidably eavesdropping as he fired up the motor, the skipper figured he knew why; the detective's answer was obviously about to tear the woman apart, and he could see she knew it when he looked over his shoulder. Shannon appeared decidedly left out of their conversation while they were distractedly wiping the blood from their hands onto their jackets.

Josey hated divulging early hunches, but they had him cornered. 'I'm sorry, Bel—'

That's as far as he got, a massive jolt brought his disclosure to a sudden end, in which he found no immediate solace given this was a deliberate attack from outside.

All eyes turned to the back window as it became ablaze with light.

'This is not good,' the skipper warned.

Shannon raised his head to see what was happening, but pain forced him back onto the rolled up blanket they'd used as a pillow, now totally bloodstained.

'We're being bulldozed!' The skipper's incredulous answer sounded like he was revealing the surprising information to himself. He wrenched at the controls and threw his machine into reverse. A hasty glance ahead with his hands cupped to the windscreen revealed the result of his action, 'Christ!'

'What?' Josey asked in an anxious attempt to help.

'We're sliding, and fast.' He didn't wait for the next question; back on the controls he shifted into first gear and poured on the power to try and outrun whatever was pushing them.

The lights at the back window receded as John's cat pulled away. It soon became clear the assault wasn't over. Before he could drive out of trouble, the lights drew back in – another almighty jolt effectively overriding the manoeuvre.

'We're in a lot of trouble here people.'

Belinda zeroed in on Josey again. 'You know who's doing this don't you.'

Ignoring her, he didn't falter in heading for the door.

'If that's true,' John told him, 'you need to tell us.'

'First let's find out if I'm right – open up.'

'Not a good idea,' John warned when he realised what Josey was planning. 'There's every chance you'll be left behind.'

'You got a better idea?' he asked impatiently waiting for the door to open.

'Here, take this,' he acknowledged as he threw Josey the flair gun. 'It's loaded.'

The door opened and Josey was gone.

As predicted he began falling behind as soon as he sank into the deep snow. Had he not grasped the ladder leading to the driver's door as the pursuing cat ground past, he would have been stranded. From this precarious vantage point, with legs still dragging in the snow, Josey could only see the driver's shoulder, but it was enough to recognise he hadn't seen the daring manoeuvre. Climbing to the second rung took every ounce of his strength. He clung there and rested before swinging his right leg up and over the third rung. This allowed him to grab the rung above and lift himself higher. He was now out of the snow and almost at the driver's window. He caught his breath. Looking ahead he saw faces at the back window of John's machine, thankfully not clearly, he didn't want them giving his position away. If he was to succeed in overpowering the assailant he would need the power of surprise. With this in mind he reached up with his left arm and tried the doorhandle - *damn – locked from the inside.*

Abandoning the element of surprise, he focussed on a snow shovel that he'd seen earlier, attached to the body of the cat just below the ladder. He had to step down a rung to reach it, but then faced another obstacle; it was frozen to the spot. He could tell no amount of yanking was going to remove it from its brackets. The flair gun came to mind, *would that work?* What it would do is alert the driver to his presence. Perhaps that'd be the lesser of two evils; at least it would put a kilter in his confidence that he had the upper hand. He pulled the makeshift weapon from his jacket, aimed, turned his head away and fired. Heat penetrated his suit, raising concern it may have breached the material at such close range, its point of impact had certainly done its job though, releasing the shovel from the ice, enough to haul it free of the mount.

With spade in hand he repositioned himself higher on the ladder and took a swing at the window.

The driver's hooded head swung round; startled by Josey's presence – not that his expression could be seen behind the faceplate of his radiation suit.

From the rear window of John's twenty-seater they strained to see past the glare of the pursuing headlights, barely able to see Josey pounding with the shovel like a crazed demon in the windswept snow.

'Shit!' The skipper's curse forced them to turn and face the front.

Shannon, who had managed to struggle to his feet, stood braced in the isle against one of the seats, panning his head left and right. 'What now?' he mumbled fixing his eyes onto the front window.

Belinda and Aaron brushed past him to reach John and

see what had him so worried. All they could see ahead was what they had been looking at for hours on end, wind and snow. The skipper had doused the headlights for some reason.

'This is not good,' they heard him murmur. 'This is definitely not good.'

Aaron frowned. 'John, what are you seeing?'

'The green line, can you see it?'

Belinda squinted. 'Yes, I see it. What is it?'

'It's a cornice,' he told her while desperately ramping up his efforts to take command of the controls, 'a cliff,' he quantified. A glance at the drama playing out at the other side of the back window told him the arsehole knew exactly what he was doing, and he voiced it.

Belinda seemed so cut up by the mere mention of the attacker; the skipper just had to point it out. 'I get the feeling you already know who's behind this. I saw it on your face when the detective tried telling you.'

Afraid to answer in front of Aaron, she steadied herself against the seats as she staggered to the back window where the surreal scene outside continued, a dilemma of her own making.

The professor followed anxiously, settling in beside her. 'Bel, is he right?' He tried reading her expression, but failed.

With eyes remaining on the man she had hired to find the culprit, reality hit – now in a very real position to kill the killer, she realised her dear detective may well *be killed instead.*

Shannon hadn't moved from where he stood in the isle, watching the events unfold like some crazy amusement-park ride.

Belinda was close to a breakdown. Aaron turned her away from the window and took her in his arms. 'Can you tell me?' he whispered against her ear. 'Tell me who's doing this.'

She turned to the drama being played out just the other side of the murky glass; a drama in which Detective Josey now had to fight for his life against a man she'd trusted. The realisation was too much. Sobbing against Aaron's chest, she told him, 'It's . . . your boss.'

He held her at arm's length to see she meant it. *'Ral* is driving that thing?' he asked disbelievingly.

Her emotional tears confirmed it was true.

Through the distorted window, the driver at the wheel of the bulldozing cat could have been anybody. Belinda's claim was beyond belief, *is this what Josey had suspected all along - jealousy?*

It occurred to him that being seen at the back window, given the glare of the headlights, and in each other's arms, it might provoke her ex-lover even further.

He drew his fiancé away from the crazy scene and they sat facing forward, their projected shadows dancing witlessly around the interior of the bouncing cat.

Josey gave up on breaking the glass, deciding it was most likely impossible, but he wasn't done. He forced the edge of the spade into the jam at the top of the glass and began prizing it. The window moved an inch, prompting the driver to search for a means of defence. It arrived quickly, a gun, gripped in one hand while he drove with the other.

Josey thought, *shoot the window out dumb-arse.*

The dumb-arse did as expected

Ducking below the shattering glass above his head, and

then shielding his eyes to dive through the open window, Josey was able to take a defensive hold on the shooter.

The assailant instinctively trod on the brake, burrowing the cat into a self-made snow bank, the driver forced into using both hands in defence against the intruder. Another shot lodged somewhere in the ceiling of the cabin.

Skipper John knew immediately that the big cat had stopped pushing. Putting the tracks into lock and reverse traction onto hold, he bolted to the back window to see why. What he saw was repeated flashes in the cabin of the stationary cat – gunfire!

We're still moving; he realised in horror, and made a hasty retreat to the driver's seat, 'Shit!'

Shannon's eyes rounded as he brushed past. 'I wish you'd stop saying that,' he requested nervously.

Belinda had pulled out of the protection of her lover's arms, and once again was glued to the pursuing cat, now gradually receding from view.

Is this the last I will see of either of them?

Joining John at the controls, Aaron picked up on just how alarmed he was. 'What's wrong?'

'We're still sliding.' The panic in his voice removed the need for further explanation.

'Get everyone to brace themselves,' he yelled – 'now!'

Outside, the stationary cleats were sliding as easily as skates, toward the edge of the cornice.

Ahead, Josey could see that Belinda's cat was fading into the blizzard. He would have preferred they stopped, but wasn't aware they were in an out-of-control slide.

The assailant's gun had exhausted its load, levelling the playing field – if only; it was then that Josey glimpsed the over snow ahead was dipping away into who knows what perils, which would soon be their own fate - they had begun breaking through their self-imposed snow bank.

His opponent saw what was happening and growled as would a cornered animal.

The voice was that of a man, but Josey already knew it would be.

Against his better judgement Josey relented, but it was too late for the preceding cat up ahead, Belinda, John, Shannon and the professor, together with their doomed machine, nosedived out of sight, into the green abyss.

The unlikely bedfellows refrained from the urge to move for fear they would shift the weight in favour of gravity. Spreadeagled across the bench seat, Josey held the man by the legs, as keen to prevent him from moving as much as hindering his escape.

'I know why you're doing this,' Josey told him with quiet assuredness.

The hollow disclosure provoked an angry defiance, voiced in what could only be described as animalistic sounds. Normal human tones were disguised by his enraged voice yelling above the scream of the storm and the massive boom of the engine.

His deliberate rebelliousness was as annoying as it was deadly. Slow as a cougar he reached beneath the dashboard and began rummaging with deft fingers inside a small box.

Josey saw his plan immediately.

With a fist-full of bullets from the box the gunman began reloading the chamber in slow and deliberately provocative movements, sensing success.

Self-preservation kicked Josey's mind into overdrive. Even as the gun was being aimed, he grappled along the gunman's legs and clamped a hand around his wrist, effectively guiding the gun away.

The snowmobile slid forward against all hope that it wouldn't, deeper into the embankment.

Fighting against Josey's resistant grip, the assailant successfully brought the barrel of the gun in line to fire.

Josey saw his finger tense against the trigger and swung away, pulling off a boot as the assailant broke free.

The bullet flew out the open window at the instant the massive cat started to slowly role onto its side, ploughing its way through the temporary safety barrier.

Like the jerk of a ticking clock, the opposing door was sinking toward the snow. The gunman knew if it reached half way through its turn his window of escape would be blocked, making his departure impossible.

Josey couldn't see if his opponent had beaten the odds when the cat finally rolled, the window became shrouded in darkness. For a moment Josey was left lying flat on the rising wall of the machine. He crabbed backward and catapulted himself clear with an almighty push, landing in a drift of snow that was being drawn along by the weight of the over snow. He saw the 20 seater disappear, as though dropping into an invisible hole.

Its departure brought the snow drift to a dubious halt.

The edge of whatever the cat had fallen into was only a foot or two from his boots; he dare not make any sudden moves. Above the wind he heard the machine hit bottom about three seconds later. To his horror it exploded, painting the storm in a red hot fading glow, as if from the innards of hell. His imagination ran wild. Had the second cat fallen on top of the first; crushing all those inside? Or, had the explosion delivered a second blow to Belinda and the others as they escaped. He looked about for any sign of the gunman, comforted by the fact being seen by him within the cover of the storm would be mutually difficult.

Still trying to comprehend the reality of the situation, Josey was left to deal with avoiding being killed, not just by the gunman, but by sliding over the edge and falling to wherever his friends lay, injured or dead. One thing was certain, there was no point in waiting for the worst, survival drove him to try and move backward without unsettling the loose snow. Having come to rest on his back, he decided against rolling over. Only able to use his elbows, clawing at the snow in miniscule progressions was his best option. Eventually his efforts brought him to a high enough point to roll onto his stomach and gain a better hold. Thinking ahead, he saw himself rounding the fissure, or whatever it was, to make his way down into it – to find the crippled machines and search for signs of life. *Life, not death – please.*

Moving faster now, he progressed far enough up the incline to gingerly rise to his feet. He stood for a moment to regain some of his strength. He prayed the blizzard would ease enough to see further than the present two feet in front of him. What he had learnt though, was the position of the hole was designated by a pale green line, which he could still see to his right. So long as he remained this side of it, he decided it would be safe to walk forward with one careful step at a time. The wind was buffering him tirelessly, threatening to blow him over the edge.

If the threat of the green abyss wasn't enough, a shot rang out, lifting a pocket of snow beside him. He looked back and saw the gunman's shadowy figure approaching, tracing the footsteps that Josey was unavoidably leaving. In spite of his extreme exhaustion, he thought to try and out-pace him, at the same time hoping the man wouldn't get in a lucky shot while firing blindly into the whiteout. In his haste he realised too late that he had stepped across the green line, the snow dropping away from under him. He fell for a second or two, landing hard against an embankment before continuing to slide, coming to rest a good fifty feet below.

On his back, he saw the green line was now above him, and realised it marked thin air, in this case, where the snow met the sky. He rolled to see if the man had also fallen and landed nearby. Visibility was being assisted by a reduction in wind, possibly caused by the wall of snow that stretched up before him. He staggered to his feet and waited to allow his eyes to scan the surrounds in the hope he might see an out of place dark shape amongst the forever-white. After a moment he thought he did, and moved toward it. Each lumbering step brought the two machines into finer detail. There was no sign of an explosion, not even a lingering lick of flame or smoke. He quickened his pace and thought to call out but changed his mind in consideration he might be heard and followed. There was no guarantee he still wouldn't be—

Then, a new noise rose above the storm. He stood still, listening, trying to decipher where he's heard the sound before. Whatever it was, it was slowly getting closer. He stepped forward until he came to within a few feet of the disabled cats. The one that had been driven by Skipper John had its door wide open. He was about to enter when he tripped and fell over something solid beneath the snow. He propped himself on an elbow and saw what appeared to be a shiny rail line, about a foot long length of it, embedded in the pockmarked snow, and presumably continuing beneath the cover—

The cause of the noise came to him with the clarity of an air raid siren right then – an approaching train! He and the crashed cats were in its path.

He yelled out the names of his friends as he clambered through the open door, hoping they wouldn't be there. He was surprised that he could see so well – see that the cabin was empty. The increasing noise made him realise the unexpected level of ambient light was coming from the train and that he needed to get the hell out.

As he exited, the light and the noise were growing exponentially. The thought occurred to him that it must be the Pan-Himalayan, which was strange because his location was above where the line ends at Lhasa.

To his right, away from the sound, there was a dark form, possible cover. He paced toward it and discovered it was a tunnel, complete with another set of train tracks emerging from beneath the snow. It gave him hope; it was the perfect place for his friends to have taken refuge after the accident. When he thought about it, there was nowhere else for them to have gone, so he went in.

The sound of the train was growing; he looked back to the mouth of the tunnel and saw the disk of light on the front of the locomotive melting through the blizzard, thankfully at an incredibly slow speed.

He stood in the middle of the track and waved his arms in the hope he would be seen. As it drew closer, the light became too blinding to see beyond it. Stepping from the tracks when it was almost upon him, he couldn't be sure that he'd been seen. The deafening squeal of brakes rang out, confirming he had. The shine of the train's light stretched the length of the tunnel now, allowing him to see there was no sign of the others.

Although approaching a stop, the train had brought a blade cold breeze with it, the persistent chill continuing across Josey's face as he pressed his body against the tunnel wall.

Scanning the illuminated windows, he could see the carriages were empty.

The last carriage approached and passed, its red lights receding to a dead stop about fifty feet along the track.

At the cessation of the train's rattle, Aaron was left standing in the glow of a nearby wall light, and beginning to wonder if this was all actually happening.

He heard a noise back toward the mouth of the tunnel and turned to see a figure standing against the dim veil of the storm.

'Josey; is that you?'

Hope and relief swept away the chill of doubt at the sound of her voice. 'Belinda, yes, it's me.'

Her being here, after the fall in the snow-cat, seemed equally surreal as the timely arrival of the train. As they approached each other, all he could think to ask was, 'Where are the others?'

Her beautiful face moved into the light and he wanted to hold her, but he mired the impulse. That didn't stop her; she wrapped her arms around him and kissed him on the mouth.

When the cat's away—

They broke off the kiss at the sound of the professor's voice approaching, not out of guilt or fear, there was more to it. When he came to their side and shook Josey's hand, it was realised - here was a man eternally glad that he and his fiancée are still alive.

Josey looked past him. 'Where are the other two?'

Belinda released a thankful sigh. 'John's with Shannon, they're both okay.'

'Someone's coming!'

Josey and Belinda responded to Aaron's announcement by following his gaze. A man was moving through the spill light from the carriage windows, approaching from the front of the train.

Josey thought he recognised the walk, and it concerned him.

Belinda saw the worry. 'What's wrong?'

'Were you out of the cat before the other one fell?' he asked without taking his eyes off the man from the train.

'We were already in the tunnel when we heard it hit. Aaron and I found our way back because we thought you might be inside. We didn't know what to expect, and finding neither of you opened up a new fear.'

Josey's eyes hadn't moved from the approaching figure, watching him all the way until he was right in front of them, moving into the light.

In total disbelief, all eyes fell on Ral, *Ral Davenport*, SciCore's Australian General Manager, the man from the train.

Josey could see that the way Belinda was shaking her head that she was thinking, *how could the perpetrator from the cat be behind them somewhere, and in front of them from the train at the same time . . .*

'Bel, I—'

'Have I got this wrong?' she asked with a deep frown.

Turning back to Davenport, who seemed to be wearing

an out-of-place grin, Josey told her, 'Yes - and no.'

'Save your breath, Detective,' Ral suggested, 'she doesn't listen.'

Davenport's comment was as inappropriate as his grin, and Belinda had her eyes fixed on him, searching for answers.

'Can we please get on the train people; we're sitting ducks out here.' Davenport gestured toward the back carriage. 'We can climb aboard here.'

Belinda went to object, but Ral once again gestured toward the carriage. 'I'm not going to hurt you.'

Without so much as a blink of an eye, she let him lead her across to the carriage.

The professor took Josey to where they had left John and Shannon, just outside the mouth of the tunnel.

'What's with the train?' John asked as they approached. 'We heard it stop.'

'It's our ride out of here,' Josey told him.

They headed back into the tunnel and to the waiting train. It hadn't occurred to Josey at first, but then he began to think it odd that Shannon was walking as though he'd never been hurt.

Everyone got settled down in the heated carriage as Davenport went to the exit, leant out and signalled the train driver to move off.

The brakes released, the diesel engine roared into life, and the wheels began to reverse, moving back down the mountain toward Lhasa.

Josey was still trying to wrap his head around the fact they had met up with the train line, he was feeling unsettled about the whole thing.

I heard the cat explode, why wasn't it there, blown

apart? And why is Davenport here with the train?

He'd been thinking this as he reached the door that led to the adjoining carriage, where he stood looking through the glass panel.

'Josey?'

He ignored her . . . All the carriages were aligned, allowing him to see all the way through to the first carriage – he thought it was strange that there were no other people on-board.

'Josey?'

This time, he turned to see what she wanted, expecting to see her sitting with the others, but she wasn't there – none of them were there. He was alone—

What th' hell . . . ?

'Josey, Can you hear me?'

CHAPTER THIRTY EIGHT
Back on the Pan Himalayan

Of course I can hear you, he thought as he opened his eyes.

She was leaning over him, looking extremely relieved. 'Thank-god, we thought we'd lost you.'

He rolled his head to the side and saw a man covered in blisters, lying on a stretcher. Looking back up at her he said, 'I don't understand – where am I?'

'You're in the hospital at Lhasa, you've been shot.'

He tried to lift himself up, but pain forced him back. He felt with his hand and realised his skull was completely bandaged.

'You've got a new part in your hair, a few centimetres closer and—'

'Bel, this is not adding up – tell me how I got here.'

'John brought us all down in the cat.'

He gave her a questioning frown. 'In the cat, the last time I saw that, it wasn't going anywhere – and the train

– what happened in the train – is that when I was shot?'

Now *she* was frowning. 'I'm sorry, sweetheart; I don't know what you're talking about. Although I have to admit you were saying *something* about a train while you were out of it.'

He thought about her answer. 'What else was I saying?'

'You mentioned Ral a few times.'

'Where's Ral now?'

'He's on the train.'

'Are you trying to confuse me – what train?'

'The train to Golmud, he's been arrested, along with Aaron and Shannon.'

Josey lifted his head, fighting the pain, and saw the Pan Himalayan waiting at the station in the glow of the platform lights, just beyond the mouth of the tunnel hospital.

'So Ral was there.'

'Where?'

'On the mountain.'

'Of course he was there, he shot you.'

Josey looked inordinately horrified. 'No, Bel, you've got this all wrong.' He managed to sit up and struggle to his feet, against her protest.

'What do you mean?'

He achieved a few uncertain steps toward the exit, sending his head into a wild spin.

'Josey, you're not well, please stay here and rest.'

He wasn't giving up. 'Talk to me, Bel – I'm missing some stuff, tell me what you think happened up there.'

'I should be asking *you* that.'

'Bel, please, just tell me what you saw.'

She realised he was harbouring a high degree of confusion and that she needed to tread carefully. 'Do you remember we were being bulldozed into a fissure and that you were trying to stop it?'

'Yes, what happened after that?'

'I saw you were being fired at as we fell, we didn't know you'd been shot until after the skipper got us out of there. Thankfully the drop wasn't much more than a couple of metres.'

Josey was doing his best to piece together what he was being told and what he remembered, he was beginning to understand why Bel thought Ral was the shooter, and he blamed himself for that. 'Where was Ral arrested?'

'Here, at the station, we gather he drove back to Lhasa after the attack.'

Noticing she had confused Josey even further she asked, 'What's that look for?'

He was beginning to comprehend what life was like for the professor, a life driven by crazy dreams.

Skipper John spotted Belinda helping Josey along the tracks and paced across to meet up with them. 'Hey, what's happening?'

'Ask him,' she answered in disgust.

'Buddy?'

Josey chose to ignore him.

With her arm hooked into his elbow, Belinda came to a sudden halt, holding Josey back. 'That's it; you need to tell me what's going on, right now.'

He stared at her before pulling free, and continued toward the train.

'I get that you're worried,' John said empathetically as he caught up, 'but these people are piss-and-steam most of the time, I think your *Ausi* mates will be fine.'

Josey realised his memory of events wasn't to be trusted, and he blamed the memory lapse on being hit in the head with a bullet, but he knew that his hunch was playing out exactly as expected. Now he had to find a way to alter the outcome – on his own. He stopped, grabbed the skipper's arm and spoke low, 'John, can you get me on the train; I promise you it's a matter of life and death.'

Belinda was beginning to really worry about Josey's state of mind.

The skipper was more countered. 'I can, but we need to be careful, you don't want to cross swords with the PLA.'

'Why would I be crossing swords with the PLA?'

'Because you're under arrest too, you all are.'

Belinda glanced around nervously, worried they were being watched. 'If you go anywhere near that train you'll end up in cuffs.' She faced John with a plea, hoping he could keep Cam from trying to get on the train. 'John?'

John trusted the detective understood what he was doing and decided not to stand in his way, but knew helping him wouldn't be easy. 'One of the porters is a friend,' he told him.

'Oh I see, this is secret-boy's-business,' she suggested, 'I'm not feeling real comfortable with this.'

They were nearing the mouth of the tunnel as Josey told her bluntly, 'Bel, you'll be a whole lot less *comfortable* if I don't catch this train.'

'That's *we*,' she corrected him; 'I need to keep my eye on you.'

He looked at her in alarm, but said nothing.

'I think you should listen to the detective,' John said buying back in, 'I've known for a while he's got this.'

'Oh, really.'

'Yes, really, Belinda,' Josey clarified with an urgency that she couldn't argue with.

'Real or not,' John warned, 'you won't get past the mouth of this tunnel unless you both listen to me.'

'Go ahead, I'm listening.'

'You need to get back to your stretcher and play dead.'

He held on the skipper enquiringly. 'You're serious.'

'I am.'

'This is not worth the risk,' Belinda protested.

'But one that has to be taken,' Josey told her. 'Come on John, let's do it.'

The skipper hooked under his arm, and against her better judgement, Belinda took the other. John had been keeping his eye on the PLA guard responsible for watching the hospital, and noted that he hadn't been paying them any attention, there was a lot of other stuff happening to take his eye.

On reaching Aaron's stretcher, they helped him down onto it. After one last glance to make sure the guard wasn't onto them, John covered Josey's face with his blanket. 'Take short shallow breaths,' he informed him. 'With a bit of luck we'll make it across to the train – ready?'

Josey answered, not realising the skipper had been talking to Belinda.

She nodded, and they took their end of the stretcher, John taking up the lead. This time, the guard zeroed in on them, watching their progress all the way to the station, making no move to interfere, or to raise an alarm via his radio.

'Okay, here's my friend,' John advised, 'let me do the

talking.'

'I'm dead remember,' came the reply from under the blanket.

'Shush!' John had again been talking to Belinda.

They approached a porter pushing a trolley, and John launched into his speal in Chinese. In consideration, the man looked across at the one Australian he could see, and down at the one he couldn't, and pointed at a small porter's room. John thanked him and they carried the stretcher inside to the warmth provided by a fireplace.

Belinda hadn't noticed the skipper covertly hand the porter something wrapped in a cloth.

'We're on our own, Detective,' John announced.

Josey felt the stretcher settle and came out from under the blanket.

'He wants us to wait until the train's loaded; there are a few guards still on the platform keeping watch. He'll signal when to get on-board via the cargo-car. You'll be walking.'

As they sat at a table Belinda announced, 'I need to go to the *John*.' She forced a chortled over what she'd said. 'I know you boys like to joke, so that's my contribution.'

They watched her go with glum faces. 'Sorry to leave you with this,' Josey told the skipper, 'she's already pissed.'

'I know, so let's see if we can get you aboard while the goings good.' He made eye contact with his porter friend at the other side of the glass—where he'd been waiting and watching from the platform—and gave him the thumbs up.

The man nodded back almost undetectably.

'I'm not sure what your plan is, Detective,' John said as

they stood from the table, 'but good luck – tread easy.'

Josey cupped John's hand with a firm grip. 'Always.'

John watched the detective exit onto the platform to meet up with the porter, who conscientiously checked they weren't being watched before accompanying his stowaway aboard.

When Belinda returned, the skipper lied to avoid a possible scene, telling her that Josey had also had a call of nature. Although suspicious, she had no real reason to argue, settling for small talk while they waited. Her demeanour changed when the train began to pull away from the station, with no sign of Josey anywhere. She squinted at John and said, 'Okay, I get it - bring your keys, you're about to find out I'm not one to be pushed aside.'

Well, he knew she'd be pissed off, but not being born-yesterday, he figured he knew exactly what she was planning to do – which in his book, wasn't a bad idea.

The baggage compartment was in the train's last car, allowing Josey to cool his heels while he tried to work out his approach to the situation. The game he was playing was a dangerous one, and he knew it. His head was throbbing like mad, but it wasn't stopping him from running over the case while he waited. The porter, who spoke no English, had set Josey up atop some mail bags, where he could wait in reasonable comfort – and out of sight. Josey figured that with the guy taking a possible risk, if someone did arrive, it would go down better for the porter if it looked as though he didn't know the stowaway was there. There was also the chance that one of the guards might look through from the preceding car.

Being able to do so was an advantage for Josey too, because when the time came to make a move, he would be able to see in advance if the way was clear.

He cast his mind back to when his hunch began to pay off; it had all come together in that hour in which communication had returned to the mountain, while they were trapped in the bowels of the ruins. Maxine had been able to connect the biker, Joseph Sheppard, to Ral Davenport's son, Lester, and Lester to *Flock Investments*, who were closely affiliated with *Davrow,* the DAV part abbreviated from Davenport, which left one last piece of the puzzle, who was the Chinese Manufacturer they were receiving components from?

Josey was fairly certain that when the skipper had spoken to the porter, he hadn't elaborated on why the stowaway was on-board the train, but the guy was clearly interested in why his mysterious visitor was constantly glancing at his phone, so much so that it looked like he was getting frustrated about it.

In fact, Josey was so irritated with the wait that he could barely refrain from making his move immediately. His moment came an hour later, and a thousand feet closer to sea level. His phone grew a single bar, then two, three and finally four – he texted Maxine.

The porter watched him anxiously punching away with his thumbs and began to understand why he had been so frequently looking at his phone; he'd been watching for tower coverage, and now spent the next hour texting and making calls. He then saw that whatever was in the stowaway's final text reply, was satisfying enough to make him smile, and clearly what was now setting him in motion.

'You go?' he asked as Josey cautiously approached the doorway to the next carriage.

He nodded and gave the man thumbs up, who surprisingly reached into his jacket and unthreateningly retrieved a small pistol, which he handed across butt first.

Josey knew immediately who'd given it to him, but wasn't sure if it was wise to take it, being caught with a loaded weapon might just be enough to get him killed. 'Is this from John?'

The man thrust the gun out for him to take as though it was a gift that could not be refused.

He reservedly accepted the weapon and immediately hid it from view beneath his jacket. A cautious glance into the next carriage indicated there were no guards within view around the entry point, but that didn't mean there weren't any. Unlike his hallucinatory experience in the tunnel, there would be some carriages where he wouldn't be able to look straight through into the preceding car, and with this one there was two blind spots left-and-right that led to the exit doors. These blind spots were to be expected and something he would have to contend with each time he entered this type of carriage.

What he was counting on was the fact he'd noticed the train was carrying passengers, not many, but a few, which gave him hope he could pretend to be one of them if seen. That ploy might not work so well suddenly emerging from the baggage compartment.

The porter startled him with a tap on the shoulder. He turned to find him thrusting a *high-vis* bib in his direction. Josey's immediate thought was *hell no; do I really want to make myself stand out?* He patted the hood of his thick jacket in refusal, indicating leaving it on was his best cover. He pointed at the door and gave the guy a shrug, which brought on a strange indifferent response.

Giving the preceding carriage one more careful consideration, he stepped onto the enclosed concertina gangway. The sound of wheels on tracks rumbled to his ears as his feet danced to the opposing movement of the adjoined car. He closed the door behind him and waited at the second door, peering in. As far as he could see there was no one in and around the exit doors. He turned the doorknob as easily as he could, hinged the door in and looked left and right – he was on his own. Looking back to the baggage car, he saw the porter still watching. It didn't seem necessary to acknowledge the guy, but gave him a wave anyway.

Moving to the right side of the train, where he knew he would find a corridor running alongside the windows, he looked around the corner and saw that no one was there. He knew from his first ride on the train that a row of small compartments branched off to the left, often housing passengers that were in clear view. He took the plunge and moved into the corridor. Inside the first compartment were two teenage local girls curled up on opposing bunks, eyes closed, presumably recovering from altitude sickness. One of them was utilising the on board oxygen via a tube that came out of the wall.

He moved on past the second compartment, which had its privacy curtain pulled across. The third compartment had an elderly man and woman sitting facing each other, local tourists in appearance, who immediately looked his way with enquiring eyes as he passed.

The fourth and fifth compartments were empty, with a toilet block between them. A guy who looked like a railway official appeared at the far end of the carriage – the bathroom becoming a timely placement. He ducked in and locked the door, listening and waiting for the officer to reach the back of the carriage.

Taking a sneak peek, and seeing that the man was out of view, he made a hasty advance to the exit doors up ahead, which were also thankfully unattended.

Repeating the same cautious procedure he crossed to the preceding car and found a single uniformed waiter preparing tables for dinner. He lowered his hood and made his way past her, receiving a warm Tibetan smile.

When he reached the next set of doors, he raised his hood and ventured across the gangway. Again, the exit door area was void of people, but the doorway in front of him presented an isle running down the centre of twin seating. A few forward facing passengers were staggered throughout the carriage, all of whom appeared to be tourists. Josey went through to the front with the deliberate persona of a passenger wanting to reach the next car, confident there was no threat—

That changed the moment he felt someone follow him through onto the gangway – standing unnaturally close at his back.

'Give me gun!' The demand was made with the thick accent of a Chinese local. 'I just want gun, then, you pass to next carriage.'

Josey had no clue who could possibly know he was carrying, other than the porter. But in a way he was happy to hand it over, provided the guy wasn't about to march him off to the authorities, or worse. The strange events on Mount Kailash had conditioned him, this event was no less alien – there was little left that would faze him. He turned with his hands out to the side. 'It's in my belt,' he told him.

'Open Jacket.'

Josey did as told, revealing the small pistol, which the man took and placed in the pocket of his own jacket. He said nothing as he returned to the carriage he had come from, and calmly sat down on his own, looking out the window like nothing had happened.

Although confused, Josey had the surreal feeling that he was somehow being helped, and decided to dismiss the anarchistic encounter as a blessing, he'd been thinking of ditching the gun anyway; the only thing that had stopped him was the possibility the weapon's registration might trace back to the skipper if found discarded.

When he made it into the next car, he couldn't resist a glance back at the gangway;

Did that just happen?

Instinctively he felt for the gun to confirm it was gone, but hated that he was having any doubt, shaking his head as if to resurrect his brain. 'Get a grip,' he told himself aloud.

As if the experience wasn't unsettling enough, the new car was one of those with a corridor up against the windows and compartments opposite. It took every ounce of control not to freeze on the spot when he saw a uniformed PLA officer enter the corridor, heading in his direction.

The hair stood on the back of Josey's neck as they brushed past each other. He walked ahead, refraining from looking over his shoulder until he reached the exit door area. Out of sight now, the man had presumably gone through to the following carriage. There was every chance that the carriage ahead, which the man had come out of, was where the arrestees were being held, along with further armed guards. Before Josey had a chance to think about entering onto the gangway, a second PLA officer entered from the other side and met up with him.

Earlier, Josey had noticed small cushioned seats that pulled down from the wall in the event a passenger or guard needed to take a seat. He pulled it down and sat on it with his head held back.

The officer expected he was looking at a passenger feeling the effects of altitude sickness, and pointed to the oxygen bottle positioned above the seat.

Josey nodded and the man lifted the container from its cradle to hand to him, which he took with clear relief there was no threat. 'Thank you, I'll be fine,' he told the helpful guy - prompting him to leave, which he did, continuing on his way sporting a knowing countenance, people got sick on the train constantly.

In actual fact there was truth in it; nausea was building in the pit of Josey's stomach. It was partly from stress, what would he find in the next carriage, and how would he approach what needed to be done. He took a moment breathing in the soothing oxygen before placing the bottle back on its cradle. What he hadn't noticed about the PLA officer was that he had locked the door he came out of, which was discovered when he tried turning the handle. This presented a challenge with no immediate answer.

Just like with the man who wanted the gun, the answer came in the form of passengers passing by the window, standing on a platform waiting for the train to pull in to a station - his plan now, being to alight and assess how he might progress further along the train.

He stepped onto the platform and into the cutting cold, tightening his hood against the night chill. He noted that people were only moving in and out of the carriages to the rear of the one that was locked, which suggested all the other carriages toward the front were commandeered by the PLA.

There was no indication of how long the train might remain at the station, so he needed to quickly find out if his plan had any chance of working. Light was spilling from some of the windows in the locked carriage; they were the ones he needed to check. At the other side of the third window of the first car to check, he was able to covertly assess the occupants. As luck would have it, Yu Chow was with them, moving about and chatting with a few of the PLA people. Step one of Josey's plan had become a reality, a possibility at least. He couldn't see any sign of the detainees, but figured they might be in the same car, perhaps behind the windows that had drawn blinds, or in an adjoining carriage toward the front of the train. Getting in to meet with Chow presented his only chance of success.

The door to the carriage was sitting wide open, with a PLA officer standing nearby having a smoke, which was a clue there might be a minute or two before the train pulled out.

The PLA soldier was completely taken off-guard when he found himself being pushed to the ground, and with no chance of gathering his wits before the assailant made it into the carriage.

The stricken smoker could be heard protesting on top of his voice as Josey appeared inside, into the wild faces of a half dozen soldiers and the very stunned Yu Chow. A quick scan confirmed Aaron and the others were not there.

The two Liberation Army guys closest took a firm hold of him, guarding against any form of attack. A third patted him down for any sign of a weapon before informing Chow that he was clean.

'Let him go,' he instructed.

Once free, Josey straightened himself and told the director, 'You're making a mistake.'

'Do you mean in letting you go?'

'I mean in arresting Davenport; he didn't shoot me.'

'Really – I'm very surprised to hear you say that, because even his fiancée has said that you claimed he did.'

'She's got it wrong too.'

'Well I'm sure that when we get to Golmud, and when all the parties involved are together there, we can sort all this out.'

'Where is he?'

'Mr Davenport? – He is in the next carriage with the others. I'll take you there to see him if you like.'

'Yes, I'd like.'

Chow moved past Josey toward the exit doors. 'Come.'

Two of the guards went to follow, but they were told to stay. Josey then followed the director across the gangway into the adjoining carriage, which was the type for seating only – and quite empty.

'Where are they?' Josey asked as he inspected the vacant seats that they were passing.

'They are in the next carriage.'

They crossed into the preceding car and found that it too appeared to be empty.

There was some disturbance building on the platform. Yu Chow shuffled between a set of twin seats and looked out. His expression changed, enough to encourage Josey to take up one of the other windows.

What he saw couldn't have been more of a surprise. Belinda and the skipper were on the platform, having an argument with a porter several carriages back. They were instantly joined by a PLA guard who proceeded to get heavy handed with John. In hindsight, Josey had no problem conjuring up the scenario that brought them there – Belinda obviously having insisted on the skipper chasing the train down the mountain in the cat.

The altercation came to an abrupt halt when a man stepped in and barked at the guard, who backed off without hesitation.

The train gave a light jolt and began moving, setting Belinda into a run alongside the departing carriages, trying to peer into the windows. She almost drew level with the car Josey was in and managed to catch a glimpse of him in the company of Yu Chow. Before she had time to assess the situation she reached the end of the platform, and the realisation the chase would need to continue on-board the cat.

Josey held on her until she moved from view, the last thing he saw was her running back toward the skipper, and whoever the other man was.

'It looks like we will have to do this the hard way.'

Josey knew why the director was telling him this; even before he turned and saw that he was being held at gunpoint. 'Yes, I guess we do,' he agreed as Yu Chow waved the gun toward the next carriage. 'Let's join your compatriots shall we.' Although confident the detective was unarmed and no threat he played it safe, backing up against the window to allow Josey to take the lead. He kept close behind as they crossed the gangway and into a carriage that was near to pitch dark, due to blinds being drawn on every window. There was just enough light to see the car was dedicated to supplies, and as cold as a refrigerator due to the lack of the trains ducted warmth - a no-go for passengers.

'I hope that you know you are to be arrested for suspicion of attempted abduction, along with your friends. Do not think that being shot puts you in better stead.'

'I'd give up on the crap if I was you, Chow; I know what your game is.'

'Stop here!'

Josey did as asked while scanning the gloomy sur-rounds for any sign of the captors. A chill ran through him as it occurred they might already be dead.

'Sit.'

Josey glanced behind him and saw he was being directed toward a metal crate, which appeared to be big enough to hold a body. He took the few steps that brought him up against it and sat as instructed. It was cold to the touch, easily penetrating his insulated trousers.

A set of cuffs landed at Josey's feet.

'I'm not the only one who knows what you've been up to,' he warned his captor.

'You are wasting your breath, Detective, your friend Davenport has been trying to scare me with what he knows ever since he was arrested.'

'I know Davenport's involved, just in case you're

wondering.'

Yu Chow raised the gun, bringing it in line with Josey's forehead, 'Put the cuffs on.'

With the gun at his head, it would have been suicide to refuse. He imagined his feet might be next.

Instead, Chow barked, 'Get up!'

Weirdly, it felt good to lift his butt from the ice-cold crate.

'Walk!'

The gun waving toward the front of the carriage demanded he go there. It had a door, but not one that advanced to the preceding carriage. The car they were in was considerably shorter than the others, indicating there might be a separate compartment.

'Slide the door!'

Josey now understood why he'd been cuffed out in front, and pushed the sliding door open, revealing the three Australian captives, who sat zip tied together around a metal pole that securely stretched from floor to ceiling. Josey thought their attitudes were classic Aussie – apologetic, rueful for allowing them-selves to be hoodwinked by a douchebag like Yu Chow.

'Good news gentlemen,' the douchebag announced sarcastically, 'someone has come to rescue you.'

Ignoring the mock, Davenport met Josey's eyes and said, 'I'm not surprised you worked this out.'

Chow shoved Josey to the floor. 'What is it you think you have worked out, Detective?'

Josey permitted himself to be a little playful. 'Oh, I don't know - does the name *Biaomi* ring a bell?'

The name rang a bell so loudly that confirmation sprang onto Chow's face, spiked with a hint of annoyance.

'It's surprising what you can learn over the phone while you're hiding in the baggage compartment,' Josey told him smugly.

'Very clever, but totally useless information – since you are all about to die.'

'Then what's to lose in talking about it.'

'Must we?' Aaron asked flippantly. 'I've been listening to my damn boss making excuses for himself ever since we became pole-buddies.'

Guilt ridden, Davenport felt compelled to elucidate. 'I gather you've worked out I was involved, but not in all of it, I knew we were dealing with Biaomi, but I had no idea about the sabotage.'

'Don't sweat it, Ral – I probably know more than *you* do.'

Yu Chow interrupted, 'This is all of no consequence; smart talk is not going to save you from what I have planned.' He faced Josey with fire in his eyes and the gun again pointed his way. 'Help your Aussie friends to their feet.'

Complying, he feigned effort as he took his time lifting himself into a sitting position, all the while searching for a way of turning the tables.

'Hurry up!' he was told threateningly.

Experience in tight spots told Josey; sooner or later their captor would make a mistake, but for the moment there was nothing other than to do as told.

On moving across to the bound trio, he saw that Verg and Shannon had been zip tied individually, while Davenport had been cuffed; obviously the one ordained to fasten the wrists of the others. A fourth zip-tie was interwoven, holding all bedfellows to the pole.

'Stand up, all of you.'

A pair of snips came sliding across the floor.

'Just the pole, if you release anyone's hands, I will shoot.'

'Do as he says,' Josey whispered to them, 'you're no good tied to this pole.'

With a collaborative effort they reached their feet.

He cut through the fourth tie, sanctioning independent movement.

Another zip tie came from Yu Chow's pocket – he seemed to have an unlimited supply. He threw it to Josey and told him, 'Tie them back together.'

At least they would be free to walk, albeit as awkwardly as a crab, no doubt part of the director's plan to explain his actions later.

'Hurry up and get it done,' he demanded, walking backward toward the exit doors.

It wasn't hard to understand his plan was to have them vacate the moving train, minus the zip ties, the plan being to self-discharge one at a time out the door, or be shot; he might even offer to shoot one of the others if they didn't abide. Josey knew Yu Chow's plan had a very obvious problem, bodies spread periodically in the snow with bullets in them, would spell out to the authorities that they had been executed one by one.

As for exiting the train, the Australians suspected that travelling downhill at a rate of eighty kilometres per hour, being thrown or indeed jumping offered no chance of survival without a snowsuit, perhaps even *with* one. Although it wasn't as cold now as it was in Lhasa, a person would surely freeze to death if an initial survival were even possible.

Driven by fear, Shannon tried to break free and took a bullet for his trouble. He fell to the floor taking the crab-like arrangement with him.

Yu Chow began imprecating in Chinese.

It was difficult to know where Shannon had taken the bullet, but he was clearly in a lot of pain. Josey felt the shooting might present no real problem for the director; because Shannon had been shot inside the train, which meant the director could just claim he was dealing with four prisoners on his own who were bent on escape. Shooting them inside the train seemed to be where his plan was shifting to.

'Move back!' he demanded.

Shannon made no sound as the bound men lifted him to his feet.

Then, with an increased awkwardness they dragged him back to the pole as ordered, just as Josey was thrown a fresh fastener. At least Yu Chow's new plan postponed being thrown from the train.

Yu Chow did seem rattled, and Josey felt he knew why. Shooting the captives inside the train had solved a problem, and yet created another. It was *the way* in which to shoot them, how to make it look like they were trying to escape. If they were clumped together, all the blood would be concentrated in one area and difficult to clean up, especially if he had to spread the corpses about the carriage.

With his body covering his actions, Josey made out like he was fastening the men back to the pole as told to do, catching their eyes knowingly. Shannon was either dead already, or playing at it, he hadn't moved since being brought back to the pole. If he was still alive, there was presently no chance to help him, his fate was in the lap of the gods—as was the case for all of them.

'You are taking too long!' Yu Chow bellowed.

Josey heard the mistake he'd been waiting for, the sound of Chow stepping closer to see what was happening, and he turned to face him, assessing the danger. The gun swung across to the professor with such positive intent, that he was clearly on the threshold of shooting the professor where he sat.

His following remark confirmed it. 'This is for giving me the most trouble—'

Standing off at this point was not in Josey's DNA, nor did he have the time to second guess whether or not Aaron would be dead in the next split second – he lunged.

Yu Chow tried realigning his weapon in defence, but his reaction was slowed by the surprise of the attack. Josey had already clamped a hand onto the would-be shooter's wrist. The gun fired aimlessly, twice, one bullet taking out a window, releasing a blast of even colder air to the already low temperature of the interior. Snow and ice swirled, driven by the movement of the train, taking on the appearance of an indoor mini tornado.

If holding the gunman at bay wasn't difficult enough in this atmospheric upheaval, the train braked as suddenly as if it had ploughed into a wall of snow, spearing anything that was loose forward, including the duellers.

The G-forces propelled Shannon's untethered body skimming to the front of the carriage, whereupon his head hit the wall solidly, extracting a yelp – *proof of life*.

Other voices, shouting, could be heard on the outside of the stationary train – *approaching*.

The new order of things had placed Josey and the director five feet apart, sprawled chaotically at the front of the car.

Verg and Davenport had fortunately come to rest with the gun at Davenport's feet, allowing him to kick it across to Josey. As smart as this manoeuvre was, Josey was pinned by a dislodged metal crate, unable to reach the weapon before Yu Chow swept it up.

Unlike the other carriages, this one had only one door in the middle on each side, which was plain to see from wherever you were. Chow had made his way to one of these doors, once again with the upper hand; except for the fact the shouting was drawing closer – definitely not something that was pleasing him. There was something *else* not pleasing him, Josey hadn't done a very good job of attaching his friends to the pole. Davenport's eye was drawn to Verg, he'd been hit; presumably by a stray bullet that had caught him in the worst possible place – the chest. If he wasn't gone, it sure looked like he might be; blood was pooling beneath him and rolling away on the sloping floor.

The scene that Chow created for himself had now become very hard for him to explain. Especially since two of the captives would be found shot while wearing ties. With the gun remaining on his captives he opened the door a slither and looked ahead, along the curve of the track; he couldn't believe what he was seeing. There was a snow-cat obstructing the locomotive, and people were running along the opposing line toward him, among them Verg's fiancée - she stood out, along with the skipper and another man that he also recognised, the same man who had shown up at the last station, and well known to him.

In his mind, he was left with little choice, leaving the Australians alive to talk was not an option. He crossed the carriage and opened the opposite door and saw that there was a substantial snow covered drop-off, a possible means of escape – but first things first. When he turned to take care of business, Josey was seemingly flying at him, defying gravity, bundling him up on his way out through the open door.

Momentum and gravity took the ensemble in a wide arc away from the bank, depositing them halfway down in deep snow.

Chow reeled back and forth looking for the gun, but quickly abandoned the search when a shot rang out, the bullet slicing into the snow a little too close for comfort.

Above, standing at the open door of the train was one of the PLA guards with his gun still aimed.

Josey put his hands up; it was difficult to appreciate who he had been firing at. He quickly learnt it wasn't the director, who was already on the move, clearing the edge of the snowdrift and making it onto solid ground.

A man appeared beside the guard at the door of the train, and seemed to have sufficient influence to convince him to lower his gun – it was the same mysterious guy that Josey had seen on the station with Belinda and John.

Josey put his hands down and looked over his shoulder, the director was still running. Although the immediate area around the train tracks was flat, the escapee was facing massive boulders and a mountainous climb, enough to test the agility of a sure footed Yak.

'Josey!'

The call came from the train. He looked up and saw the

skipper standing in the doorway.

'He's got nowhere to go; I'll pick him up in the cat. I'll swing by you.'

Josey gestured in understanding.

John was right about the director having nowhere to go, he was operating on autopilot with no chance of reaching the boulders before either running out of steam, or being picked up by John.

He wondered what was going on inside the carriage. Was Belinda there? Was she being forced to deal with the death of her fiancé in front of her former lover? Perhaps blaming Ral instead of the gunman?

Adding to the questions, the mystery man in the doorway, whoever he was, presumably carried a high degree of clout with the authorities; a PLA officer came to his side and appeared to accept an instruction, after which he hurried away.

Josey waited in the snowdrift, recovering from the knowledge two men had been shot, and from the adrenalin rush that stemmed from his having prevented further casualties. He was still having trouble believing that an intelligent man like Ral Davenport, could allow himself to be drawn into a conspiracy against the one person who he should have supported. To have involved his son in it was even more astounding. Josey had a few questions for him on that score; he would deal with that when he got back home.

Just above the crest of the snow bank, he could see John and a PLA officer board the cat that had been parked across the track, an idea that he felt may have come from Belinda; people do desperate things in desperate times. Of course it would have been up to the skipper to assess the feasibility of coming out of it alive. It was clearly a high risk decision, because it looked like the train had only managed to come to a stop a few feet from the parked over snow.

A brief cloud of black smoke emitted from the cat's exhaust as it left the tracks and drove down to where Josey sat in the snow waiting.

'Let's get you in out of this before you freeze,' John was saying as he jumped down from the machine to help him to his feet.

He had a point, even with the heat of exertion; the cold was beginning to penetrate his woollens. 'Is Belinda up there?'

'She is,' he answered as he helped Josey up the stairs.

'Is she all right?'

'I won't lie, it's pretty heavy going.'

Josey's reaction faltered when he got inside and saw that the mystery man was on board.

'I can see you are wondering who I am,' he said with smiling eyes. My name is Professor Huang, Lui Jie's uncle.'

Josey's mind raced through the facts, responding with, 'This explains a lot.'

'I hoped that it would.'

'Sit tight folks,' John announced.

Josey dropped into a seat just in front of the professor as the cat jolted away in pursuit of the SciCore director.

Minutes later they were inside torrential rain, not just rain, golf ball sized hail began smashing against the windshield, providing even less visibility than the worst of what the blizzards had dished out. The skipper had to bring the cat to a stop yet again.

'Wow, how bad is this.' Josey was making a statement, and an obvious one.

John had tapped into a meteorology site. 'Take a look.' He had drawn their attention to the disturbance on the console's computer; black swirling patterns covered the entire area.

Around the cat, ribbons of lightning joined the mix, confirming the interface wasn't lying.

'We're not going anywhere are we,' Josey surmised, having considered the extent of the disturbance. 'Will our friend survive out here?'

'He might - or he might freeze to death if we're lucky.' He threw the cat into a three sixty turn and began following his own tread marks. 'Sorry for the rush guys, but these caterpillar tracks will be gone in minutes.'

CHAPTER THIRTY NINE
The Nitty Gritty

When Josey returned to the train, he found people had been moved into the warmth of the dining car. Belinda faced him, looking like she'd cried herself out of tears. Yes, she was full of sadness, but also happiness as she told him, 'He's alive.' Aaron's head was cradled in her lap. He was conscious, although his cognitive powers were noticeably weak.

Beside them, Davenport appeared shamefaced, perhaps laden with feelings of responsibility. Josey decided this was neither the time nor place to address the rights and wrongs of his behaviour. 'Good,' was all he could think to say, emotion had made the comment sound slightly cryptic. It also wasn't the time to divulge that this whole episode wasn't even close to being over. For now, that could wait.

Professor Huang appeared through the door as Josey moved to sit next to a local woman who was tending to

Shannon, one of the on board nurses that had been procured to attend to the wounded. 'English?' he asked the young nurse quietly.

She looked up from the patient and nodded.

He asked her, 'Will the man with the Australian woman be all right, do you know?'

'Yes, it is very fortunate that the bullet did not hit his heart. It would have been so sad if he had died; I am told they are to be married.'

Huang had moved into the carriage and crouched beside Belinda. 'We have a helicopter arriving,' he told her, 'it will take your fiancé the rest of the way to Golmud. Although I suspect its arrival may be delayed until this weather has eased.'

'Thank you so much, professor.' She looked over at Josey sitting beside Shannon and the nurse. 'What about the other man shot – will he be looked after?'

He reflected on the wounded reporter and explained, 'What he has done is of no consequence to the treatment he needs, and to be perfectly clear, the trouble you Australians are in with Beijing, pales into insignificance when one considers the trouble that besets us here in China; our part in sabotaging the satellites is inexcusable, not to mention our aspersions on Professor Verg's reputation. I also must apologise personally for Yu Chow's behaviour throughout this ordeal.'

Her expression acknowledged his acceptance of blame, trying to blink away tears of relief that it was Chow, and not Ral, who tried to murder them all on the mountain. She forced her attention to Ral, who appeared repentant for not recognising the level of corruption.

'I'm truly sorry, Bel, I didn't mean for this to happen.'

Huang saw the anguish. 'In spite of the part you played Mr Davenport, we understand you are not directly involved.' He glanced over at Josey. 'You can thank that detective over there for - how you say . . . watching your back; he fully explained your involvement to me. But at the same time, he assured me you are an honest man.'

Belinda knew this to be true, but told her ex, 'Lives have been lost, Ral – that's something you will have to live with the rest of your life.'

'Hopefully time will permit forgiveness,' the professor offered.

Unprepared to forgive himself, Davenport knew when to say nothing.

Huang stood and moved to where he could face all the occupants of the carriage. 'I will be taking the injured and the other Australians in a helicopter to Golmud. We must all make ourselves ready to go at a moment's notice.'

For a half hour they sat in silence, waiting for the sound of the approaching rotors, but it was another sound that dashed the helicopter's early arrival. The hail and lightning had subsided, but the torrential rain and wind had strengthened with a vengeance, making it impossible for a chopper to land.

During the delay, no one noticed that Ral Davenport had slipped away. That is until Skipper John heard the familiar rumble of his over snow starting up, the noise coming from the front of the train where he'd left the machine with the keys in the ignition.

John's sudden departure from the carriage brought all those who could, heading for the door to see what had him so startled.

Josey descended the steps and was quickly hot on his heels. 'John, what is it?'

'Someone's in the cat!'

Huang heard what he said from the open door of the train and hastened to join them. 'Where's Davenport?' they heard him yell over the storm.

The answer came as they rounded the locomotive and saw the cat powering off the railway tracks, with Ral at the controls.

John ran after it with no hope of catching up, finally stopping and throwing his arms in the air in disbelief. 'Where the hell does he think he's going?'

Josey and Huang joined him in his helpless study of the receding cat. The intensity of the rain had eased, and the latest news from the helicopter was that it would be arriving within half an hour; perhaps the reason Davenport felt it was time to make himself-scarce.

'Did he not want to face the authorities?' Huang asked short of breath.

Josey guessed otherwise, 'I've a feeling he's gone after Chow.'

John considered his suggestion and told him, 'He's travelling blind - unless he lets-up he'll hit the boulders. Do we have anything on the train that we can follow with?' John asked.

Huang was shaking his head. 'There are some skidoos, but I cannot allow—'

'That's my cat out there, professor,' John warned as he walked away. 'Show me where they are.'

Josey caught up. 'You've helped enough, skipper. Isn't this a bit risky?'

'You *betcha.*'

'Then don't do it.'

The skipper lowered his voice so that Huang, who was following a few steps back, wouldn't hear. 'If I get out there and find my machine smashed against a rock, I'll kill him,' he promised figuratively.

Against Huang's better judgement, and John's unwavering insistence, he was permitted to head out on the skidoo five minutes later. Not one to take a back seat, Josey joined him on a second machine, travelling blindly as John had warned.

'Stick close, Detective - be ready to stop in a hurry!'

Josey knew why, somewhere up ahead was the cluster of snow covered boulders, making them almost invisible now that the rain had given over to another windswept blizzard. John had a mental picture of the terrain in his head, and he'd calculated when to slow down based on the distance to the outcrop and his speed.

Easing up, the ghostly mounds appeared before them – as predicted.

The rumbling idle of Skipper John's all terrain could be heard nearby – also expected.

What wasn't expected was the sudden bright orange flash that burnt out of the white, the gunshot seen and heard as the skidoos were sliding to a stop beside each other – the bullet, taking out a headlamp on Josey's bike.

The gunman, embedded in the sleet, barely recognisable as Chow, had his attention and his aim on the interfering arrivals.

Davenport lay on his back nearby; it was reasonable to assume Josey and the skipper had interrupted Ral's execution, and invited their own.

'Split up!' Josey shouted urgently as he powered the

skidoo away to the left.

John speared to the right intuitively.

They heard two more shots as they raced into the veil of the blizzard. Each could only hope the other man hadn't been hit. John heard Josey's motor go silent and understood he should follow suit. The blanketing blizzard was their friend now. Their advantage blossomed when Yu Chow fired blindly, giving away his position.

Josey hoped John knew not to call out. He got off the skidoo and began closing in on where his mind told him the last shot had been fired from, his eyes peeled for the first sign of movement. He'd taken maybe a dozen steps before he saw something. It didn't make sense; the vague shape that he was seeing was too big to be Chow. It crossed his mind that it might be an animal, a large one. He almost wished Shannon was there to bring him up to speed on the Tibetan wild animal population.

He was close to talking himself out of the possibility one such animal was somewhere close, when the thing let out a frightening roar.

Dropping his guard, John shouted from behind, 'What was that for shit's sake?'

The gun went off – not at John.

Another mighty growl was followed by a bloodcurdling scream of pain – Yu Chow's pain? Or was it Davenport? Among the desperate screams were what sounded like pleas for help – and then silence, except for the slurping sounds of something - *feasting?*

Thankfully, Josey thought, *John knew not to call a second time.*

They remained quiet, listening to the graphic sounds, which now seemed to be moving away. The beast, or whatever it was, could be heard dragging its catch through the snow.

Josey and John didn't move for several minutes, thankful they couldn't see what was happening. With a picture of where this carnage had taken place, Josey moved forward until he reached the blood drenched snow.

Although paled by a constant layering of fresh streaks of powder, the substantial patch of blood looked to be smeared, the disappearing drag marks leading away.

On the spot where Davenport had been awaiting execution, there was no evidence of his having walked away, but one way or the other, he was gone.

'Josey, where are you?' John asked forcing a whisper through the blizzard.

He spoke back just loud enough to be heard. 'Stay with the bike, I'll come to you.' He backed away from the grisly scene until he came up against his waiting skidoo.

John heard the bike start-up, and Josey telling him, 'There's nothing to be done here.'

John fired up his bike and headed over to the sound of Josey's motor. 'What'd you see?'

'Blood and nothing more.'

'They've both been taken?'

'They're both gone, that's all I know.'

'Let's not stick around to join them,' John suggested.

'My thoughts exactly.'

'I'm taking the cat back and leaving the skidoo here,' he told Josey as he edged his bike toward the sound of the cat. 'You can dump yours too and join me if you'd prefer.'

Josey couldn't see the train through the blizzard and

immediately opted to take up the offer.

Back on the train, they were immediately swamped with questions, which they answered truthfully. Josey knew Belinda would be concerned that Ral was somewhere out there with a killer beast, but there was no real way to withhold the information.

Money could have been put on Shannon knowing what the beast was. 'It sounds like an Asian Black Bear to be honest; they *are* known to have attacked, but I have to say though, it's rare – apparently there are only twenty of them left in the wild.'

'Is Ral still out there, Josey?'

'I'm sorry, Bel,' he told her apologetically, 'there's no way of telling.'

'Either way, I'm not leaving here until we know,' she responded defiantly.

Huang quickly nipped that in the bud. 'Ms Baxter, once the helicopter arrives; staying will not be an option.'

She gave him a decent glare. 'No?'

'I am afraid not, my orders are to return you all to Golmud for interrogations. For your own safety, I strongly recommend that you abide by this ruling.'

There was nothing more to be said, at least by the Australians. 'I'll keep looking,' John offered, 'as soon as the weather clears.'

Belinda shook his hand, 'John, we have a lot to thank you for; not the least being for keeping us safe in that magnificent machine of yours.' On impulse she gave him an embrace. 'I hope things get better for you up here.'

He looked at her fiancé lying on the stretcher at their feet. 'I'm certain that it will.' He gave Belinda a peck on the cheek and shook Aaron's upstretched hand, promising, 'I'll keep in touch with Professor Huang and let him know if we find your friend.'

Twenty minutes later the weather took a turn for the better and John kept to his promise, heading out among the boulders to look for Ral Davenport, the disgraced SciCore manager.

With the break, the helicopter was able to land, settling down on the tracks a short distance away from the front of the train. The PLA soldiers assisted with getting people aboard, including some sick passengers that had been added to the manifest.

Aaron and Shannon's stretchers were taken up by PLA officers and carried toward the waiting chopper.

Josey quietly approached Huang and asked, 'Will I be able to talk with you before we leave for Australia?'

'Try to leave without doing so.' His toothy grin was reassuring - sort of. It wasn't completely clear whether or not arrests were off the table.

With everyone aboard and belted up, the chopper twitched into flight in a windstorm of its own making, heading in the direction of Golmud – and to uncertain conclusions.

On the flight, Josey and his client took their first chance to have a decent talk since Yu Chow's escape; although *escape* was hardly the right word given he'd probably been taken by a black bear.

Belinda was trying her best to put the black bear out of her mind. 'Please tell me John will find Ral,' she pleaded.

Josey understood where her loyalty was coming from,

in spite of what Davenport had done, that's just the kind of person she was. 'John says he hasn't given up looking, I trust him to do as he says.'

'I hope so, I can't rest without knowing.'

'I hear you.'

'Anyway, I can't wait to hear how you finalised the case. I feel guilty for putting you off the scent with Ral.'

'Who says you did? But listen, don't feel guilty, he only played a small part. At least he didn't know about the sabotage.'

She drew a deep breath. 'Are you sure about that?'

'I am; thanks to what Max and Carl discovered. We know Flock Investments handled the money side of things, and Ral's company Davro - built the chips for the satellites. What wasn't known until a few days ago was that certain specialised parts for the chips were coming from China. I actually got that message while on the train out of Lhasa. It all started to fit together. I got quite a bit of work done in that baggage car. With Max and Carl's help we found out exactly where the Chinese parts were coming from, and that Yu Chow was one of the directors of the company making them, an electronics firm called Biaomi, operating out of Nanjing.'

She was wearing a frown.

'Problem?'

'How did you make the connection to Chow?'

'He had a fifty one per cent share in Biaomi, which SciCore knew nothing about.'

'And that was enough to convince you?'

'There was a little bit of hacking involved, but you didn't hear that from me.'

She grinned at that. 'Apart from money, what the hell

was he getting out of doing this?'

'The money was billions, if not trillions. I don't think we can minimise it.'

'How was the money made?'

'As you know, for the conspiracy to work, Aaron's satellites needed to fail, and that's where Biaomi came in. Their firmware allowed for remote control of the satellites, which took in navigation, atmospheric testing and ozone monitoring. By the same token, Yu Chow was able to cause Aaron's satellite to explode on command, using a laptop from here on the ground. Even some very common sun lotion companies were inadvertently benefiting from the manufacture of sunscreens, and probably still are.'

'Why *inadvertently*?'

'Because in most cases, no one at these companies had a clue about the conspiracy, it's the perfect cover. There's nothing wrong with the potions they make, it's just that they wouldn't be needed if there wasn't an ozone problem. We found out, Yu Chow had a finger in no less than a dozen other companies involved in sun-protection, things like clothing, building materials – even cancer research.'

'Wow.'

'These companies didn't, and probably still don't, have any idea about the conspiracy. SciCore itself had no clue.'

Belinda seemed reasonably satisfied with Josey's explanations, and he hoped she wouldn't be asking any more difficult questions for now, because there was still something about the case that hadn't been resolved, and he couldn't make mention of it until he had proof, but he was very aware of the fact that even with Yu Chow gone, certain people were still very much in danger.

'I didn't do this alone,' he told her. 'I had a heap of help from Maxine and Carl back home. Max approached Davrow and explained to them what was happening at Biaomi, and that to avoid potential prosecution they needed to cover their arses by conducting tests on the parts coming from China. The reaction she got was nothing short of cooperative. They hired an independent company to conduct the tests, indicating they personally had nothing to hide. They were as shocked as anybody when firmware was found to be imbedded in the parts – firmware capable of being manipulated wirelessly.'

Josey noticed Belinda's frown had deepened. 'You still look worried.'

'Well, you know, I can't see how this indemnifies Ral.'

'It doesn't,' Josey agreed, 'but the paper trail clearly shows that Ral's only gain was from bonuses bestowed on him by SciCore; as I said he knew nothing about the affected parts. The only way he was involved was in accepting money to discourage Aaron from trying to work out what was wrong with his satellites – on the basis natural depletion was bad for the company.'

Belinda's brow arched. 'So he's not exactly innocent.'

Josey considered her conclusion. 'Sadly, no.'

'Bloody hell,' she breathed in sheer annoyance.

'I've spoken with his wife by the way, while we were waiting for the chopper.'

'Really, how'd that go?'

'Not good at first, but after she'd settled I learnt that the police cleared their son Lester of any wrong doing. Max helped them with that. He apparently was a bit smitten by his friend the biker . . . This is not over,' Josey told her, 'the shit will hit the fan if it's all brought to light.'

'It will be brought to light if I've got anything to do with it,' she promised.

Josey gave her a sly grin. 'You might have to talk with your favourite reporter about that.'

She wobbled her head in recognition that he was probably right, and looked across at Shannon lying quietly on his stretcher next to her fiancé – both of them out of ear shot. 'I guess we can't deny, if he hadn't taken the trouble to give you guys heads up at the ruins, this may have finished very differently.'

Josey bunched his eyebrows, feigning surprise and merit for her forgiving attitude. 'Bel, you astound me - it's very generous of you to point that out.'

'Shut up,' she ordered with a wry grin and a titter.

From his stretcher, Aaron looked across at the love of his life, spending time with her old boyfriend, and couldn't deny a pang of jealous uncertainty.

Aaron and Shannon were put under guard in Golmud's public hospital. Exhausted following their respective operations, they slept most of the following day. Both injuries were flesh wounds only, having narrowly missed vital organs and bone, but in Aaron's case it was touch and go for a while because of the extensive loss of blood. He'd raised everyone's spirits when he was coming out of the anaesthetic after his emergency operations, by saying, 'I thought I was supposed to s-save the world.' He had his eyes on Huang, who told him, 'Perhaps you still might.'

Josey had something far more positive to say. 'You've had the worst case of mistrust dropped on you that I've ever seen in all my years as a detective. Business is one thing, but friendship is another. With what we now know, your satellites work – meaning you have come up with a way to not only detect ozone loss, but to repair it. After what I've just been through up on that mountain; I would undoubtedly call that, *saving the world.'*

Emotional tears welled in Belinda's eyes; prompting her to gently rest a hand on Josey's arm in a gesture of thanks.

Following the interrogations, as Professor Huang had called them, Josey and Belinda were invited to attend a meeting in his office at the university. There was no PLA involvement, which was a calming sign, yet an expectancy of disclosure hung in the air on both sides.

The first revelation came the moment they walked in, Huang had a visitor. The way he was dressed was a dead giveaway, or at least Josey believed so. On the other hand, Belinda knew exactly who he was, even though this was the first time she'd seen him.

Huang gestured to the man, seated to the side of the desk. 'I am most happy to officially introduce to you, someone who I am sure you are already very familiar with - please meet renowned Scientist, Dr Zanchu.'

The mutual voices in the visitor's heads were, *'really'.*

Huang could tell they were thinking it.

'It is true; we have worked together for many years. Our main interest has been the environment, and specifically – its decline. But, as I am sure you are aware, people change. Zanchu and I began to move down very different roads some years ago – and yet, with very similar goals. Zanchu had left the world of science to become a devout Buddhist priest.'

The little monk stood from his seat over by Huang's desk, and approached the visitors. He extended his hand in a greeting, which was first accepted by Belinda. 'I must say, this is a surprise.'

Josey took his hand in turn. 'I was beginning to wonder if you were real.'

'You know, it is funny,' the monk responded with a beaming smile, 'a lot of people say that to me, I have no idea why.' He gave a polite laugh. 'I have been very anxious to meet you, Detective Josey. You have been most influential.'

Josey felt it was impossible to pull his eyes away from the smiling face. '*Influential?*'

Zanchu turned to Huang. 'Perhaps we should begin to explain,' he said as he regained his seat over by the desk.

Josey was thinking he would be the one expected to begin explanations; he had a lot to elucidate.

The Australian guests sat in single leather armchairs that were placed neatly against the wall of the small room, appropriately cluttered with books. Given their recent experience on the mountain, it was disconcerting to see the sun cutting harmlessly across the faces of their hosts. Of course, the news that the radiation had subsided on Mount Kailash was well known now – and a welcome relief.

For some, the reason for the vortex was unknown, having closed as mysteriously as it had opened. Scientists and those closest to Professor Verg understood there was no mystery. They knew that the sun had experienced the biggest solar flare in close to five thousand years.

Huang moved his eyes from Josey to Belinda. 'All of this started when I received a call from Professor Verg's father, informing me of the work his son was doing, and he asked if I could connect him with Zanchu, the Grand Master. Adam Verg was still quite well at the time. It saddened us to hear of his cancer.' He looked across to his friend. 'As it turned out, Zanchu already knew of Professor Verg, having been told by Abbot Le Camus who he was. Zanchu took it on himself to go to Australia and personally invite Aaron to join The Observers. And here we are.'

For Josey, at least Huang's explanation explained Abbot Le Camus, but mostly it only covered the timeline. 'I have to ask,' he said apologetically, 'I'm still trying to get my head around the *observer thing;* and the mummies for that matter.'

Their hosts stared at him blankly, Huang finally asking, 'What exactly would you like to know?'

Josey sensed Belinda was staring at him as well, but he pushed on. 'No, I mean, what's the connection?'

Huang felt he understood. 'Do you mean the connection with Aaron?'

Josey turned to Belinda and thought he saw an almost undetectable message to hold his tongue. Then, she picked up the thread, saying to Huang and Zanchu, 'Detective Josey is a very practical man—'

'Ms Baxter, you do not need to explain.'

Following a long drawn breath, Zanchu addressed the Australian by saying, 'Whatever you believe about what has happened to Professor Verg here in our respective regions, believe that spirits have interwoven irrefutably.

As scientists,' he glanced at Josey, 'and people of considered thought, I think I can speak for us all in saying, there are things about the cosmos, that are outside of our understanding.'

This sounds familiar, Josey thought.

'It is my firm belief that, collectively, we have all made a difference to that understanding. Please know in your hearts, you have done a good thing.' He stood from his chair and took in the faces one by one, including his good friend, Huang. 'Well, anyway, this is what I believe . . .

'And now, it is time for this servant to leave you, and to wish you all, much happiness.'

They all got to their feet when the old monk stood and presented them with a reverent bow, which they returned with the utmost respect. The little man said no more. He stepped quietly to the door and left.

Josey's eyes fell on Professor Huang. 'Wow.'

'Wow-indeed,' Huang agreed before adding, 'But Mr Josey, I must say to you, that you have remained very open minded during your experience here. And in so doing, you have uncovered the culprit for the sabotage – have you not?'

Belinda accepted his point enthusiastically. 'He's got you there, Cameron. If you hadn't taken on the case, the sabotage might never have been uncovered.'

'Ms Baxter is right; all that Zanchu and I were sure of was the science. We knew that Professor Verg's satellites should have worked, but were unable to ascertain why they did not.'

Josey had seen some complex orchestration in his time, but this gambit took the cake.

'Detective, I must assure you, I had no knowledge of

the stone tablet, or the prophecy, but to be honest I am not surprised.'

Josey couldn't deny the amulet had opened the door in the ruined monastery, and it obviously fitted into the tablet like a glove, seemingly making an ancient prediction about the present—

He stopped himself from thinking about it.

Huang was patiently eyeing him in wait to hear what else he wanted to know.

Josey decided to leave it there, and couldn't fathom whether or not he had been drawn into their world as well, although - given that Belinda was the one who hired him, it seemed unlikely, unless she was part of it. Okay, he'd found the main perpetrator in the end, but somehow it felt like these two Chinese scientists had been a step ahead of him the whole time. He decided to leave that question alone as well, but there was one thing he desperately hoped they could answer. 'The fellow who took my gun on the train – he was working for you, right?'

'After your assistant Maxine called me from Australia, outlining what you'd already found out, I had to be sure you remained safe while you, how do you say, did your thing – finding the bad guy. Suffice to say, you have witnessed the work of The Observers. I hope it did not cause you any stress.'

'Frankly I'm glad he took the gun, or I might have shot someone.'

'Yes.' A moment of reflection and silence descended while Huang gathered his thoughts. 'There is something else,' he finally told them soberly.

The room fell silent for a moment.

Belinda's heart began to pound, especially since Huang had his eyes fixedly on her. 'What's happened?'

'We are not exactly sure why, I can only tell you that your friend John has not been able to find Mr Davenport.'

'Is it possible he might still be alive?'

'We may never know for sure, but certainly not until the summer returns and the snow is gone.'

Josey gripped Belinda's hand.

'The American over snow driver continued to search for two days,' Huang divulged, 'travelling beyond what would be humanly possible for Mr Davenport to have walked.'

In Josey's mind, Ral was almost certainly dead, but he had no intension of mentioning this hypothesis in front of Belinda.

'We will continue to look for him,' Huang promised. 'There are many people on the mountain now; and we can be thankful the radiation has subsided—'

The conversation was interrupted by Huang receiving a notification on his computer. 'Aah, I think that this might be for you. Rotating the laptop to face them he said, 'Lui Jie would like to give her wishes.'

And there she was, via zoom. 'Hello, I am glad not to have missed you.'

A chorus of hellos greeted her and brought a glowing smile in response. 'I have heard from my uncle the good news in solving your case, Detective Josey. Please accept my congratulations.'

'Thank you, Lui; I wasn't alone.'

'Of course; well I have some good news too; my precious mummies are going to Beijing, to the museum. It is very exciting for me.'

'That's great,' Josey told her.

'Belinda, I have had a long talk with my uncle about your fiancé's mission here. If he has any doubts about some of what has taken place at Kailash, please be assured that, in time, he will make complete sense of it. Do not allow him to doubt that he is a special person in the eyes of my people, the Tibetans. His visit here will be remembered forevermore; it will be spoken of for generations to come.' She smiled broadly and added for Belinda's sake, 'I hope that you and Aaron will live a long and happy life together.'

'Thank you so much, Lui Jie; we will always remember your friendship.'

'Good, good. But before you go, I have a request.'

Belinda mirrored her smile, wondering with anticipation.

'I would like to invite you all to a first showing of my mummies, at the museum in one weeks' time. Do you think you will be able to come?'

Josey and Belinda looked at each other in consideration. 'Try and stop us,' Belinda accepted happily. But then she realised a week was too soon for Aaron to attend, and was forced to decline. She suggested there was no good reason why Josey couldn't go.

'I'd be very honoured to attend,' he told the matriarch.

'Excellent; well, I must go now.'

'Lui Jie,' Belinda offered quickly, 'I'm so sorry for the loss of your mentor. Mr Leung's passing must hang very heavily on your heart.'

'Yes, it does, but he had a very good life, and I am so pleased that he was alive to see our mummies. When you see Professor Verg, please pass on my sincerest wishes for a speedy recovery. Perhaps he will be well enough to come to the museum before you leave for Australia.'

Belinda held Josey's hand. 'We will pass on your invitation.'

Even via the computer, Lui Jie saw that Ms Baxter may be in love with more than just one man, she made no judgement. 'Yes, I know you are all very good friends – Goodbye for now.' She focused back on Huang, 'Uncle?'

The professor swung the computer around to see his niece. 'We will meet each other in Beijing,' he assured her.

'Yes, I am looking forward to seeing you again, Uncle.'

They were walking on air when they left the university, headed for the hospital; they felt the professor's promise of a blessing was already attributing some sort of feeling of wellbeing. Belinda hooked her arm in Josey's, her second most favourite man. 'They took a real shine to you, Detective Josey,' she told him. 'You might end up getting an invitation to join the Observers.'

'Yeah, well, forget that; I'll settle for just being observant.'

She snuggled in against his arm, keeping her smile from view.

The mummies became known as the Kailashians, fast tracked to the National Museum of China. To say it was popular is an understatement. Mums, dads and academics alike rolled up in their numbers to take a look.

A few days later, Lui Jie received news from Belinda that her fiancé had insisted she attend the museum in the company of the detective.

As ordained, Belinda and Josey arrived in the great hall and stood with Lui Jie to once again *lay eyes* on the ancient trio. They foreigners shared the enquiring glances as well. Whisperings circulated about who the matriarch was, and who the Australians were.

Jack Pearson had postponed his departure to Boston so that he could see what all the fuss was about. He was seeing the mummies for the first time under the carefully thought out lighting, a far cry from the dim abode in which they were found.

The small one year old baby, with brown hair protruding from under a faded red and blue felt cap, attracted the most interest. People were fascinated by the fact that all the mummies were found wearing the clothes they died in – forty thousand years ago.

Mesmerised like all the others, Belinda and Josey stood in front of the trio, accompanied by the matriarchal Archaeologist.

'Congratulations,' Bel told her, 'This must make you feel very proud.'

She was beaming—

'Lui Jie, forgive me for interrupting.' It was her uncle, Professor Huang. 'The president would like to have his picture taken with you now.'

'Oh, yes, of course.' She bowed politely to her guests. 'Can you please excuse me; I must take care of business.'

They bowed and she glided away with her uncle.

Belinda noticed an unsettling in Josey. 'Are you feeling all right, you've been very quiet?'

He brought his mind back. 'I'm fine, just missing home I guess.'

She understood. 'When are you going back?'

'I'm booked to fly out Saturday week.'

He wasn't looking at her; she was worried about the way he was glancing around the room. He'd been acting nervously since they arrived. 'Would you like to join me for a coffee?'

His phone rang on silent. He took it from his coat pocket and checked the screen. 'You go ahead, I better take this – it's Max.'

She took a couple of steps back. 'Come over when you're finished.'

He was nodding as he spoke into the phone. 'Max, talk to me.'

Belinda picked up on his business like tone as she headed toward the coffee table – worried. She found a table for two and waited. She could see him through the milling visitors taking his call; he looked as serious as hell, not his usual persona when talking to home. She was so worried about him that she found herself shifting in her seat every time he disappeared from view. Her heart was leaping and falling each time.

The obstruction became a little too persistent for her liking and she stood up to gain a better point of view. She couldn't see him. She hesitated, feeling foolish for worrying. The traffic between them thinned to the point that she should now have been able to locate him, but he must have moved from where he was. She left the table and walked across the floor until she reached the exact spot where he had been standing – right in front of the mummies.

'Fabulous aren't they.'

The male voice was right at her shoulder and she turned to face Russel Sleeman, the Australian SciCore Director.

'Oh, hello, I didn't know *you* were coming.'

'I wasn't, but my flight got cancelled, so here I am.'

'Right.'

He saw she was on edge. 'Is there something troubling you?'

'No, not really, I was about to have a coffee with Josey, but I've lost him.'

'I just saw him out on the garden terrace,' he told her pointing over his shoulder—

'Russ, can I have a quick word?' It was Pearson. 'Sorry Belinda.'

'One second,' Sleeman said. I was just about to help Ms Baxter find her *boyfriend*.'

Annoyance shot through her veins, *cheeky bastard.*

'That's all right, you guys go ahead,' Jack told them. 'Russ, I'll be over by the wine table.'

Belinda wanted to refuse the help, but he was already leading her away by the arm.

'Thanks,' he told Jack, 'I won't be a moment.'

They came onto the terrace and panned their eyes in search of Josey.

'He was here a minute ago talking on his phone.' His attention fell to the garden below. 'There he is.'

She turned too late to see him.

'Come on, I'll show you.' He led the way with a gentle touch to her elbow.

There was no real reason not to follow, so she did, down the stone staircase and into the garden.

Josey had finished his call with Max and was inside looking for Belinda, she wasn't at the table where he'd seen her earlier. He thought to call, but got interrupted.

'Hey, buddy.' Pearson announced, 'You look lost.'

'Not me, I'm looking for Belinda.'

'Funny that, she's looking for you.'

'Where'd you see her?'

'You look worried, what's up?'

'Was she with anyone?'

'As a matter of fact she was. I just saw her heading into the garden with Russ.' He pointed to the exit that led to the terrace, 'Through there—'

Josey bolted away, leaving Pearson gobsmacked. The terror on Josey's face prompted him to follow.

Josey took only a moment to glance down into the garden from the terrace before bounding down the wide steps.

He paused uncertainly at the edge of the greenery. Sweat was building on his brow.

Pearson arrived above, leaning against the balustrade and calling out. 'Josey; Can I help?'

He wanted to shout back, *I don't know*, but moved on, taking a stab at which direction to go. The garden wasn't particularly open, with lots of places to go out of sight if that's what you wanted.

Pearson heard the detective shouting Belinda's name while entering the cover of dense bushes, his voice facilitating a point of reference to follow. His behaviour was unsettling enough to warrant backup, and Pearson barked orders into his earpiece to get it organised.

Up in the main hall there was a buzz of confusion building, drawing in Lui Jie and the museum's own security people. They, along with Pearson's bodyguards, gathered on the terrace to exchange intelligence.

Deep into the garden, only fleeting glimpses of the museum could be seen.

Pearson had caught up with Josey. 'I've got help on the way. Tell me what's happening.'

'It's Sleeman, he's lost his mind.'

'What th' hell you talking about?'

'Sleeman's in it with Chow.'

'You're shitting me.'

'He's got Belinda, and if we don't find him she's dead.'

Pearson passed the information onto his people back on the terrace and clearly received a response. 'Hang on,' he said trying to keep pace with the detective, 'They say there's an old crypt around here someplace. Getting little response he barked an order into his pager. 'If anyone knows where this damn crypt is get your asses down here pronto.'

Josey wasn't waiting for anyone, but he did stop yelling, figuring it might be exacerbating the situation, signalling for Pearson to do the same.

That's when they both heard a weak cry. Ironically it came at an impasse, a fork in the gardener's trodden track. He couldn't have been certain which path to take except for one thing – a scarf - a blue silk wrap that he had noticed her wearing, now strategically positioned on a branch.

He'd only traversed fifty feet before he came across the outside of the crypt, almost overgrown by a section of dishevelled garden.

Its black entrance yawned at him in welcome.

Suddenly it felt like he was standing under spotlights, the dimly lit garden standing in total contrast to the crypt's interior.

He thought, *I could stand here all day worrying about entering, but how much time has Belinda really got?* He went in.

The walls of the crypt were like the inside of a Mayan ruin, infiltrated by the encroachment of the garden. He stopped and listened. It was so quiet; he should have been able to hear breathing. There was nothing. He ventured further and stopped again.

Was that a glint of light?

Yes.

What caused it?

He looked over his shoulder and saw that he entrance to the crypt stood out like a dim grey section of vegetation. He turned back to the black and saw the faint flicker again, a small glow; *reflecting the dim grey of the crypt's entrance—?*

He saw it again, and he knew what it was, the face of a watch, *Belinda's watch!*

This told him that he was standing out like a silhouette against the pale exterior. Meaning, Sleeman could see him approaching, and probably was presenting some threat or other to keep Belinda quiet.

There were obvious questions; did he have a gun, *a knife?* There was no choice, he had to find out.

'Sleeman I know you're in here,' his voice echoed dully in the dank blackness. 'Let Belinda go, it's your only way out of this.'

He heard him laugh.

'Bel? Are you all right?'

'She can't answer you, she's dead—'

'I'm not, don't listen to him.'

Josey's heart had popped like a champagne cork and landed in relief, almost in the same instant.

'Okay, I'm letting her go, but first can I ask what put

you onto me?'

'Maybe it was your ties with the *Puerto Rico Bank*, or your sweeping international money laundering, your tax evasion, or your global payment transfers between your financial institutions. Shall I go on?'

'I'll tell you what you *can* do; try backing up and letting me out of here – it's either that, or you come in and find Baxter dead.'

'Let him out, Josey.'

'Listen to your girlfriend.'

'I'm listening, and I'm doing what you ask. But if you hurt her I'll see you dead.' He took his phone from his pocket, knowing Sleeman could see it. 'All I have to do is call for backup and game over. I'm moving back. When you get out here, I want to see Belinda in the land of the living. Have you got that straight?'

'That's what'll happen, just as soon as you backup.'

Josey set the ball rolling, stepping backwards to the entrance and a good ten feet out into the garden.

He stood staring at the black interior, waiting for a sign that Sleeman was playing his part in the deal.

From the blackness, emerged the captor and the captive, Sleeman with a knife to Belinda's throat.

'Take the knife off her and you're free to go.'

'No tricks, Detective.'

'You have my word.'

He was about to clinch the deal when a shot rang out. Blood splattered across Belinda's face as Sleeman took the bullet in the head, like Josey told him – he was free to go, but someone else had other ideas.

The surrounding bush came alive with armed men, PLA, Museum security and American bodyguards. The smoking gun belonged to Pearson's guy, a marksman if ever there was one.

Pearson caught Josey's eye and told him. 'I don't like to take chances.'

Belinda was standing with her arms out to the side, like she'd been hit in the face with a blood pie.

Sleeman saw none of this.

Josey rushed forward and with his trusty handkerchief, began cleaning - what was Sleeman's - from her face.

With Sleeman dead, the final piece of the puzzle was put in its place.

The retelling of their day at the museum, as told to their friends in hospital, came across like fiction. The only part they had little trouble believing was that Sleeman was a rogue. No one was prepared to say that they were glad he got his comeuppance aloud, yet visibly thinking it.

Prior to the drama at the museum, several happy snaps had been taken in and around the Kailashians, and some smiley shots of everybody with each other, and oddly even with Director Sleeman before they knew what he was. His shots were unceremoniously deleted from phones ahead of showing the remainder to the hospital staff.

Before Lui Jie returned to Mount Kailash, she also had dropped in at the hospital to say goodbye to Professor Verg.

He promised her that he would go to the museum as soon as he was free of the hospital.

Josey soon discovered that she had something on her mind that was worrying her 'I know that I said to you there was no need to concern yourself with my abduction, but—'

'Let me stop you there – the answer's yes, I know who it was.'

'Are you able to tell me?'

'At that stage, Yu Chow wasn't in a position to show his hand. He had several people working for him that he could rely on to do his dirty work.'

'Do you know why he wanted to abduct me?'

'It was purely your connection to your uncle; he was paranoid that professor Huang was getting too close to learning the truth about the satellites.'

'Are these people any further threat to me?'

'Their source of income is gone. You have nothing more to fear.'

Her relief was palpable, so much so that she just had to kiss him. 'You are a wonderful man, Belinda is very lucky.'

Josey suddenly thought he may have given her the wrong impression about Belinda. 'Lui Jie, I have a wife back home.'

She smiled. 'Yes, she is very lucky too.' She bowed and walked away, leaving Josey enchanted by her candour.

The Australians stayed in Golmud another three weeks, long enough for Aaron and Shannon to be able to travel. The reporter could hardly believe the change in attitude toward him, and really loved the attention. He couldn't imagine that they would ever have agreed to divulge the corruption, and the truth behind the environmental cataclysm.

But, they only had a week to go before leaving when a new disaster beset them, not just them, but the rest of the world. The planet had entered into a sudden lockdown, preventing their departure. It was a pandemic, believed to have originated in the very country they were trapped in – China.

On the day Shannon was due to be discharged from hospital, Josey and Belinda went to visit the two injured Australians as usual. While they were visiting Aaron, who was still laid up, a sense of foreboding began to sweep through the wards – at first the problem was incomprehensible due to the exclusive adoption of the Chinese language in their presence.

Aaron's nurse finally told them the bad news; the world had a new virus that they were calling Covid-19.

Of course as expected, Shannon knew a little about the Coronavirus. 'It was originally named *Sars-Cov2,*' he told them. He would have went on for hours about it, if they'd let him.

Because of the international lockdown, it was predicted that none of them would be allowed to leave China for close to a year, a year in which Professor Verg was invited by Huang to continue his work on the satellites at the University of Shanghai. They'd planned to make some amazing developments to Aaron's satellite design, in complete cooperation with the parent company in Boston.

Josey kept in touch with Max, and from within his expatriated situation was ready to help solve an Australian case during the first week of international isolation.

Belinda and Shannon were about to become EASI's foreign correspondents working out of China, covering exclusive developments in finding a vaccine for Covid-

19.

But, none of these plans were to come into fruition. Political relations between China and Australia became suddenly toxic. In less than four months since the virus set foot on the planet, and against regulations, Professor Huang strongly advised they leave for Australia, which as far as Covid-19 was concerned, had to be the best place in the world to go. He secretly got them into Hong Kong, where they were lucky enough to be included on a special Qantas flight organised by the Australian Federal Government. Josey rang Rebecca and let her know they were returning home. Her relief filtered through the phone.

Australia wouldn't be Aaron and Belinda's final port of call, but they would have to wait another two years before they could pull up stumps in Australia and resettle in Boston.

Russel Sleeman's family were refused access when they requested the return of his body to Australia, and he was buried in an unknown location in China, with no headstone. He wasn't missing anything from his old life though; the Australian branch of SciCore had been shut down for good, as promised by Jack Pearson.

Of course CorpCause, the Sydney based demonstrators, took the credit for the closure.

This news reached the stranded Australians while they were still overseas. The only thing that upset Aaron was the loss of jobs at the debunked Research Centre. He promised himself that he would personally help each and every one of the staff find new positions when he got back home, especially the field ops.

On the day Josey and Co departed China, none of them

could possibly have imagined the event that was taking place one kilometre away from the Pan Himalayan train tracks, high in the mountains of Tibet.

*

Ral Davenport could barely keep his eyes open, let alone lift his head to see who was there. Even with eyes open he wasn't able to see clearly, the movement around him was vague and shadowy, but he recognised it was people; about five or six of them. They appeared to be clad in ankle length tunics, with fleecy over-jackets adorned by fur lining.

Nearby, against the protection of a black boulder, a motionless mound, frozen by the sub zero wind, nestled against its snow stripped face. At its crest, behind a thin layer of ice, the face of a Chinese man had crystallised in his last moments of terror, held by the sub zero wind. Snow cover concealed vicious wounds beneath, depicted only by the protrusion of a single hand that lay severed beside him.

With his eyes rested upon this, Ral realised they had been sitting opposite each other, propped against their sarsens of choice – a choice of where to pause, and where to die.

He passed out; unaware he was being placed onto a makeshift travois. He saw nothing of the monks dragging him across the snow covered terrain, a distance of twenty miles to their monastery, and a day's walk from Mount Kailash.

As they approached its sanctuary he didn't see the superficial destruction of the stone fortress that stood rebelliously against the elements, or the secret tunnels that led to a hidden subterranean structure away from the harsh exterior, a warm abode where he might seek life; and perhaps forgiveness.

His new home finally stole the cutting wind from his face, bringing him to full consciousness. He looked up into the face of a small man standing over him. He had no idea who it was, but he had a kind face, and in time, he would come to know him as Zanchu, prophet and spiritual leader of the secret society of *The Observers*.